VOICE OF DOMINION

THE SPOKEN MAGE SERIES

VOICE OF DOMINION

THE SPOKEN MAGE BOOK 3

MELANIE CELLIER

LUMINANT PUBLICATIONS

VOICE OF DOMINION

The Spoken Mage Book 3
First edition published in 2019 (v1.1)
by Luminant Publications

ISBN 978-1-925898-07-1

Luminant Publications
PO Box 203
Glen Osmond, South Australia 5064

melaniecellier@internode.on.net
http://www.melaniecellier.com

Cover Design by Karri Klawiter
Editing by Mary Novak
Proofreading by Deborah Grace White
Map Illustration by Rebecca E Paavo

For my niece, Cressida Bella,
who is already on her way to being
a strong and adventurous young lady

ROYAL FAMILY OF ARDANN

King Stellan
Queen Verena
Crown Princess Lucienne
Prince Lucas

MAGE COUNCIL

Academy Head (black robe) - Duke Lorcan of Callinos
University Head (black robe) - Duchess Jessamine of
    Callinos
Head of Law Enforcement (red robe) - Duke Lennox of
    Ellington
Head of the Seekers (gray robe) - Duchess Phyllida of
    Callinos
Head of the Healers (purple robe) - Duke Dashiell of
    Callinos
Head of the Growers (green robe) - Duchess Annika of
    Devoras
Head of the Wind Workers (blue robe) - Duke Magnus of
    Ellington
Head of the Creators (orange robe) - Duke Casimir of
    Stantorn
Head of the Armed Forces (silver robe) - General Griffith of
    Devoras
Head of the Royal Guard (gold robe) - General Thaddeus of
    Stantorn

CHAPTER 1

I stood outside my childhood home and tried to view it with the objective eyes of the mage girl beside me. Coralie had been my closest friend for two years, but she had never visited Kingslee before.

I hadn't seen my house in nearly a year, and yet I could have closed my eyes and pictured every scratch and bump on the wooden door. Nothing had changed, although the curtains looked a touch more faded.

But would my family inside be equally unaltered?

"Is this it?" asked Coralie, looking between me and the door in confusion. No doubt my Academy friend thought I had gone mad and forgotten my own home.

The other possibility—that she might think me embarrassed of my family's house—made me shake myself and step forward. Before I reached the door, however, it swung open, and a tall, slender girl came rushing out. We collided, nearly tumbling to the ground together.

Clutching at each other, we both staggered and regained our balance.

"Elena!" she almost screamed, letting go only to grab me in an even tighter hug.

"Cl...Clemmy?"

My eyes felt as if they were bulging out of my head as I tried to crane my neck back far enough to get a good look at her. Surely this tall girl—graceful somehow despite gangly limbs—could not be my baby sister.

I tried to hide the painful contraction of my heart as I remembered how long it had been since I last saw her.

"Yes, it's me." She pulled free and did a twirl, grinning at me with satisfaction. "Aren't I enormous now?"

"Absolutely enormous. I can't quite believe it." I shook my head. "Jasper was back here for Midsummer—why didn't he tell me you'd become a giant?"

I had spent our time apart trying to picture my sickly sister in full health after her healing a year ago. But I had never imagined her like this. Freed from whatever weakness had plagued her system, she had grown strong beyond even my hopes. Moisture gathered in my eyes.

"I'm fairly sure she's grown a full inch since he was here, and that was only a few weeks ago," said a gruff voice from the doorway. "Welcome home, Elena girl."

I spun around.

"Father! You're home."

He held out his arms, and I ran forward for an embrace. He clasped me quickly and then let go, turning to offer a welcome to my friend.

"We heard you were both arriving today, so we left Thomas to mind the store. Your mother will be home any minute."

I smiled and ushered Coralie inside as I performed all the necessary introductions, forcing myself not to wonder if his hugs had always been that short.

"I've been dying to meet you all and see the famous Kingslee," Coralie said once we were settled and had deposited our bags in the loft which had once been my shared bedroom with Clementine.

I watched my father closely for his reaction. Did my parents resent my bringing a friend home with me? Invading their house and making them uncomfortable in their own space?

My father murmured further polite welcomes, but I knew him too well to miss the uneasiness in his eyes. I bit my lip and turned away to hide my face. Perhaps I shouldn't have let Coralie badger me into bringing her home. I already struggled to fit in here now that I had become a mage—how much worse had I made it by bringing a true mageborn with me?

My mother arrived in a storm of activity, hugging us all, even Father and Clemmy, almost before I'd drawn a breath. Her welcomes to Coralie were long and effusive, and she didn't pause until everyone was sitting with a cup of tea in their hands.

But instead of alleviating my worry, her efforts only exacerbated them. My mother wasn't usually so…intense.

"I was horribly disappointed when Jasper showed up for Midsummer without you," Clemmy said, pouting out her bottom lip, her mischievous manner reminding me that she was still only thirteen, and half child as much as she had suddenly become half woman.

"I'm sorry," I said. "I would have come if I could. I'm sure Jasper explained the situation."

Clemmy's good humor faltered, and I tried to think how to smooth over the awkward moment. Clearly she did know the reason for my absence—and I never wanted her to get the idea that I resented her for it. Not even for a moment. Because for all the trouble it had caused me—and might still cause me—I had never second-guessed my decision to enlist in the Armed Forces in her place. Even if my role as a private meant I could only receive a maximum of two weeks leave a year—and even then, only at the discretion of my commanding officer.

Lorcan was my current superior, despite his lack of rank in

3

the Armed Forces, and I did wish he had let me take my leave at Midsummer. But the Academy Head was far too obsessed with studying me and had put my trip off until the week before classes resumed, when other tasks at the Academy required his attention. Apparently he had thought my week spent at Coralie's home in southern Abalene celebrating her eighteenth birthday to be plenty of frivolity to keep me going until the end of the break.

My mother only made the moment worse by lurching to her feet and pulling me into a suffocating hug.

"My girl. My dear girl. What you've done. And here you are. Not on the front lines at all."

I fended her off and grimaced apologetically at Coralie. My mother might have spent years expecting me to disappear to the front lines as soon as I turned eighteen and enlisted in Clementine's place, but she wasn't usually so emotional. Certainly not in front of outsiders.

My actions seemed to remind her that we had a guest, and she hurried off to boil yet another kettle. Something had certainly put her on edge and off balance. But surely it wasn't my presence. I couldn't bear the thought that I might not have a place here anymore.

Something almost like fear lingered around her, and she wouldn't meet my eyes for more than a second. Surely she couldn't have heard that the third and fourth year Academy students were to visit the front lines this year?

And even if she had, she would no doubt think us safe there, unlike the normal soldiers. To my mother the world of the mageborn was one of privilege and safety—she couldn't even begin to imagine the complexity of the dynamics among the great mage families and the ten mage disciplines. How could she? She had no way to know of my precarious position, balanced between my role as a trainee under the Academy Head, Lorcan, and my new role as a private under General Griffith, the Head of the Armed Forces.

News of my unique powers had apparently made its way throughout the kingdom—or at least the capital. In our world of written power, I was the only Spoken Mage. And when you suddenly found yourself the hope of your kingdom, everyone had an opinion on how you could best be used. It didn't matter that being a weapon in someone else's hands wasn't where I wanted to find myself.

"I've been trying to convince Mother and Father to take me to Corrin for Midwinter since it's been so long since we were all together for a festival." Clemmy's bright voice tried to recapture the earlier mood. "Tell them they have to take me."

My mother flinched, although she tried to hide it by bustling over the tea. Was she concerned that the capital was too dangerous for someone with my sister's weak health? And then I remembered Beatrice and Reese had healed her.

I tried not to think about why else my mother might not want to have the whole family together in Corrin. Not when I was the only one of us who had changed. Instead I changed the subject.

"I suppose it was the healing that made you grow so much?"

Clemmy shrugged, bouncing on her seat with an irrepressible energy that went a long way toward driving off the shadows filling my heart. Whatever changes I had undergone—and whatever they cost me—they were worth it to see Clemmy so well.

"Who knows?" she said. "Maybe?"

Our mother directed an affectionate look her way. "You certainly seemed to shoot up not long after. Mayhap the old weakness just delayed your growth somewhat."

"Did you ever find out who was behind sending Beatrice and Reese to heal her?" asked Coralie.

"You don't know?" my father asked, a sharp edge to his voice. "I've been thinking you were behind it this whole time—or your important friends at any rate."

"I thought it was our friend Finnian at the time," I said slowly. "His father's Duke Dashiell, the Head of the Healers."

"His father, a duke." My mother murmured the words, half shaking her head as she bent over the stove. I tried to ignore the tremor in her voice.

"But then it turned out it wasn't him," said Coralie. "So it was all a great mystery."

She looked at me with raised eyebrows. But a slight twinkle in her eyes made me wonder if she suspected the truth.

"A mystery?" My father frowned. "I don't like the sound of that. To owe so much to someone unknown?"

"We don't owe him anything," I said too quickly, and then bit my lip. Would I ever learn to bite my tongue and keep my silence?

"So you do know who it is." Coralie's smile only reinforced my earlier impression.

I tried to correct myself. "Well, we don't owe him anything for Clemmy, is what I mean. Of course we do owe him in general. Well, not him, more his family. And not owe exactly, but—"

"Who are you speaking of, Elena?" asked my father, cutting me off.

My eyes slid away from his. "It was the prince. Lucas sent the healers."

"Prince Lucas!" My parents exchanged a look, and there was no mistaking the discomfort now. "He did this...for you?"

"No! I mean...yes. Sort of. It's complicated." I knew my attempted explanation was weak, but I subsided into silence despite the interested eyes watching me with varying levels of fear, mistrust, excitement, and pleasure.

I could hardly admit to the truth. The strange, impossible, tangled truth. Lucas had remembered I had a sickly sister. He had cared enough to send healers, had cared enough to try to save me from conscription. But he had not cared enough to save her from conscription—if I had been heartless enough to consider Clemmy's new strength reason to leave our family's conscription responsibility to her. Lucas had no younger siblings, so perhaps he had truly not understood how impossible such a thing would be for me. Or perhaps it proved that his actions had been driven more by strategic thinking where the Spoken Mage was concerned than love for me.

He had kissed me, certainly, and assured me of my importance to him. But then he had let me walk away. His love for me was forbidden, and apparently his feelings did not run deep enough to counteract the barriers that stood between us.

Sometimes I respected him for his duty to our kingdom, for his desire to end this never-ending war and all the death it brought. Other times I railed at him silently for being so focused on the war that he refused to work to bring about the changes needed in Ardann. For believing that unity in fighting Kallorway required he put aside any thought of fighting for the rights of all his subjects, including the commonborn. And sometimes I could think of nothing but the pain that I would never be first for him. That at the end of the day, we could never be together unless laws against the commonborn were changed—something he would not do. He would not fight for me.

The one thing I had not managed to do was succeed in putting him from my mind. None of which boded well for classes resuming in less than a week. How would I sit across from him every day and act like nothing had changed?

"I think coming into Corrin for Midwinter is an excellent idea," Coralie said to Clemmy, saving me.

"Thank you!" Clemmy looked up at Coralie with a slightly bashful enthusiasm. She at least didn't seem to share my parents' strange discomfort.

"Let's go into Kingslee," I said, standing abruptly. When I received several odd looks, I tried to smile normally. "I want to show Coralie the village."

"Can I come too?" Clemmy leaped up, clearing our mugs from the table with such an excess of enthusiasm that she nearly sent two of them crashing to the floor.

7

"Of course," I said, and ushered them both out of the door.

I just need some fresh air, I told myself, as we started down the dirt road toward the distant clump of buildings. *That's all. And then I'll realize I'm being foolish. I could never be unwanted and out of place here. This is my family.*

CHAPTER 2

*T*hree days later, standing in my parents' store, I no longer felt so sure.

The bell above the door clanged, and three women walked in, gossiping among themselves, their hands flying as they punctuated their words with exuberant gestures. But they made it only a couple of steps into the store before they looked up and saw me.

Their movement faltered, and fear transformed their previously animated expressions. The one in the front cast an agonized look at the women behind her, and one of them spoke up quickly.

"Oh! I've just remembered that I have some turmeric at home after all."

The three of them turned tail and fled from the store, not even acknowledging my mother as they went. My eyes flew to her. The stoic cast to her face did nothing to reassure me. Three years ago, one of those women had endured a flare up of her arthritis. She had come to the store for herbs to alleviate it, and I had seen my mother pack twice the weight of herbs in her package as the woman could afford. There had been no fear in her eyes then.

The third silent one had been the Kingslee midwife. Her hands had delivered me and my parents before me. And yet now she turned from us all.

My hands balled into fists before a sudden memory made them begrudgingly relax. Duchess Phyllida, Head of the Seekers, had said once in my presence that she had visited Kingslee herself after my powers appeared. That she had interviewed the midwife who delivered me. Could I blame the woman for turning away now, when I had been responsible for bringing the Grays down on her? The Head of the Grays herself, in fact. Had the midwife's own business fallen off at this sign of mistrust from the most feared branch of the mages?

I had wanted to help out with shelving and serving customers, like I used to do, but I might be more help just by taking myself back to the house. Just by being here I was losing business for my parents. Should I head home, so they could salvage the rest of the day's sales?

I had secretly hoped that my presence might help them, since the half of Kingslee that didn't fear me seemed to hold me in excessive reverence thanks to my newfound *hope of Ardann* status. But whether fear or respect, the end result seemed to be the same. No one wanted to come near me.

The bell sounded again, making me flinch. A young local boy I didn't even recognize wandered in alone, and my body only relaxed when I saw his age. He was here to gaze with longing at the large jars of candies and couldn't care less about the Spoken Mage.

Coralie's face lit up when she saw him, and she hurried over to intercept him at the counter. No doubt he would soon have his desired treat despite his lack of coin.

I seized the opportunity. It wasn't easy to get a private moment with my parents when Coralie knew no one else here and slept in the same room as me. I joined my mother where she was stacking shelves.

"Mother, can I talk—"

"Oh, Elena. There you are." She turned and thrust a small box into my arms. "Could you take this to the back room for me?"

"Of course, but I just wanted to—"

"I need to get this shelf finished off, so could you bring a crate of soap back with you?"

The bell rang again before I could make any further attempt to bring up the question I needed to ask her, so I ducked my head and hurried for the back room, hoping the newcomer wouldn't see me. As I passed through into the safety of the crowded rear of the store, I chewed on my lip.

I needed to ask my parents about my ancestry and why my blood suggested I wasn't fully Ardannian. But my mother and father seemed to be colluding in their efforts to prevent any private talk between us. At first I had put it down to their desire to be polite to Coralie, but I was finding it harder and harder to make excuses to myself. My parents didn't want to talk to me.

When I returned with the soaps, my mother had moved on to another shelf, so I unpacked and arranged them myself. My thoughts swirled, an unsettled feeling gripping me. If I wasn't Elena of Kingslee, who was I? My family had always been my anchor, and I could feel myself starting to come adrift.

"Elena!" The excited voice pulled me up short, and I turned warily. When I got a good look at the speaker's face, I nodded a greeting.

"Alice. Good afternoon."

She smiled brightly, and I tried to hide a wince. She obviously didn't fear me, but I wasn't sure I had the patience for adulation either. Not when I was already feeling on edge. Alice was my own age, but we hadn't spoken since the night I accidentally opened my mouth and discovered a power no one else possessed. And back at that last meeting—when I was just an ordinary girl, like her—she hadn't shown me any great respect. How different would our interaction now be?

"I heard your friend's a mage," she said, watching Coralie deliver yet another candy to the small boy who had successfully wrapped her round his finger.

"Yes, she is," I said warily.

Alice watched for a moment in silence as the little boy laughed before toddling away with a treat grasped in each grubby hand. Coralie pretended to give chase, demanding the return of her candy while the boy squealed in glee.

"She's not like I imagined," said Alice, after they disappeared out of sight down one of the rows of shelves, the laughter floating through the store.

I made myself focus on the other girl. She had chosen to approach me and had no sign of fear on her face. But she didn't have the fervent light of admiration in her eyes either. The one that made me want to go hide under a rock at the weight of expectation.

No, she merely looked intrigued. A slow smile spread across my face. Intrigued I could handle.

"How are you, Alice?" I asked, meeting her eyes for the first time.

"Well enough." She shifted a little nervously and then her face suddenly brightened. "Oh, I almost forgot. The reason I came to find you. I wanted to thank you, for what you did in Abalene. I have cousins who live there."

"I didn't know that."

"Yes, my mother's sister moved down south before any of us were born." She paused, and then spoke all in a rush. "We were all so relieved when we heard what you did. It was amazing."

I shook my head. "Don't believe everything you hear. I didn't turn back that epidemic all on my own, or anything. There were a lot of mages helping, and many of them were far more skilled and important to the effort than me."

"But you helped? Right? You helped heal the commonborn who were sick."

I nodded reluctantly, and she shook her head, the first note of wonder creeping into her expression.

"How incredible," she whispered. "Who would have ever thought someone from Kingslee could do so much good?"

Her voice sounded wistful, and I fixed my attention on the boy and Coralie who had rounded the far end of the shelving and come back into sight, heading toward us. Her emotion rubbed at something painful inside me, something I usually tried to ignore.

I had escaped Kingslee, I had expanded my world beyond anything I could have dreamed possible. But it had been an accident, one I still didn't understand. One no one understood. There could be no equivalent escape for Alice. If she wrote so much as a single word, she would destroy herself and those around her in a fiery explosion. For all the marvels I had managed to achieve, for all my unique power and remarkable control, I could do nothing to change that fate. Alice, and untold others like her, could never read and write. Could never transform themselves into something more than they were born.

The guilt ate away at me. Why me? Why was I so special?

Living in the world of the mages, it was all too easy to forget how the rest of the kingdom lived. But I had sworn to myself to be their champion. The problem was, I didn't know how.

"Johnny!" A sharp voice sounded from the doorway of the store, and the little boy froze. "Get over here at once!"

He hesitated, looking down at the candies in his hands and then up at Coralie who had now caught up to him.

"Johnny!"

Coralie gave him a gentle push toward his mother, whispering that he could keep his prizes, and he cheerfully trundled away. The woman stepped forward and bundled him into her arms, casting quick, nervous glances in our direction. She murmured in his ear as she hurried out of the store, no doubt warning him to keep to his own kind.

I sighed. "We should go back home," I said to Coralie.

Her mouth twisted, but she didn't protest. Coralie came from a minor mage family, rich by our standards, but nothing compared to the great families. She understood the value of money, and I didn't have to explain that my family couldn't afford to have us linger here, driving away customers. Jasper still needed to be funded through a final year at the University, and after three days my presence had already caused more than enough disruption for my family.

"I'll walk back with you," said Alice, as if nothing untoward had happened. I could read in her face that she understood, however, and I wished I could thank her for not sharing the woman's fear and mistrust. But that would no doubt prove far too awkward a conversation for both of us, so I let it drop.

We strolled down the dirt road, Alice talking about her southern cousins and asking Coralie questions about Abalene. Coralie responded in a friendly fashion and kept shooting me small encouraging smiles. They were easy to read. *See*, she was saying, *some of your old friends can still treat you normally.*

"So, do you have a young man here in Kingslee?" Coralie asked, bumping against Alice's shoulder in a teasing way.

Alice glanced quickly up at me and then away, and I remembered how she had been with Samuel the last time I saw her—alone together on a secluded walk near the bank of the local river. Samuel who had a loose tongue, an ugly temper, and a tendency toward bullying. Alice deserved better.

"None at the moment," she said lightly, then paused. Turning to me, she said, "I stopped walking with Samuel after that, you know. It wasn't right, the way he treated that child."

I smiled at her. "I'm glad to hear it. For your own sake."

She nodded, but her eyes strayed toward the river off to our left, and she sighed. "There isn't a great deal of choice here in Kingslee."

Coralie made a sympathetic sound in her throat before pausing and turning in the direction of the river herself. Several clumps of bushes stood between us and the water, and she cocked her head to the side, frowning in concentration.

"Did you hear that?"

I followed her gaze but could see nothing. "No, what was it?"

"I don't know, but it sounded like—" Her words cut off abruptly as she stiffened and then toppled sideways into the dust.

Alice screamed before the sound choked off in her throat, and she too toppled to the ground. The rush of power surrounding them both had come too quickly for me to recognize its approach, but as Alice thudded against the road, I was already yelling, "Shield!"

My own power blossomed around me just as a third wave of power crashed against me. This one felt different from the workings that held my two companions frozen, but I couldn't identify its purpose. The attack ebbed and dissipated, some of my strength draining out as my power kept it at bay.

At the end of second year I had thought myself skilled at the shielding composition. But my skill then was nothing to my current ability, thanks to weeks of grueling one-on-one tutoring with Lorcan. The politics of the upper court had shifted, and I was no longer perceived as a threat, removing the need for Lorcan to keep his distance from my training. And he had apparently been determined to make up for lost time over the empty summer weeks following Coralie's birthday.

We had uncovered no new secrets about either my powers or their origin, but I could now do a single word shielding composition almost without thought. The skill saved me now, and I swayed for a moment with shock as I stared at the two bodies beside me.

To my relief they both still breathed, their eyes staring frantically up at me, although their lips appeared as frozen as their limbs. I stepped toward Alice, who lay closest to me, my shield moving with me, and then thought better of it.

Instead my hands balled into fists, and I took off running for the bushes. I could only guess that Coralie's sharp sense of hearing had precipitated the attack, and perhaps if our attackers weren't fully prepared, I could catch them off guard.

I crashed through the greenery, my shield doing nothing to protect me from their scratches, since I had limited it to magical attacks. I didn't know how much strength I would need before this was over.

"Quick! Grab her! Stop her!" The rough, accented voice hit my ears a moment before my eyes took in three figures in front of me.

A middle-aged woman pointed in my direction, and I could feel the power trailing off her in the direction of my friends. Had she tied their binding to her own energy? A foolhardy move, if so, and perhaps it might allow me the chance to overwhelm her. I narrowed my eyes and focused in on her just as a pair of strong arms grabbed me from behind.

I used my momentum to hurl myself forward, and the man, unprepared, toppled with me. Twisting as we fell, I thrust up my knee, connecting with his stomach. When we landed, his weight drove him hard against my knee, the force of the blow leaving him gasping for air. As he struggled to breathe, I pushed myself back to my feet and spun lightly just as a second man lunged toward me.

"Block," I yelled, and his attempted blow stopped short in mid-air. The crunch of bone sounded from his hand, followed by his scream.

Another rush of power swept over me, and yet more of my energy drained away into my shield.

"I need support," the woman yelled, retreating backward toward the water, her eyes on me. She already held another intact parchment, and as I watched, she ripped it, sending another rush of power my way.

My shield held, but my steps faltered slightly as a wave of fatigue washed over me. Whatever those workings were meant to do, they were powerful. Some of the most powerful I had ever felt.

I glanced quickly back at the road, but the bushes now obscured Coralie and Alice. I hesitated, but the sound of approaching steps drew my attention back to the retreating woman. She already held yet another parchment, and a man had appeared behind her. He held one in his hand as well.

I needed to act quickly and incapacitate them both.

Before I could speak, however, yet more pounding feet approached, this time coming from behind me. Whirling, I saw two newcomers—both robed mages—racing toward us, each with a composition already in his hands.

I was surrounded.

CHAPTER 3

$\mathcal{I}$ had no time to consider the consequences of attempting to incapacitate so many attackers at once. I might not have the strength for it, but if I didn't speak a composition now, I definitely wouldn't once those four attacks hit.

I formed the words I needed in my mind's eye, layering the full sense of the limitations I wanted built into the working over them. But I was too slow. I hadn't spoken even the first word when the two newcomers ripped their compositions.

Two fresh streams of power raced toward me, and I braced, trying to reform the words which had vanished from my mind. But no force hit my shield, both workings brushing past me without contact.

I spun, following their trajectory in time to see the woman's shocked exclamation cut short as both she and the man with her collapsed. No new power whirled through the air, only the weight that hovered over the two of them, holding them down. The thread that had connected the woman to the distant road had dissipated.

My friends.

But I lingered still, properly considering my two attackers

now that I had a moment to do so. Both wore the clothes of commonborn, although they were clearly mages. And the woman had spoken with a distinct accent.

"Elena, are you harmed in any way?" asked one of the robed newcomers, coming up to stand beside me. I turned to get a proper look at him and his companion. Now that I had a moment to think, I could see the differences between these two and the two on the ground. The most obvious being that these wore the robes of Ardannian mages.

And silver robes, too. Officers then, in the Armed Forces. Belatedly, and with reluctance, I straightened and gave a salute.

The second man reached and passed us, going to kneel beside my attackers. He glanced back up at me and signaled for me to be at ease. I let my hand drop and glared at them both.

"What exactly is going on here?" I asked, exhaustion adding extra bite to my voice.

"That's what we intend to find out," said the kneeling one in a grim voice as he moved to examine the second attacker. Already he had stripped the first one of a small pile of compositions, and he now added more to their number. If they all held the strength of the ones used against me, it must have taken a very long time or a small army to produce them.

The mage beside me looked considerably younger than his companion, although still a number of years older than me. He had a pleasant face, darkened from recent days spent in the sun.

The older one looked up and saw him still standing there. Grunting, he jerked his head to the water behind us. "They must have a boat stashed back there. I can't imagine they meant to try to get her out while she was still conscious."

The younger one glanced at me, uncertainty clear on his face, but the older one just jerked his head again.

"Get on with you, Martin. You already saw she can take care of herself well enough."

"Yes sir, Captain Carson," said Martin, his words appropriately respectful, although he winked at me in a friendly manner before obeying his orders.

I watched him walk off, still somewhat dazed, until I started and looked around me.

"There were two other men. I don't think they were mages, but—"

"We dealt with them already," said Captain Carson. "That's what delayed us."

"And my friends?" Even as I said the words, my feet started moving back toward the road.

The captain looked up sharply. "I'd prefer you stay here, Elena, if you don't mind. You might be able to protect yourself, but you must be closing in on exhaustion after that performance." His cool eyes weighed me. "Those workings carried a hefty weight."

I just shrugged, uncomfortable discussing my unnatural strength with a stranger.

"And if I do mind?" I asked, instead.

His hands stilled, and he turned fully toward me. For a long moment our eyes held as we each measured the other's resolve.

"Well, I suppose I'd have to issue an order...private."

My eyes narrowed. So that's how it was. I took a backward step, not taking my focus off his face, to test his reaction. He frowned, and I weighed up my need to check on my friends against the determination I read in his expression.

"Elena!" A breathless cry and hurrying footsteps behind me relieved me of the need to choose. Both Carson and I relaxed, looking away from each other.

Coralie threw her arms around me, and I felt the slight tremble shaking her body.

"Thank goodness you're all right," she said, drawing back and looking in confusion at the scene around me. "What happened? Who are they?"

"I'm just glad you're all right. Both of you," I added, nodding toward Alice who hung back, her eyes round and her face white. "Did that attack hurt you?"

"We'll have a few bruises from landing on the ground, I'm sure," said Coralie. "But that's the worst of it, thankfully. A simple incapacitation, no doubt aimed at you. But what happened?" She looked around again, her gaze jumping from the captain to Martin, who had reappeared from his search of the riverbank.

"All I know is these two attacked us." I gestured at the still prone figures. "And these two saved me." I pointed at the robed mages. "They appear to be officers of ours."

I wrinkled my nose. "And presumably my watchers. Or protectors. Or whatever the Mage Council are calling them this time."

"But I thought Lorcan said you'd come far enough in your training that he'd let you go home this time without them? Since no one had attacked you in over a year."

"Apparently he lied." I could hear the hardness in my voice, but I made no attempt to soften it. I didn't like being lied to. And I had thought the Academy Head and I were past such deceptions.

"Don't look at me," said Martin cheerfully. "I just follow orders."

"A good thing we were here, in the end," said Carson, with a significant look at the two still unconscious mages.

Some of the shock of the attack had started to fade now that I knew my friends were safe, and I nodded at both Martin and Carson. I hadn't seen any sign of them in the last three days which meant they must have been camping out somewhere under constant cloaking compositions. It couldn't have been an enjoyable assignment.

"Yes, you have my thanks, both of you. I don't know what would have happened without you."

"Nothing good, I imagine." Carson nudged the woman at his

MELANIE CELLIER

feet. "We heard this one yelling out. She sounded Kallorwegian to me."

I shivered. I had never met a Kallorwegian in my life and didn't have the experience to recognize their accent. But the captain had the hardened look of someone who had spent more of his life at the front line than anyone should have to, and I didn't doubt his assessment.

"Well you have double thanks from me, then," I said.

"And from us," added Coralie. "I'm Coralie, by the way. Of Cygnet." She named her family, a minor one.

I expected to see hidden contempt from the two officers since Devoras currently ruled the Armed Forces. They tended to consider themselves far too important for anyone not from one of the four great families. General Griffith's twins, Natalya and Calix, had been two of my staunchest enemies in my first two years at the Academy.

But both of the men nodded politely.

"Captain Carson of Callinos," said the older one.

"And I'm Lieutenant Martin of Ellington," said the younger.

Of course. I was letting my exhaustion cloud my thinking. Every discipline included members from across the different families. A Devoras might command the Armed Forces, but the family didn't own them. After I finished being angry at Lorcan for lying to me, I might thank him for at least being considerate enough to assign a Callinos and an Ellington to my detail.

Callinos and Ellington might be great families, but their members had always treated me with more respect than the members of Devoras and Stantorn. And that was aside from the fact that Devoras and Stantorn had both voted for my execution in first year, only for me to later briefly see one of my subsequent attackers among the Stantorns. Lucas had convinced me not to mention it to anyone, that I would never be believed, but that didn't mean I had forgotten. He might trust Devoras and Stantorn, but I did not.

"You were right, Captain," said Martin. "There's a boat tucked away back there, snug as you please. From the looks of things, they've been holed up here for some time. Observing, waiting for the right moment, perhaps."

I frowned. "Coralie heard them. In the bushes. I think it pushed them into acting before they were ready."

Carson's eyebrows rose. "Might explain the poor execution of the abduction attempt."

"Are we sure it was an abduction attempt?" I asked.

"No question," said Martin, holding up a length of rope and a gag he hadn't been carrying when he headed for the river. "No doubt the Kallorwegians are itching to get their hands on our Spoken Mage." He said the words with a slight proprietary air that made me twitch uncomfortably.

Carson gave him a depressing look, and the lieutenant made no more guesses as to the intentions of my attackers.

After a moment of silence, I sighed. "So, what now?"

"Our bindings will hold for some time longer." Martin glanced back toward the bushes where the other two must have been left. "So I suppose we need to find some sort of transport that can get us all back to the capital."

"Too risky," said Carson immediately. "Four prisoners to transport as well as two trainees to protect, and only the two of us?" He shook his head. "And it's already getting on toward dark, too. No. We hole up here for the night and send for help. Reinforcements will be here before morning, and we can head out at first light. With proper transport."

"Hole up?" I asked with a sinking feeling. "And where are we going to do that?"

Carson glanced in my direction. "Your parents' house is big enough for the purpose. And isolated too. No need to go searching for somewhere."

I frowned. That's what I had been afraid of. They obviously

feared a further attack, and they wanted to put my family right in the middle of it.

I opened my mouth to protest when a ray from the lowering sun glinted off one of their silver officer robes. Angrily I slammed my mouth shut. I had already seen enough of Captain Carson to know that protests would be useless, and the gray soldier's uniform back in my wardrobe at the Academy bound me to follow his orders. I would just have to convince my family to spend the night in Kingslee in the store. It might not be the most comfortable, but at least they would be safe there.

Several hours later, I huddled in my family's loft, resting my heavy head against my mother's shoulder. My father sat on my other side, the three of us watching Clemmy and Coralie as they slept in the two loft beds.

I should have known better than to think I could convince them to leave. Even Clemmy had protested so loudly and so long that my parents had relented and allowed us all to stay together.

"That captain seems to know what he's doing," said my father. "He'll keep us all from harm, I have no doubt."

My mother nodded her agreement, having uttered hardly a word since we had arrived in procession at her door. Two girls— Alice having hurried back to the village—two silver-robed mage officers, and four bobbing, unconscious bodies floating beside us. Even I found the sight unnerving, and I had studied the composition that caused it.

After examining the house, Carson had determined that Coralie, my family, and I were to shelter in the loft. He and Martin had produced four fresh compositions which he claimed would keep the prisoners asleep all night. A fifth one had sent power encircling the house, ready to act as an alarm if anyone approached, and a sixth sent a puff of power whooshing off in the direction of the capital.

He had spoken into the final ball of power first, and it had folded itself around his words, carrying them to an officer in Corrin who stood ready to receive such messages. My parents had looked at him as if he were mad, unable to feel the power that his composition unleashed or the way it interacted with his words. But I had been fascinated. I had read about such compositions and been wanting to see one in action for some time.

"A neat working," I said as he directed us all toward the ladder in the loft.

"It has its uses," he replied, "and its limitations. Only works if there's someone ready to receive it on the other end. Too easy to get lost in the noise otherwise."

I began to ask another question, but he gestured more firmly toward the ladder, and I subsided. As I climbed slowly upward, I heard him issuing quiet orders to Martin. The prisoners had all been piled into my parents' bedroom, and he planned to keep all the internal doors of the house open. Carson would position himself in the main, front room of the house, and Martin would take the remaining room.

I might have doubted their ability to stay awake and alert all night except that I couldn't imagine sleeping a wink myself.

Coralie had been far from her usual bubbly, talkative self, and a bruise was already blossoming on one of her arms where she had taken the brunt of her fall. Every time I saw it, I winced, knowing she had only ended up in danger because of her proximity to me.

Clemmy had looked half excited, half terrified, and though I wanted to comfort her, taking on the role seemed to settle Coralie, so I left it to my friend to murmur reassurances to my sister. My parents had expressed no fear aloud, but the uncharacteristic way my mother clung to me did the talking for them. And although my head rested against her shoulder, I had never felt so distant.

My stomach clenched. Did I need any more proof that I no longer belonged in their lives? In only three days my presence had completely overset their ordered, safe world.

"I'm sorry," I said, the words such a faint whisper that only our proximity and the quiet of the house let them hear them.

"Sorry?" My mother pulled away to look at me. "What nonsense is this?"

"I'm sorry for bringing danger to your house." In spite of my resolution to be strong, my voice wobbled. "I'm sorry for being a mage. For changing so much." There, I had said it. I held my breath as I felt their eyes meet over my head. Any moment now they would speak and finally confirm that they had been pushing me away because I was no longer the daughter they raised.

"Oh, girl of mine." My mother sighed. After a breath of silence, she gathered me all the way into her lap. I didn't fit there, curled awkwardly in on myself, my arms and legs overflowing in every direction. But the move was so unexpected that I didn't protest.

For a moment I closed my eyes, and none of this had ever happened. My life was simple again.

Then Coralie whimpered in her sleep and rolled part way over. Reality came crashing back in. Simple meant no Coralie. No Finnian or Saffron. No Lucas. And it meant no written words. No wonder of reading, no exhilaration of composing. It meant words that were only dull and flat and lifeless. It was a past that had become too foreign to comprehend.

But still I craved the old easy assurance of my parents' love.

"Elena girl, you are a wonder," my father said quietly. "You and your brother. And your sister too. You need never apologize for who you are. Not to us. Not to anyone."

"But you've..." My voice dropped. "You've been avoiding me ever since I got back."

"Because we're afraid," said my mother. "And hasn't today shown we have reason to be?" Her arms tightened around me. "Just imagine if those officers hadn't been there. And even aside from the dangers..."

She hesitated, and I extricated myself from her lap so I could see her face.

"What do you have to fear aside from the danger?" I asked. "Aside from me?"

My mother shook her head. "I hope one day you will be a parent yourself, Elena, and then you'll understand. We fear losing you. You live in a different world now. One of power and gold. With duke's sons and a prince. How can anything here compare? How can we compare? I suppose you're right, and I have been avoiding you. Because I didn't want to hear you tell me you no longer fit here with us. You only made it back for a week this year. I was afraid to hear next year you wouldn't be coming back at all."

I stared at her in shock. I had spent three days stewing over the change in my parents, and this explanation had never occurred to me. I had doubted them, and I felt ashamed of it now in the face of their unwavering love.

"You could never lose me," I said, looking between them. "You're woven into my heart far too firmly to be removed. And no duke's son could compare."

My mother gave a half sob and pulled out a handkerchief, but my father watched me with eyes that were far too knowing.

"And what about a prince?" he asked, his voice hardly more than a breath. "Could he compare?"

I flushed and hoped the darkness would cover it. He nodded once, slowly.

"Watch yourself, Elena girl. Don't get in over your head."

I tried to think of a response but couldn't. It was already far too late for such advice, but I could hardly admit as much to him.

Silence enveloped us, broken only by the deep breathing of

Coralie and Clemmy, and the occasional rustle of movement from the officers downstairs. Released from my previous worries, I felt exhaustion pulling at me. Perhaps I could sleep after all. I swayed, my head pulling me downward toward my pillow until I suddenly remembered the reason I had been trying to get one of them alone ever since my arrival.

I sat up straight again and turned toward my father. When day dawned, I would have to leave for Corrin with the officers, cutting short my stay. This was my last chance.

"You said never to apologize for who I am. But who exactly am I?"

CHAPTER 4

$\mathcal{M}$y mother straightened, her voice sharp despite the low volume. "You're our daughter, that's who you are. As I told you when they first dragged you away. The mages themselves came and questioned us and confirmed it the truth."

"Aye, that you are," said my father. "You're our blood, right enough, despite the wonder of you." He paused. "Why do you ask? What lies have they been telling you?"

"No lies," I said. "Unless my blood itself can lie." But my own words fell on my ears with a false ring. I hadn't tested the blood for myself—I wouldn't even know how to begin such a task. My information came from Lorcan, and from Jessamine, the University Head.

And Lorcan had proved himself less than trustworthy.

I could think of no reason why he would lie about this, however. And he and Jessamine had been eager to hear if I could shed any more light on their information. It would have made no sense for them to lie.

"Blood? You are of my blood and your father's. I swear it," said my mother.

"That's not in question, Mother. The issue is before that."

My parents exchanged a confused look, although my mother looked somewhat relieved.

"You mean your grandparents?"

I shrugged. "Maybe? All I know is that my and Clemmy's blood showed that we are not fully Ardannian. Or at least, our ancestry isn't."

"Not Ardannian?" my father asked in astonishment at the same moment as my mother said, "Clemmy's blood?"

I bit my lip, a faint ghost of my former anger tainting my words. "They took both of our blood for studying. Don't worry, I've let them know it can't happen again. Not without our knowledge at least."

My parents exchanged another look, but it didn't hold the anger I had expected. Whatever passed between them flowed too quickly for me to interpret, and then my father was turning back to me.

"What do you mean not Ardannian?"

I shrugged. "That's all I know. Something in our blood showed we have ancestry from outside Ardann."

"Sekali ancestry or Kallorwegian?" He looked as if he meant to spit at the mention of our enemies, as so many commonborn did, but a single glance around made him hesitate. We had brought extra sleeping pallets up to the loft, cramming them into the limited space, and there was no safe target to direct his ire toward.

I shrugged again. "I told you. I don't know. I was hoping you would know."

"Your grandparents were all born right here in Kingslee," my father said, sounding angry that anyone could question that.

The officers had snuffed out all the candles to give them a better view out the windows, so only the dim light of the moon filtered through to the loft. I could barely make out my parents' faces and movements, so I nearly missed the subtle hand my

VOICE OF DOMINION

mother placed on my father's arm, or the brief look she flashed
at him.

He took a breath and calmed somewhat.

"You know, I remember your mother telling me a story once,"
she said to him. "It was so many years ago now I'd completely
forgotten. She was telling me all about the romance between
your father's grandparents. How he left Kingslee and spent a year
roaming Ardann. His parents despaired that he would ever
return and take his place running the family store, but he eventually reappeared, and with a wife in tow. Said he found her in the
northwest where her family had been killed by some illness. It
was quite the scandal at the time, I believe, as he was considered
one of the most eligible young men in Kingslee before he left."

My father's brow crinkled. "My mother never spoke to me of
any romance that I remember. But now that you mention it, I do
remember she used to make little remarks about my father's
grandmother being an odd woman. You think perhaps his grandfather traveled beyond Ardann?"

My mother looked thoughtful. "It's possible, surely. Or that
his grandmother crossed the border herself. Those northwestern
forests extend far beyond the border on both sides. And although
the border with the Empire has always been closed, there was no
war with Kallorway back in those days."

My father's hands balled into fists at the mention of our
western neighbor, no doubt giving him the physical outlet he
couldn't get through spitting.

"I suppose it's possible," he said reluctantly. "But we are
talking about a great many generations back. I am sure we are
hardly the only family to have such intermingled history. There
can be no question of treason in such a thing."

"Treason?" I stared at him. "No indeed. We don't even know
for sure that she was Kallorwegian."

"Yes, calm down," my mother murmured, almost too quietly
for me to hear.

"Well, I suppose that explains that mystery," I said. But what relevance could such a thing possibly have to my abilities? And even if it was somehow impossibly connected, why did my siblings not possess the same capability? Or my father?

I frowned. "There was one more thing."

My mother flinched, and this time it was my father who reached over a steadying hand. My frown deepened.

"They said they found some sort of...markers in my blood. Whatever that means. I don't think they know themselves. Markers that they didn't find in Clemmy's."

A hiss like an indrawn breath sounded.

"Mother? Do you have any idea what could cause a difference between my blood and my sister's?"

She was shaking her head before I had finished speaking.

"You are my blood and your father's, as I already said. As is Clementine. As is Jasper."

"We know nothing of blood markers," my father said, his voice curt. "And we should all be getting some sleep. Those officers want you all on the road by first light."

I looked slowly between the two of them. My mother met my eyes almost defiantly, while my father turned to busy himself with his sleeping pallet.

"Very well then," I said, reluctance making my voice slow. "I can let them know about your father's grandmother at least."

"Let them spend their time searching out our ancestry if they so desire," my father said, still not looking at me. "And good luck to them. My great grandparents were an odd couple by all accounts, but it's no nevermind of mine."

I didn't answer, slipping silently down to rest my head against my pillow instead. But it took a long time for sleep to come.

I had learned nothing that seemed to shed any light on my mysterious abilities. Nothing except that my parents appeared to have a secret. One they weren't willing to share with me.

As it turned out, we were all woken before dawn by the arrival of troops from Corrin. The two silver-robed officers leading them had brought a cart to carry the prisoners, a carriage for Coralie and me, mounts for Martin and Carson, and a whole squad of commonborn soldiers.

The racket of their arrival was enough to wake even Clemmy, who my mother had informed me was now a deep sleeper. The four officers conferred and loaded the prisoners into the cart before permitting us to come down from the loft. The first rays of dawn were piercing the windows by then, and it was only with reluctance that Carson agreed to allow us to eat a quick breakfast before departing.

When the carriage door closed on us and the vehicle lurched into motion, I looked across at Coralie. It was our first chance to talk alone since the attack.

"Don't look at me like that, Elena," she said.

"You hosted me for a week at your home at the start of summer, and it was one of the best weeks of my life. I host you and it's, well, not."

She snorted a brief laugh. "It wasn't that bad!"

"Wasn't it?" I raised an eyebrow at her. "And I'm not just talking about the attack."

She shook her head. "I loved meeting your family—especially Clemmy. You talk about her so much. And seeing Kingslee. It's so much smaller than Abalene. I've never spent time in a fully commonborn village like that..." She trailed off.

"And was it everything you imagined?" I asked, dryly.

"I don't know what I imagined, to be honest." She chewed on her lip and shifted a little in her seat. "You're always saying we should make more of an effort to understand the commonborn. So I thought it was a good place to start."

So that was why she had insisted on accompanying me. Once

again demonstrating how much more open-minded Coralie was than most of her peers. And that difference in attitude made even more sense to me now that I had spent more time in her family home. As a minor family, the Cygnets seemed a great deal less formal than their counterparts among the great families, and they interacted freely with their commonborn servants, even assisting them in their tasks when needed.

"Well, it turned out we weren't the only mages in Kingslee," I said, a sour note in my voice.

"No. I admit the visit would have been improved by the absence of a Kallorwegian attack."

I winced. "I'm so sorry you got caught up in that."

"It's hardly your fault that you're so extraordinary everyone wants you." She gave me an exaggerated wink, and I laughed reluctantly.

Her face fell into more serious lines, and she hesitated before speaking.

"It wasn't right for him to lie to you, but I have to admit I'm glad Lorcan sent officers to watch over us. As it turned out." She looked at me tentatively, and I forced myself to nod.

She was right, of course, and her hesitation hurt me more than I cared to admit. Coralie was my best friend, and she seemed to expect me to fly off the handle. Lucas was always telling me I overreacted, too. I just wished either of them could understand what it was like to be so constantly beset on every side, out of place wherever you went. Threatened, mistrusted…

I gave myself a mental shake. I had a family who loved me, powers no one had ever dreamed of, and access to unlimited words. Alice's face formed in my mind, shaken and white, defenseless against our attackers, and then before that—wistful but hopeless.

A whole kingdom of commonborns would never have the opportunities I'd been given. I had a duty and a responsibility to them, and I couldn't advocate for them among the mages if I continued to let my unruly tongue get the better of me. It was time to overcome that particular weakness.

"You know…I'm glad, too," I said. "If he hadn't sent them, I'd be on my way to Kallorway right now, and for some reason I vastly prefer being here with you."

"Goodness, I can't imagine why," she said in a joking voice, and we both laughed. The release of tension lightened the air in the carriage, lifting the cloud that had hung over us since the attack.

The day was still only beginning when we rolled into the capital. The small houses on the fringes slowly grouped closer together as I watched through the window, pressing against each other into a solid mass of building. Unlike the year before, the weather was already starting to cool, and I saw the occasional tree in one of the small parks already stripped of most of its leaves.

The tall row houses gave way to elegant storefronts as a growing feeling of homecoming rose in me. Was it possible to feel at home both in a simple three-roomed house on a dirt road and in a crowded city among mansions of white marble and red sandstone?

It was only the streets that felt familiar in this part of the city, though. I had never actually been inside one of the mageborn city estates.

Still, the sight of them signaled the approach of the Academy, and not even the beautiful, elegant palace towering above us could lessen the pleasant glow of turning in at those familiar gates. If I was fortunate, I would have no cause to visit the palace this year. I certainly couldn't imagine Lucas would be inviting me to his Midwinter birthday celebrations.

The thought of the prince made my stomach clench and my eyes turn glassy, as I imagined an altogether different scene from the one visible out the carriage window. Was he already here? Would I run into him in the corridors? In the dining hall?

What would he do? What would I say? I didn't dare hope that he might have changed his mind over the summer break, that he might have decided he was willing to fight for change after all.

"Elena?" Coralie peered up at me from outside the open carriage door. We had stopped in the Academy courtyard, and she had alighted without my noticing. I jerked and scrambled quickly down.

"Sorry, my mind was elsewhere."

"It's strange how much more familiar it grows every year, isn't it?" She joined me in my contemplation of the square building of white marble. "And even stranger to think that next year will be our final year at the Academy. After we graduate, we won't have any reason to return. Well, not until we have children old enough to attend," she added, with a giggle.

Children. The idea felt too foreign to even contemplate. Before I could get married, I would have to forget about a certain tall, dark-haired, green-eyed year mate. Unthinkable. An impossible task.

I shivered.

"Let's get inside, shall we?" Suddenly contemplating the future was the last thing I wanted to do.

Coralie followed me eagerly enough, and we found the entryway deserted, due no doubt to the early hour. Together we headed for the broad, elegant stairs. Climbing past the instructor suites and classrooms on the next level and the fourth-year suites on the level above them, we stopped on the third years' floor. We had finally achieved enough seniority to spend the year in suites rather than the single rooms that filled the higher floor for students in the two junior years.

I had been living in mine for some weeks now, but Coralie wanted to examine every inch of hers, exclaiming at the extra space and the simple yet elegant furnishings.

"It will be so nice to have proper study space in our own

rooms." She patted the enormous desk. "There's enough space that we could study together in the evenings."

I nodded, murmuring something noncommittal. My head said it was a very good thing indeed. If only my heart wasn't telling me how much I would miss nights spent studying in the library with Lucas. But being alone with Lucas in the depths of the library in a single shared circle of light seemed like more than a bad idea.

I extracted myself as soon as Coralie would allow it. I didn't doubt that Lorcan now had a full account of the attack, since Captain Carson and Lieutenant Martin had continued on to the Academy with us while the newer officers split off with the soldiers and the cart of prisoners.

Like many other mages in positions of authority, Lorcan's wont had always been to question other senior mages about happenings of interest rather than me—even if I was the sole witness. But I wanted to talk to him, even if he didn't want to talk to me.

I let myself into the receiving room outside his study and hesitated before the door. It stood partially ajar, and I could hear no sound of voices. The officers had already left, then.

"Come in," called Lorcan as I raised my hand to knock.

I rolled my eyes and pushed the door open. The bookshelves that lined two of the walls of the large room no longer impressed me as they had done on my first day at the Academy. But I still appreciated their presence, along with the tall windows that gave a view over the gardens to the rear of the Academy. Combined, they gave the room a pleasant aspect that had made the long hours I spent here over the summer more tolerable.

"Ah, Elena, I was about to send for you," said Lorcan.

So he had intended to speak to me directly. Progress, then.

"I wanted to find out if you had a chance to speak to your parents about any known irregularities in your ancestry."

I blinked at him for a moment. So much for the progress. I

considered protesting and bringing up the attack or Captain Carson and Lieutenant Martin's presence in Kingslee, but I remembered my resolution in the carriage.

"There is some question as to the origins of my grandfather's grandmother."

He raised an eyebrow. "That is a great many generations back."

I shrugged. "Everyone since then has come from Kingslee, apparently. They were all as Ardannian as you." One side of my mouth quirked up. "Unless there's something you haven't told me."

"Very amusing, Elena." He drummed the fingers of one hand lightly against the desk. "Your grandfather's grandmother." He murmured the words, shaking his head. "I cannot see what relevance that would have to the…" His mutterings dropped so low I couldn't catch the words.

I walked over to one of the windows to look at the view, leaving him to his musings. The last of the summer flowers had died in the week I had been gone.

"Will we continue our training now that the year has begun?" I asked without turning back around.

"What? Oh. No, you will need the time for your regular studies, and I will be busy with my own duties. You've come a long way, and Jessamine and I will need time to consult before we have any more experiments for you to try. And perhaps it would be worth looking into this ancestor after all. Perhaps Jessamine will…"

I sighed and glanced over my shoulder at him. He had taken up a pen and begun to scribe something on a piece of parchment before him, still muttering indistinguishably.

Shaking my head, I crossed over to the door but paused with my hand on the latch.

"Lorcan."

He looked up.

"Yes, Elena."

"The Kallorwegians tried to abduct me yesterday."

"Indeed, I had the full report from Captain Carson. He says you performed admirably."

I gave him a flat look.

"You needn't feel any concerns. You are perfectly safe here at the Academy. After the incursion in your first year we have been to considerable pains to shore up our protections. No trainee under my care is in danger, I assure you."

"You told me you weren't sending mages to watch me."

For the first time he had the grace to look uncomfortable. "Consider it a test. To see how you performed when not under supervision."

"And I performed admirably, you said." My voice was expressionless.

He nodded, still looking uncomfortable.

"Then I can assume there will be no more secret tests?"

"No, indeed," he said quickly. "I can foresee no need for such a thing."

"That's good." I paused for a moment as if the topic were done. "Oh, I hear General Griffith is eagerly anticipating the completion of my time at the Academy. I wonder what plans he has for my next posting after I am no longer under your command?"

The general was a Devoras, and I didn't trust him one bit. And that was on top of his desire to use me as a weapon. I would never willingly choose the Armed Forces over the Academy, but thanks to Lucas, I had never actually told Lorcan of my suspicions regarding Devoras. He no doubt considered me just rash enough that I might throw myself at the front lines if he offended me enough. And the Academy Head wouldn't want to lose his most interesting subject of study—any more than a senior member of Callinos would want to lose a pawn as significant as me to a Devoras.

I looked at him for a long moment, meeting his eyes without backing down. His gaze changed from uncomfortable to considering, and then a calculating gleam filled his eyes. I pulled the door open before pausing a second time.

"Don't lie to me again, Lorcan. You might not like the consequences."

"Very well, Elena," he said, his voice as serious as my own.

But as I stepped out of his office, I saw the beginnings of a satisfied smile. Almost like that of a teacher whose pupil had made him proud. Finally I was learning to play the game.

CHAPTER 5

innian and Saffron, my Callinos friends, didn't show up in the dining hall until breakfast on our first morning of classes. Our other year mates had moved up to the row of third year tables as soon as they arrived, but Coralie had been insisting we eat with some of the first years.

Her younger brother Arthur—whose enthusiasm for the Academy had known no bounds on the previous occasions I had met him—was now trying to act as if his entry to the Academy was no big deal. But Coralie cheerfully overrode his protests as well as his requests that she would, "Go sit with her own kind." And so we ate all our meals until the start of classes with him.

And from the way he kept looking at me and then quickly away, and then back again, and then at the other first years who had arrived early, I wondered if perhaps he didn't mind our presence after all. The sixteen-year-olds in his year seemed torn on their opinion of me—but opinions they all seemed to have. And Arthur personally knowing the one and only Spoken Mage clearly gave him a position of some interest among them.

I tried not to dwell on how utterly strange such a thing felt. If being an object of awe and terror among my old friends in

Kingslee had been strange, this was even stranger again. And when I got called to Lorcan's office from lunch one afternoon, it struck me as I left the dining room that I felt no surprise or trepidation at the summons. Some of Arthur's year mates had looked nervous at a summons from the Head—even if it wasn't for them. It was easy to recall that I would have felt the same when I first arrived—magnified many times in fact.

Less easy to pinpoint was the moment when I started to belong. When a call to the Head's office evoked no more extreme reaction than mild irritation that I had not yet finished my meal.

And when Lorcan told me the purpose of our meeting, a further sense of satisfaction swelled in me. He had called for me in order to update me on information regarding my attackers. It seemed my earlier challenge had generated the desired effect.

Less satisfying was the news itself. All four of them had been questioned under the influence of carefully crafted compositions that compelled them to speak truth. They were intelligence agents, smuggled across the border with a raiding party. Their sole goal had been my abduction, and they knew nothing of the reasons for it. They had no links to other Kallorwegian intelligencers in Ardann, and they knew nothing of the overall plans for the war. Lorcan assured me that they would have been carefully chosen with this lack of knowledge in mind.

"So they knew there was a good chance they would be caught?" I asked.

He nodded, and I frowned. Two mages—trained intelligencers, too—seemed a big sacrifice just for a chance of stealing me. But was it possible they had already tried without a mage and failed? I had never believed Kallorway was truly behind my abduction attempt in first year. Particularly not once I saw one of my abductors with the Stantorns. But was it possible the man had been an intelligencer placed with the Stantorns by Kallorway?

But, no, that made no sense. He had been arrested and apparently died in prison. I still didn't know how he had faked his own death, but the Stantorns would certainly have noticed his unexpected resurrection and return.

Unless they had been the ones to make it happen, of course. And my abductors in first year had used inside knowledge of my exams that Kallorway could not possibly have acquired. No, despite Lucas's insistence, I still believed at least one of the great families had chosen to act against the ruling of the Mage Council. Traitorous behavior Lucas believed to be impossible.

The thought gave me no joy, and I wished I could talk to my friends about it. But I had never wanted to burden them with my fears. Especially when I had no proof.

The arrival of Finnian and Saffron at breakfast the next morning cheered me up, however.

"Welcome, welcome, welcome." Coralie bounced over to Saffron and gave her an enthusiastic hug. When she turned to Finnian, however, she paused, almost imperceptibly. He didn't seem to notice, swooping her up and spinning her around before putting her back on her feet. He turned immediately to me and did the same thing.

"Someone's awfully happy to be back in class," I said. "Terrible up north, was it?"

I rolled my eyes at the other two girls, and Saffron shook her head, a smile tugging at her lips. Coralie smiled as well, a beat late, before taking a seat at one of the third year tables. I watched her with narrowed eyes, but I couldn't say anything in front of the others, so I simply sat down beside her.

"Cutting it a bit fine," I said to the Callinos cousins. "When did you get in?"

"Last night, late," said Saffron, filling her plate with enthusiasm from the platters a servant had already delivered. "Our families wanted us to stay until the last possible moment."

"Was your father home for the summer then?" I asked Finnian, aware that his father's role as Head of the Healers often took him away from their northern home in Torcos.

"For a few weeks. But it was my mother who wanted me to stay." He smiled at us all. "It wasn't too bad, though, since I had Saffron to keep me company."

"Finnian's estate is about twice the size of ours," said Saffron. "I think Aunt Helene gets lonely. Plus my mother has a number of health concerns, so we often spend as much as half the year there. They're sisters," she explained to me, "and they both married into Callinos, so they've always been close."

That explained why Finnian and Saffron were so close—more like siblings than cousins.

"It's sweet that they love you so much and didn't want to miss any time with you," said Coralie.

"More like anxious than sweet." Finnian frowned. "It's these rumors of the front line, they have them on edge."

"Is it true?" Saffron directed the question at me. "The third and fourth years are to go to the front lines to train?"

I shrugged, raising both hands. "Don't look at me."

"I thought you spent most of the summer here training with Lorcan," said Finnian. "Coralie wrote to us about it."

I directed a curious look at my friend, but she didn't meet my eyes, her attention firmly focused on her plate.

"I wasn't the one asking the questions," I said. "But—" I hesitated. "If you want my guess, I think it's true. There must have been an officer here visiting with Lorcan once a week over the summer. The colonel from the main training barracks even came herself several times."

"What? Colonel Jennica?" Finnian raised both eyebrows. "Then it must be true. What else would Lorcan need her for?" He glanced around the table at us. "No one else has more experience with raw recruits."

When none of us responded, he pointed his fork at each of us, ending with himself. "That's us. The raw recruits. If you didn't pick it up."

"We got it, thank you," said Coralie, in a voice of long-suffering.

Finnian looked at her with a gleam in his eyes, but his response was lost in the sound of the bell. At least half of the trainees remained in the dining hall, so we weren't the only ones caught off guard. Obviously many of our fellow trainees were having the same difficulty as us getting back into the rhythm of our usual schedule.

And one trainee had yet to show up at the Academy at all. But I was determinedly not thinking of him, so I pushed the thought back with all the other thoughts I was determinedly not thinking.

"Ugh, Thornton will have us all running extra laps now," said Saffron as we rushed out to the training yards behind the Academy. Our combat instructor had no patience with tardiness.

"You're forgetting," said Finnian with a grin. "Thornton will be with the first years this week. We're in the clear."

"You'd better watch out, Finn," said Saffron with a shake of her head. "The junior instructors for the third years might not find you as charming as the second year instructors did."

"Impossible." He placed his hand on his heart as if wounded while winking at Coralie and me.

I groaned but smiled back at him. Coralie, on the other hand, just looked away. Finnian watched her, a slight crease between his brows, but we arrived at the yard before any further words were exchanged.

As Finnian had predicted, the junior instructor accepted our late arrival without complaint and soon had us running the normal number of warm up laps. I moderated my pace and let our two Callinos friends draw ahead.

"What is going on with you?" I whispered to Coralie.

"What do you mean?" She tried to sound innocent, but she still wouldn't meet my eyes.

"You've gotten weird ever since Finnian and Saffron arrived." I prodded her lightly. "Well, let's be honest, I don't think it's Saffron that's the issue."

Dariela passed us, her long legs having already lapped us around the yard. I fell silent for a moment until she continued on out of ear shot.

"You wrote to them over the summer?"

Coralie flushed. "Remember how they stayed on for a couple of extra days after you left to come back here after my birthday?"

I nodded.

"Well, Finnian and I might have...well, we might have kissed." She finished the sentence in a rush.

"What!?" I squawked the word so loudly I drew a reprimand from our instructor and quickly lowered my voice again. Thank goodness we didn't have Thornton today since he would never have countenanced our obvious distraction, and this wasn't a story I could wait to hear.

"You and Finnian. Kissed! We've been together for over a week now, and you never told me! Coralie!"

"Sorry!" She grimaced at me apologetically. "I didn't know what to say. It's not like we're a couple now." Her eyes strayed over to where Finnian ran effortlessly beside Calix. "At least, I don't think. He never said anything about..."

"I'm going to smack him around the head." I glared in his direction.

"No!" Coralie turned and grabbed my arm, slowing our pace enough to earn another rebuke from the instructor. We both sped up, but she kept her pleading eyes fixed on me.

"Don't say anything to him. Please don't. It was just a summer kiss. And I'm going to go back to being normal and all of us friendly just like always. I just...Seeing him again...I need a day to adjust."

"I thought you liked Edmond," I hissed.

"I do, he's very nice. But it was never serious between us. Or anything at all, really. I haven't even seen him since your birthday celebrations last spring."

"So, if you like Finnian now, why does it have to go back to like it was before?" I asked, more confused than ever.

We slowed down as we approached the end of the final lap.

"Because it wasn't serious with Finnian either. We spend all day together every day here. If we tried being a couple, and it didn't work…" She shook her head. "Better to wait and leave serious relationships for after we graduate. Finnian feels the same way. I swear."

She dropped her voice and threw me a conspiratorial smile. "I'd just forgotten how utterly delicious he is to look at."

I raised both eyebrows at her, and she giggled. Rolling my eyes, I let a smile tug up one corner of my mouth.

"I suppose he is easy enough to look at," I whispered as we joined the others. "But don't think you're getting out of telling me every single detail later."

I gave her a mock glare, and she laughed at me. I turned away, a smile lingering on my own lips, only to find a pair of brilliant green eyes fixed on my face.

Lucas looked away quickly, but my smile had already disappeared. Why was it suddenly hard to breathe? I had to restrain my hands from reaching for my throat. Where had all the clear air gone?

The instructor ordered us to begin a series of stretching exercises, and I fell into place, a step behind everyone else. Suddenly Coralie's behavior made all too much sense.

Finnian was handsome, with his golden skin, twinkling eyes, and dark, silky hair—but he couldn't compare with our prince. I had thought I could perfectly recall his image, but I found now I had forgotten something of the breadth of his shoulders. Not to mention the intensity of his eyes, or the way his dark hair framed his strong features.

Or maybe it wasn't the way he looked at all, but an ineffable something in the way he carried himself. All I knew was that despite thinking of little else for days, I wasn't in the least prepared to be standing mere feet away from him again.

Coralie had claimed she only needed a day to adjust. I could only hope I regained my equilibrium that quickly. I had positioned myself behind him and to one side, but my eyes must have been burning into his back because he turned to glance at me, his eyes going straight to mine.

This time I was the one to quickly look away. I wished I could read his expression, but I had never been much good at that, and when I dared to look again, I could see only a sliver of the side of his face. But it was enough to know his usual court mask was back in place.

At least the exercise could be blamed for the flush on my face. Although with the way Natalya was watching me with narrowed eyes, I should probably be working on my own impassive expression.

"You'll begin in the arena tomorrow." The instructor's words broke through the haze that had taken over my mind, and I looked up quickly. So soon?

At her announcement, every trainee in the year—save one—turned to look at me. I glanced from left to right, wondering if I'd missed a question directed at me, but the instructor continued on with further details of our weekly schedule, and gradually they all looked away.

I slunk down into myself. Of course. The last time we had all been in the arena I had done the impossible and defeated the two strongest trainees in our year with a single word composition. I had almost let the familiar environment of the Academy make me forget. My status had changed. I was a wonder. An impossibility. A weapon. In a kingdom trapped in a decades-old war.

I dreaded finding myself back in the arena with my year mates. I had actually enjoyed the days my training with Lorcan took me there. Stretching my power to its fullest extent against

the strongest of opponents had been more satisfying than I anticipated. But in truth, my year mates could no longer challenge me.
And even the prospect of pummeling Natalya or Weston held no
appeal. Not when we would be so unevenly matched.

The thought bothered me all the way back to the Academy
building, and I trailed behind my friends, too lost in the turmoil
of my own thoughts to contribute any coherence to their conversation. But voices from several steps behind me broke through
my perturbation.

"You're late," said Calix to whoever he walked with.

"I had royal business to attend to."

I sucked in a breath, my posture stiffening and then slumping
again as I told myself to act naturally. Little hope of that, it
seemed. I just wished I knew if he was affected the same way.
And also if my emotions were broadcast across my face—I wasn't
sure I could bear the humiliation, if so.

"Will Their Majesties permit you to accompany us to the
front lines?" Calix asked after a moment's silence.

"Of course." Lucas sounded faintly surprised. "I'm a third year
and must complete the required course work just like everybody
else."

"I'm surprised old Thaddeus hasn't put his foot down and
forbidden it." I could hear the mocking smile in Calix's voice. I
should recognize it since it had been directed at me often
enough.

"Who says he hasn't tried?" If there was amusement in Lucas's
voice, it was harder to detect. "But since it's his duty to protect
me, the Head of the Royal Guard could hardly advocate for my
failing the Academy."

I knew he wasn't serious, but just the idea made me shiver.
For my year mates, failure meant incarceration. And the vision of
Lucas in chains made me want to cry. He was already bound
enough by his birth and position, never free to follow his own
inclinations. I had only seen his true intensity and power break

through his careful mask a handful of times, and it had always taken my breath away. Normally he kept it tightly under control. If only he could truly be free.

I risked a single glance back at them. Utter foolishness. Lucas smiled lightly at General Griffith's son—the closest anyone in his world came to being his equal—the image of royal privilege and confidence.

If he saw me looking, he gave no sign. Instead it was Calix who met my eyes this time, and what I saw there unnerved me almost as much as Lucas's presence. Because it wasn't disgust. Or anger. It carried no threat that I could perceive. Instead his gaze looked considering, almost as if it asked something of me.

And that felt more threatening than anything else.

I sped up, joining my friends and driving them on faster. Coralie glanced behind us once, but when she saw who followed us, she made no protest at the quicker pace. And later when we shared cups of tea in her suite and giggled about Finnian, she asked me no questions, for which I blessed her. Our friend we could laugh and joke about, but the prince was out of bounds. In every way that mattered.

CHAPTER 6

The next morning I remembered to let my friends know that the rumors about our trip to the front lines were true. As son of the Head of the Armed Forces, Calix would know. The topic occupied us all on the walk outside, but we fell silent as we crossed into the arena and took our places just outside the bubble of power that always enclosed the arena floor.

To our surprise, Thornton awaited us. He usually spent at least the first week with the new first years, but he offered no explanation for his presence, and no greeting for the new year. Instead he announced that the first bout would be a display exercise between Lucas and me.

Every muscle in my body seized, and I might not have made it to my feet without Coralie's prodding. Slowly I climbed down the stairs from where I had been sitting in the tiered arena seating. Was Thornton trying to torment me?

The sad answer was probably yes. At least based on his past behavior.

But when I reached the rough arena floor, I realized Lucas had made no move to step into place for a bout, and his sword remained sheathed at his side. He stood expectantly in front of

Thornton, his focus on our instructor. I joined him, trying to pretend I wasn't acutely aware that we stood so close our arms almost brushed against each other.

Thornton handed us each a parchment, and I scanned it with furrowed brows. Slowly they lifted as I skimmed down the paragraphs. It was possibly the longest composition I had ever seen, taking up both sides of a full parchment.

The nature of our bout became clear as I deciphered the intention behind the working. Lucas, on the other hand, displayed no surprise—likely he had already been aware that our studies were to look a little different this year.

Thornton directed us both where to stand, one on each side of the small section of seating taken up by our year mates.

"For the purpose of the display, please talk at a sufficient volume for all to hear," he said. "You will release the compositions on my mark."

I frowned at him even as my hands gripped the parchment, ready to rip. Did he think Lorcan had already prepared me, as Lucas had clearly been prepared? Or did he hope for me to fail?

But he had called this a demonstration bout, which meant he intended everyone to learn something from it. And if there was one thing Thornton cared about, it was preparing his trainees for the front lines. He wouldn't waste a composition like this on humiliating me.

"Mark," he called, and I ripped the long parchment in half, letting the pieces flutter to the ground in front of me. They glowed a hazy green as five life-size figures—a little fuzzy and indistinct, but clearly human in form—sprang into existence. Three men and two women, all dressed in green uniforms, arrayed themselves in a defensive position around a green crown that rested on the arena floor some distance away. Two carried bows and quivers of arrows, and the remaining three clutched spears and small round shields.

Across the empty arena, five equally transparent figures dressed in yellow formed a ragged line.

"Advance on the crown," called Lucas, in a loud voice, as instructed.

"Archers, shoot when ready," I called to my own troops.

Each of my archers obediently drew their bows, waiting for the yellow uniformed figures to come into range of their arrows. I glanced across at Lucas. Surely he did not mean to send his soldiers marching in a row to their deaths?

But he pulled a much smaller parchment from a pocket in his white robe and ripped it. Instantly a roiling dark smoke filled the space between our opposing forces, washing over and entirely obscuring his transparent troops.

I narrowed my eyes. Unlike real people, his counterfeit soldiers had no need to breathe and were presumably undisturbed by the screen he had created. Meanwhile my own archers had let their bows drop uselessly to their sides and stood motionless, awaiting further instruction.

An arrow flew from the smoke and cut down one of my spear-wielding men. He toppled over before dissipating into nothingness. I ground my teeth, my mind racing as I tried to think of a relevant composition.

Almost fumbling the binding words in my haste to speak them, I muttered a composition to clear smoke. Thornton might have instructed us to speak loudly, but no one could read what Lucas had put on his parchment, and I didn't intend to be disadvantaged.

My power rushed out, pushing the smoke with it, and as soon as the yellow figures re-emerged, my two archers drew their bows again, firing arrows with perfect aim. Two of Lucas's soldiers went down, and he called loudly for a retreat.

His next composition sent a small forest sprouting out of the earth, providing cover between his troops and mine. I called for mine to close in more tightly around the crown, forming into a semi-circle facing toward the new greenery.

When Lucas called for his archers to take up position out of sight in the treetops, I erected a simple wooden wall around my troops. I hadn't done any studies in the creator discipline, however, and in the time it took me to come up with the words and then speak them, one of my archers was killed.

We went back and forth in a slow battle of attrition as we each tried different tricks. Finally, with only two soldiers remaining on either side, Lucas yelled a sudden order for his to charge. I called for my own two remaining men to defend, but the yellow-garbed attackers had been moving closer and closer throughout the bout and had almost no distance to cover.

Fire had already destroyed the wall protecting my men, and one of them was cut down before my defensive orders had been received. Together Lucas's remaining men took my lone survivor prisoner, proudly lifting the green crown above their heads.

The scene froze for a moment, and then the figures, their weapons, and the crown faded away. Thornton stood and ripped a short parchment. Power raced around the arena, removing the other debris from our extended battle.

Thornton nodded at Lucas, the victor, and then turned to our seated year mates.

"At the front lines a mage does not work alone. Each mage officer commands a squad of commonborn soldiers. Each of you must learn to command your own forces, must learn the most efficient use of your compositions to enhance their effectiveness. Each of you will have a turn across the coming weeks to complete a bout. In future, your commands may be whispered so as not to give away the element of surprise. Afterward, we will discuss the various strategies used and where they could be improved."

Without thinking, I looked over at Lucas, exhilaration gripping me. In an instant, combat class had gone from the most dreaded part of my week to the most anticipated. He had commanded his troops well, and I was already going over it in my mind, thinking through what I could have done differently and how I might have effected a different outcome.

I could only imagine he was analyzing his performance the same way, despite his win, and for a moment I forgot everything else and grinned at him. His face still held its usual detached expression, but his eyes gleamed with the same elation. When our eyes latched, something heated and intense passed between us, locking them together.

With enormous effort, I tore my gaze free and forced my legs to climb the stairs back to my friends. Between the mental intensity of the bout, the energy I had expended on my compositions, and the shared moment with Lucas, my whole body trembled. But at least I didn't need Acacia, the Academy healer, as I had after my first arena bout the previous year.

And as my nerves settled, Thornton's words washing over me as he continued to discuss our bout, I realized he had done me a favor, after all. Caught up in the bout, I had forgotten my history with Lucas and had remembered only the many hours we had trained together. I had proven to myself such detachment was possible. Somehow I would regain my equanimity around him and make it through the next two years.

As soon as Thornton dismissed us, I rounded on my friends.

"Did I miss something? Did we know that was coming?"

They all shook their heads and protested their lack of foreknowledge.

"We don't normally do command bouts until fourth year," Finnian added. "I'm guessing they've moved it forward due to our upcoming trip to the front lines."

It made sense and explained why Lucas hadn't been caught unawares. Once again I lacked the general knowledge of their world that my friends so effortlessly shared. And yet the cool look that Dariela gave me as we passed each other on our way back to the main building reminded me that somehow I was succeeding without it.

Because that hadn't been a punishment from Thornton. He had merely called his top two students to demonstrate the upcoming exercise to the class. And those two positions no longer belonged to Lucas and Dariela.

Something in the Ellington girl's eyes told me she wasn't going to forget it.

It amazed me how quickly we fell back into the routine of classes. Many of the third year composition classes were taught by junior instructors while Redmond focused on the newer students since they were the most dangerous ones, their control still being established. The instructors worked in small teams to allow more opportunity to provide personalized instruction, working through the more complex problems that arose.

And unlike Redmond, who had always left me to my own devices, the other instructors actively sought opportunities to assist me as I adapted the day's exercise to my spoken limitations. They asked me more questions than I asked them, their curiosity and thirst for knowledge reminding me of the University mages who had sat in on classes in order to study me in first year.

Lucas remained in the same seat he had always occupied, and if he didn't feel the need to move, I wasn't going to concede defeat by being the one to do so. And so we remained a short aisle apart, as we had always done, and over time I grew more accustomed to his presence.

We studied a more varied range of compositions than we had done in previous years, although the classroom setting limited us somewhat. At least the others could sit in class and compose a composition to bring rain, waiting to test it until later. I had to leave such experiments to my own time when I could escape into the garden.

But oftentimes the instructors picked smaller versions of the compositions we studied, wanting the other trainees to tear their creations on the spot to demonstrate whether or not they had successfully completed the working.

I struggled more on days when I had been one of the trainees chosen to direct an attack in the arena, my energy already vastly depleted. My strength at compositions allowed me to exercise far more power than a standard mage my age, but even I had my limits. As a spoken mage, I had to expend my energy in much more concentrated bursts than my year mates, and the workings required of me now as a third year far exceeded those in my first year. On days when I was particularly tired, I even thought longingly of first year when we spent every combat class beating each other with sticks.

On one such afternoon I stared at the example working handed out by the composition instructors in dejection. It was a creator composition, since we were focusing on manipulating physical mass, and it looked exhausting.

I had once seen a creator reshape an entire room of the library that had been blown to pieces by my uncontrolled power. Compared to that, building a tiny structure from stone should be simple. It didn't even have to be structurally sound—that sort of expertise was left to those who studied the creator discipline. We just needed to demonstrate that we could lift the stones supplied by the Academy into place, fusing them into a solid mass without the aid of the mortar employed by commonborns when building their homes.

But even that much felt beyond me.

Coralie had already succeeded, writing one of the longest compositions I had yet seen. After she released it, she admitted to me in a whisper that the resulting creation looked more like an unstable hovel than the elegant doll's house she had been picturing.

Dariela and Lucas had both produced structures that Clemmy would have loved to claim for her dolls. Lucas's creation looked like a simple replica of the palace, made miniature, while Dariela had recreated the block-like Academy. I tried not to glare at either of them, directing my ire toward the pile of stones in front of me instead. They looked only slightly heavier than my head felt.

"It's not all about brute force, remember," said Lucas's quiet voice to my right. He sounded cool and detached. "Consider it an exercise in finesse. You've mastered speed, but you're still limited by energy. Working out how to achieve the same result with less energy and force will serve you well."

His familiar voice jolted through me, piercing my mental fog. He had always been a good teacher. I bit down on my bottom lip, chewing it as I considered the problem before me.

Picking up several small blocks of stone, I stacked them on top of each other, building a rudimentary structure. Coralie watched me with two raised eyebrows, but I ignored her. Once all the pieces were in place, I ordered them to fuse together, power rushing through them and sealing them against each other. It required a great deal less energy than would have been required to shape the structure with power.

"Uh, I think that might be cheating," said Coralie.

I grinned at her. "They told us to produce a small structure. Voila. Here is a small structure, formed via composition."

"Was it, though?" she muttered.

A small sound, almost like a choking laugh, drew my attention to Lucas. Amusement glimmered in the depths of his eyes, although his face remained impassive.

"That's not quite what I had in mind," he said.

"Wasn't it? I thought it was an excellent suggestion."

He shook his head. "You've always thought differently, Elena. It's one of your strengths."

An instructor moved between our desks, and Lucas fell silent while she examined my and Coralie's creations. She offered only minor suggestions for improvements before moving on, although the tilt of her lips suggested she had witnessed my shortcut.

Lucas spoke again when she moved out of earshot, his voice much quieter this time.

"You could make a difference, you know. To the war. Your power is more flexible, and you learn more quickly than any mage I've ever heard of. If you bent all your energies on the war, who knows what breakthroughs we might achieve?"

My stomach dropped, the traces of light-hearted humor from my small cheat dissipating instantly. For a moment I had forgotten why Lucas and I no longer trained together. Although he had made no effort to renew any romantic interest in me, I should have known he wouldn't abandon his efforts to convince me about the war.

"What would have happened in Abalene last year if everyone was putting all their effort into winning the war?" I whispered back at him.

His mouth twitched again, this time into a slight frown, but one of our instructors called our attention to the front of the room, so I didn't get an answer. My mind kept circling back to his advice, though. For all my joking in class, he was right that I could benefit from learning finesse in my compositions.

In the days that followed, I made myself pause before every composition, considering first if there was a more efficient way I could achieve the same result. And whenever I had particular success, I caught myself looking reflexively toward Lucas, wanting to share the victory.

The stab of pain always came a moment later when I remembered the barrier that stood between us. He had chosen the war, and I had chosen change. I needed to forget the connection we had shared. But while I lived and studied beside him at the Academy, it was proving far too difficult to do.

Sometimes I caught him listening to my conversations with the instructors, and on those occasions, he usually had some helpful suggestion to make for whatever task I was attempting. But all too often we remained in close proximity without speaking, his attention taken by Natalya and Lavinia—who seemed to lurk closer to him than ever before—or by Calix and Weston. And I could only be glad Lucas and I refrained from speaking—I had nothing I wanted to say to him within ear shot of the four of them.

Natalya and Lavinia continued to look down on me, despite my position at the top of the year, although their manner had mellowed somewhat. Due, perhaps, to the obvious tension between Lucas and me. Weston's hatred, on the other hand, didn't seem to have abated a jot. I only had to look at him to remember everything I most disliked about the Stantorns.

But somehow I still preferred seeing the three of them to observing the change in Calix, Natalya's twin. Occasionally I caught flashes of his old contempt, but those glimpses were slowly decreasing, replaced with a calculation that edged over into greed. General Griffith's younger son was far too much like his father for my comfort.

Coralie had done a better job of masking her emotions than me, and I rarely saw any sign of her discomfort after the first day. But I caught her gazing at Finnian when she thought no one was looking just often enough to tell me she hadn't truly forgotten their romantic encounter.

Finnian himself paid her even more extravagant compliments than was his previous wont, but it was hard to take it seriously since he did the same to me.

"Your mere presence delights me," he assured me, slinging an arm over my shoulder and pulling me tight against his side. "You cannot possibly think of leaving me in this cruel manner."

I snorted while Saffron gave an impatient huff.

"It's our rest day, and you heard Damon, Finnian. There's a package from home waiting for us. Come on!" She smiled apologetically at me. "There might be cookies in there. Finnian's family chef makes the most divine cookies."

"You mustn't delay then," I said, attempting to extract myself from under Finnian's arm. "Just save me one, if there are some, will you? It can be my reward for making it through this assignment."

Coralie grimaced at me in sympathy. My friends had continued to study the armed forces discipline with me, the specter of the front lines providing ample motivation. But they had all chosen new disciplines to replace healing this year, placing them back at beginner level and leaving me the only one struggling through the current advanced essay on healing.

Finnian just gripped me more tightly, bemoaning that the three of them couldn't possibly sacrifice me to study. Someone passing by bumped him roughly as he hurried down the corridor, making solid contact with his shoulder.

Finnian narrowed his eyes at the retreating back, and I took the opportunity to slip away from him. But while Finnian's attention returned to our friends, mine remained on the disappearing figure. Lucas.

He had been moving toward the stairs. Away from the library. Which meant now was my perfect opportunity.

Next to me, Finnian put his arm over Coralie's shoulder and began entreating her to convince me.

"I really must get to the library." I sent a mock stern look in Coralie's direction. "Don't let them eat all those cookies, Coralie. I'm relying on you."

"I will not betray your trust," she said with the utmost seriousness.

I nodded. Cookies were serious business.

"Come on!" repeated Saffron with even more insistence, and

the three of them moved toward the stairs while I hurried off in the opposite direction.

Stepping through the double doors of the library, I paused to breathe deeply the smell of parchment. I had missed this place for more than just my evenings studying with Lucas. This was where I had learned to read, opening a whole new world for myself. Walden's office in the back was where I unlocked my power, and I had spent more hours than I cared to remember browsing the untold wealth of knowledge weighing down the many shelves.

But entwined with all of that was the prince. Always the prince. From the beginning of our first year, Lucas had made the library his domain. And if I was honest, that was why I found myself behind on the assignment now. I had been avoiding the library as much as possible.

I raced between the shelves, hurrying for the section on healing, but a voice pulled me up short.

"Elena!"

I turned and smiled at the library head, Walden.

"We've missed seeing you around this year," he said. "I used to like it when a few of you studied in here in the evenings. I know I wasn't officially supposed to let trainees remain here at that hour, but how could I say no to anyone so eager to delve deep into this realm of knowledge?" He gestured around him at the shelves, then dropped his voice to a conspiratorial whisper. "Plus, it always made me feel like a bit of a rebel."

He chuckled, and I had to smile at a librarian's idea of rebellion. But my mind had snagged on his earlier comment. Had Lucas stopped frequenting the library at night as well? Was he trying to avoid *me*?

"I'm sorry," I said, dragging my mind back to the present. "It isn't the library, I promise."

"Oh, I quite understand," he said. "From what I hear you're outshining all of us these days. And while I sometimes miss the challenge and the mystery of your first year when we were trying to unlock your power, I wouldn't have it any other way. We must always be moving forward, you know. No point in standing still."

"Well perhaps you could help me again now," I said.

He brightened visibly. "Nothing I would like more, I promise you. As long as it's within the confines of my library, of course." He shook his head with an amused smile. "You won't find me of much use to you out on the combat field."

"Oh no. It's this healing assignment." I grimaced guiltily. "I'm afraid I've left it a little late, and the other students have most likely stripped the relevant shelves clean. I don't suppose you could point me to any remaining texts?"

"Now there is a request I can fully support." Walden smiled. "I'll even pretend I didn't hear you say you were running late with it."

He led me down the row of shelves and across to another one, muttering to himself as we got closer. Running a hand along a shelf just below eye-level, he stopped with a satisfied exclamation.

"Ah huh! Just what I was looking for. There are some older texts tucked away here that don't tend to be as popular. They're focused more on the history of healing. But the secret is our methods really haven't changed all that much. You can still get most of what you need from these."

"Thank you!" I stepped forward to peer at the section he indicated.

"I won't give you the books themselves, you'll have to look through and choose those for yourself. I have to keep it a challenge somehow, hey?"

He turned to leave and then glanced back. "You wouldn't go amiss starting with that one, though." And with a wink he pointed at a large tome on the end of the shelf.

I murmured further thanks and began to look through the titles, eager to be done and back to the safety of my suite. But as I continued to browse, I slowed, losing myself in the familiarity of the exercise. I found the book I was looking for, but two more caught my eye. And at the back of one of the shelves I found an ancient looking scroll.

It felt brittle in my hands, and I didn't trust myself to take it back to my rooms, so I carried all my findings to one of the desks which ringed the rows of shelves. Sitting down I began to read it, comparing its pronouncements against my stack of more modern books.

Unlike my year mates, I had to deliver my essays to Jocasta or Walden verbally, and I couldn't take notes as I read. Between our new command and strategy exercises in combat class, the increasing complexity of the compositions I had to memorize for composition class, and the advanced level of my healing and armed forces studies, sometimes lately it felt as if my mind was so stuffed with information, I couldn't fit a single new word inside.

But reading about some of the more ancient approaches to healing fascinated me, and the core argument for my assignment soon took root. I noted the names of each of the books so I could reference them, but it was the scroll that fascinated me most. After a lengthy discussion of various antiquated methods for first surveying the damage to internal organs and then healing them, the scroll veered off topic.

The author noted that some of the more complex healings needed to be completed in a single working, and that only the strongest and most skilled healers had the capacity to compose them. The matter of energy limits, and the effect these had on mages' ability to compose, had obviously been a subject of interest to the author, and she diverted into a description of various experiments she had conducted to see if it was possible for one mage to replenish the energy of another.

If such a thing were possible, she posited, then two weaker mages working together could manage the more draining compositions required for the healings she had just outlined. I already knew she had failed—energy was one thing the use of power could not supply to mages—but her process still interested me. I struggled more than most mages with the dangers of burn out since I couldn't prepare my compositions in advance. I would never have the opportunity to build up the arsenal that some mages possessed.

When I got to the end of the scroll, I became aware that time had passed more quickly than I realized. The small number of other trainees using their rest day afternoon to study had disappeared, leaving me alone in the library. I hurried to replace the scroll, wondering if the dinner bell would soon be sounding.

But as I turned back around, I started, stepping backward and colliding with the shelf. I wasn't alone after all.

CHAPTER 7

"I haven't seen you in here much this year," said Lucas, his eyes pinning me in place.

I swallowed and shrugged. "I've been studying in my suite. I have a suite of my own this year, too." Lucas had been given the largest suite on the fourth-year floor from the moment of his arrival in first year.

Lucas ignored the irrelevant jibe, stepping forward, his eyes not leaving mine.

"It's been lonely studying on my own." There was no one around us, but he still spoke in quiet tones, his husky voice sending shivers racing up and down my spine.

I tried to regain my earlier calm, but it only slipped further away when he stepped closer again. I could think of no answer to give him.

"I've missed you, Elena," he said, so close now I could feel the heat radiating from his broad chest and smell his unique scent. It brought back memories not only of evenings studying in the library but of late nights secretly training in the arena, the moonlight our only illumination.

I swallowed again and licked my lips, and his gaze immediately dropped to them.

I knew I should say something discouraging, but his nearness wiped my mind of everything but the unvarnished truth.

"I've missed you, too."

He took the final step forward at that, resting one hand on the shelf behind me. Always the gentleman, he left the other hanging at his side, leaving me a way out if I chose to take it. But I had never been as good at walking away from Lucas as I should have been.

I didn't move.

"How is it that you grow more beautiful every year?" he whispered, our faces a mere breath apart. "And more brilliant. Sometimes I think you must do it on purpose to torment me."

I squeezed my eyes closed to escape the fire in his. I told myself this exquisite pain wasn't worth it, and I should take the opportunity to escape.

Still I didn't move.

He gave a soft sigh. "And then I remember that you never did any of this for me. Or any of us. You did it for yourself, and your family, and the other commonborn." His voice dropped again. "It's one of the many reasons I love you."

My eyes flew open again. He had never used that word before. It wasn't something I would have forgotten. If Prince Lucas spoke that word to me while I lay unconscious, I would sense it even in my comatose state. I was sure of it.

But opening my eyes had been a mistake. The intensity of his expression robbed me of breath.

"This is torture, Elena. To be so near you constantly, and yet so distant."

I shook my head slightly. That was my line, wasn't it? He had given no sign that he struggled as I did. A lifetime of training at court had stood him in good stead, it seemed.

Just the thought of court acted like a dousing of cold water. I found the strength to raise both hands and push him away from me.

"I know you hate me for the choices I've made," he said, his words fast and low, his face pleading, "but I keep hoping you'll see I'm right. That I would change things if I could. That I will. When we're not trapped in this war."

I froze, both hands still flat against his chest, fire racing from his bunched muscles through into me. How I longed to nod, to fall into his arms.

But he was waiting for a day that would never come. The war with Kallorway was never-ending, and while Lucas was worth waiting for, I couldn't wait forever. Not when more common-borns suffered and died every year for the heedless ways of the mages. Not when there was so much good that could be done even while the war continued to drain us. The epidemic in Abalene had proven that.

When I was a child, I used to live in constant hope that the war would end before I grew old enough to need to enlist. I would wait eagerly for news of changes at the front. And yet every fortunate soldier who made it through his term and returned told the same tale. Nothing had changed.

Eventually I grew old enough to give up childish dreams.

Lucas had grown up knowing that he would spend two years at the front. But he had also grown up surrounded by royal guards whose sole job was to protect him. His line had been care-fully bred for strength and power; he himself had been trained from the youngest possible age. His future conscription had not been a millstone around his neck as it had been around mine. He still had hope that the war would end, that victory could be imminent, because it had yet to be beaten out of him.

But I knew better. And without change—the change he would not fight for while the war raged on—Lucas could never openly acknowledge his love for me. A prince was not permitted to love a commonborn girl, no matter her unique status. I refused to embark on a relationship that could have no future outside of the impossible dreams of a prince.

"The commonborns need change now," I managed to say in a voice that shook. "Not in a future that may never come. And if it's this hard to walk away from you now, how impossible might it become years from now?"

He traced one finger lightly down the side of my face, and I could feel the same tremor in his hand.

"But you're not walking away."

He swayed toward me, and I somehow forced myself to step away from him.

"No, but I should be."

"You underestimate yourself, Elena. You always have. With you on our side—if you dedicated yourself to the effort with single-minded focus—we could win this war." His voice turned rough. "I know you want me to fight for us—but perhaps you're the one who needs to fight."

I drew in a sharp breath. As a private in the Armed Forces, I was already at a disadvantage in my struggle not to become a mindless weapon in the hands of the Ardannian army. He might not mean that he wished me to become an instrument of death and darkness, but surely he could see that's where such a path would eventually lead.

And had he really deluded himself enough to think that I could do alone what a whole kingdom of skilled mages had been failing to do for thirty years?

His words gave me the strength to turn and walk away, but his voice pulled me up short.

"Elena!"

Reluctantly I glanced back at him. For a moment I saw his passion blaze hot, but then it flickered and died, his expression forming back into his usual detached mask.

"We'll be at the front lines ourselves soon enough." His words were quiet, but they pierced me just the same. "And you'll see that I'm right. You'll see that this war needs everything we can give it, or it will bleed us all dry."

I turned and almost ran from the library, his voice echoing after me.

"You'll see that I'm right, Elena."

My hurrying feet took me straight to my suite where I locked myself inside and stood with my back to the door, ignoring the sound of the dinner bell.

Was it possible? Could he be right? Would seeing the death first hand open my eyes? Would it unleash a darkness in me strong enough to turn me into a killing machine?

And if I did come to think Lucas right, would it be too late for his love? The disappointment in his voice as I fled from him haunted my sleep and told me it would.

I woke in the morning unrested and immediately made a new goal for the year. I must ensure I never found myself alone with Lucas again. I had many conflicted feelings for the prince, and the one thing they had in common was that they were far stronger than they ought to be.

I halted briefly in the doorway of our composition classroom the next afternoon before forcing myself to continue to my usual seat. It seemed I would no longer have to struggle with Lucas's daily proximity in this class, at least. He had taken up a position on the far side of the room, a new desk mate acting as a wall between us.

I turned my back on the prince and Natalya and tried to focus on our assigned composition, but my mind felt sluggish and slow. It had been my turn to bout in combat, and I had overextended myself, failing to allow for my lack of sleep. The resulting exhaustion was an entirely valid cause for my distraction which had nothing whatsoever to do with the fake giggles Natalya kept projecting around the room.

One of the instructors asked me to temporarily swap places with Araminta so that Dariela and I could complete the composition in tandem while they looked for any differences in the result. Reluctantly I moved forward, not receiving so much as a nod from my new desk mate. With my foggy mind, I worked at half speed, struggling to complete the working at the Ellington girl's level.

She continued to ignore me, neither taunting nor encouraging. But I thought I detected a faint smugness to her expression when my second attempt at the working produced much weaker results than her own torn composition had done a moment before. Of course, she had not spent the morning composing as I had done. A surge of resentment made me want to lash out at her, but I restrained the impulse, knowing she wasn't the true target of my frustration.

Someone—Finnian or Coralie most likely—had once told me that although the Ellingtons currently held the balance of power on the Mage Council, thanks to Duke Lennox of Law Enforcement and Duke Magnus of the Wind Workers, they had always been the least powerful of the great families. Politically powerful, at any rate.

But since I had also learned that most of them were enormously wealthy, I hadn't exactly wasted any pity on them. I had been here long enough to understand more of how these mage families worked now, however. Long enough to understand the value they placed on position and power and prestige. And while most of the Ellingtons I had met, like Walden and Acacia, had been friendlier than the majority of their mage counterparts, Beatrice—the most empathetic healer I had met, despite being a Stantorn—had taught me that every family held a range of attitudes.

So, while Acacia longed for greater strength so she could do good on the front lines where healers were most needed, Dariela had never displayed much interest in anyone else at all. From the first day I met her, she had always been cold and detached. Alone, even among her true peers. And watching her now, I thought I could understand why. She had a drive the other Ellingtons seemed to lack. And she had the potential to shoot straight to the top—not just among the Ellingtons but among all the mages.

She had no friends because she had no time for them. She didn't allow herself time. Already brilliant, talented, and powerful, she had always worked with single-minded focus to ensure she remained top of the year. She even managed to provide true competition for Lucas, despite his extra year, royal tutors, and natural strength.

And then I had come along. Appearing from nowhere, I had risen from the very bottom of the class to overtake them all. Armed with a mysterious power none of them could match, I had taken everything she worked for away from her.

Somehow I couldn't find it in me to resent her coldness now. And since I couldn't imagine she would want my pity, I had been sticking to keeping my distance. Now I just had to make it through this one class, and I could go back to that approach.

If only the irritating sound of Natalya's giggle didn't keep piercing the room.

I wasn't the only one to have noticed the change in seating arrangements, and one of the instructors was watching the prince and the general's daughter with a curious eye as he approached Clarence at one of the front desks.

"Here, let me check it over for you," he said, reaching down to take Clarence's parchment with only half his attention.

Clarence, a scholar with only middling strength, had a tendency to go long on his compositions, using twice as many words as the rest of us. But this instructor had been working with the fourth years and was new to our class.

"No, I'm not finished," said Clarence sharply, grabbing at the parchment as the instructor tried to pull it away.

The instructor focused on him, realizing his mistake too late, and time seemed to slow. Everyone in the room turned toward them as the ominous sound of tearing parchment cut through the usual noise of the room.

"No!" called one of our regular instructors, one hand diving inside his robe.

But there was no time. He had no hope of finding and identifying the right composition, even if he had one on his person.

I leaped to my feet, my chair clattering loudly to the floor behind me, as three words blazed across my internal vision.

"Shield us all," I screamed across the room, my hands pushing out as if to assist the dregs of my strength as it rushed out to envelop the fifteen people present.

Almost instantaneously the ripping sound finished, and unconfined power burst through the room, released prematurely from the incomplete composition. Desks and chairs exploded, ragged spears of wood shooting in all directions. Chunks of stone from the ceiling shattered and crashed downward.

The initial fiery force sent me reeling as it battered against the shields I maintained around Clarence, his desk mate Calix, and the new instructor. My faltering strength had cocooned each person barely inches from their skin in tight balls that protected the smallest possible area. Yet as each shard of stone and sliver of wood collided with my working, I felt more and more of my faltering energy drain away.

I swayed, my vision going blurry and then darkening from the edges inward. I couldn't hear any more crashes, but a ringing had started in my ears, so it was hard to tell.

"Easy," said a familiar voice.

Strong arms circled me just as my knees gave way. I searched for Lucas's face, but I could no longer see clearly enough to make out his features.

"Sorry I couldn't save the room as well," I murmured, and then the darkness enfolded me.

CHAPTER 8

"*S*orry I couldn't save the room? Really?" Coralie's exasperated voice greeted me as soon as my eyes opened.

"Personally, I thought they were inspired final words," said Finnian beside her. But his words held a hidden bite. "If final words were truly necessary, of course."

"What he's trying to say is that he'd prefer you didn't kill yourself—even if you're going to do it in style," Saffron interpreted.

I tried to sit up.

"Whoa!"

"Whoa, whoa!" All three of their voices overlapped as they all lunged forward to try to push me back down onto the pillows.

Faced with such united opposition I sank back down onto the bed.

"Goodness, there's no need to get excited." I surveyed the room, recognizing the small alcove in Acacia's healing rooms. I'd woken up here before.

"Actually, there is at least a little need," said Acacia in a flat voice.

She appeared behind my friends, pushing through to stand beside my bed and gripping my wrist between her fingers. We all remained silent as her eyes fastened on the blank wall for a moment.

"Your heart is beating strongly at least. Now." She gave me a stern look which melted into a long-suffering sigh. "None of the other students give me as much trouble as you, Elena. It's always you."

I grinned weakly at her. "You're welcome. I wouldn't want your life to get boring."

She chuckled before turning serious again.

"You're fortunate to wake up at all. You came very close to draining yourself completely. This isn't the sort of thing you can recover from all in a moment. I have already issued strict instructions to all staff that you are not to attend classes, study, or attempt even the smallest composition for at least two days."

She glowered at me. "Two full days. I want your word."

I nodded. Since my head spun, and my entire body felt as if I had run a marathon where the finish line was a brick wall, I didn't have it in me to protest.

She turned to go but paused to look back at me. When she spoke, her voice was quiet.

"You've been unconscious for approximately thirty minutes. The result of your burn out."

I nodded slowly, and she replied with a single nod of her own before disappearing off to the far side of the room.

Finnian gave me an odd look, but none of the others seemed to have noted our interaction, and I offered no explanation. I had never told my friends the real reason for the medically induced sleep Acacia had put me in for my two days of recovery after I burned out in first year. I had only discovered in second year that it had been less to ensure my full recovery, and more so that Lorcan and Jessamine could harvest my blood for testing purposes without my consent or knowledge.

If I had needed proof that my status both at the Academy and among the mages had changed, Acacia's assurance was it.

"You nearly killed yourself, Elena," said Coralie, and this time there were tears in her voice. "You were stupid."

She threw herself half onto the bed so she could give me a tight hug, moistening the blankets that had been tucked around me with her tears.

"Any one of us could have died without you," said Saffron quietly.

"Thank you," said Finnian, "for being you. And doing what no one else could."

I shifted uncomfortably, awkwardly patting Coralie's back.

"I only did what any of you would have done. If you could."

"Yes, if we could. A fairly major distinction." Finnian shook his head before looking down at me, a slightly wicked gleam in his eyes. "You know a number of fairly important people now owe you."

I snorted. "Yes, because I can see Natalya and Calix being eager to repay that debt."

"Next time, if it comes down to you or them, feel free to leave them out of your shield," muttered Coralie darkly, sitting up and mopping at her eyes.

"Coralie!" I poked her. "Didn't you just hear? They're Fairly Important People."

She giggled a little wetly. "It's just...after the way they've treated you..." Her face tightened. "It makes me angry. And you know they won't be properly grateful."

I smiled, touched at my friend's defensiveness on my behalf. "Then it's a good thing I didn't do it for their gratitude." I grimaced. "To be honest, I didn't think at all, I just reacted on instinct."

"A generous impulse that might get you killed some day." Finnian met my eyes with no sign of his usual lighthearted humor in his own.

I bit my lip and looked away, unable to hold his gaze. Was he right? Would I end up reacting one day to something too big for me to recover from? Every time I reached new heights of my power, I found new limitations, new dangers—all unique to me. If only I could store up my power somehow, like normal mages did with their written compositions.

Acacia bustled over to banish my friends, but Coralie begged to be allowed to stay, and the healer relented. And I appreciated her presence when Acacia eventually permitted me to leave the healing rooms for my own suite.

I had to lean on my friend's arm all the way up the stairs, and I made no protest when she insisted I go straight to bed. Frustrating as it was, I was clearly going to need the two days' rest Acacia had prescribed.

Coralie tucked me in, fussing around the room closing curtains and ensuring I had a glass of water within reach before she would leave. But as she gave the blankets a final pat, she glanced at me sideways.

"Lucas carried you to Acacia himself. He wouldn't let anyone else touch you. I just thought you might like to know."

I made no answer, so she crossed over to the door.

"And I've never seen him look so white."

"Goodbye, Coralie."

"Goodbye, Elena." She shut the door, clearly suppressing a smile.

My mind clung to her words and tried to process what she meant them to convey to me. But sleep dragged me down too quickly for me to come to any satisfactory conclusion.

I slept on and off throughout the next day. Coralie and Saffron took turns bringing me food, and Acacia stopped by once to check I was obeying instructions. In the unfeeling way of healers, she was delighted to find me bedbound.

All for my own good, she assured me. I'd feel better in no time. But it was hard to believe that when I barely had the strength to feed myself.

And yet, when I woke up on the second morning of my convalescence, the heaviness of the day before had almost entirely lifted. The idea of beating any of my year mates with a practice sword—as we did on non-arena days—held no appeal, but otherwise I felt almost normal.

When I opened my door to head down to the dining hall for breakfast, however, I found a tray outside my door.

"Well-meaning, over protective…" I mumbled to myself as I carried the food back inside my suite for a solitary meal.

I spent the time considering which of my assignments was in most urgent need of work until I remembered that Acacia's prohibitions had included study. I let my eyes roam around my suite. It was a pleasant space to spend an idle day.

Two hours later I had changed my mind about that. With no books allowed, the confinement was going to send me out of my mind. My thoughts only wanted to circle around to the one topic I had sworn not to dwell on, and watching the tiny figures of the other trainees battling it out in the distant exercise yards could only hold my interest for so long. Idly I picked out my own year mates, and then the first years. Thornton didn't seem to be with either group, so he was no doubt in the arena with the fourth years.

A knock on the door mercifully cut short my boredom, and I hurried to answer it. When the door swung open, I realized I had been wrong. Thornton wasn't in the arena, after all.

"Elena," he said with a nod.

I blinked at him in confusion, but when he raised both eyebrows, I hurried to invite him in and offer him one of the chairs in the living portion of my suite. He declined it, however, insisting I sit instead.

"You are the one recuperating, after all." He crossed over to take my place at the window, surveying his classes below.

I had no idea what had brought him to my suite, but I was trying to learn to listen before I spoke, so I said nothing, letting him take his time to reveal his purpose. After what felt like an excruciatingly long wait, he turned back to me.

"I thought," he said, directing a stern look at me, "that we had covered the issue of energy expenditure in your junior years."

Any thought that he might wish to congratulate me for saving my year mates died.

"Yet it seems," he continued, "that you are in need of the most basic lessons on the matter. Every living person can access power through words—written, of course, for everyone except you—but only mages can control that power. But channeling power comes at a cost—a cost of energy. For a commonborn, it makes no matter that accessing power burns their life energy. The act itself consumes them with explosive force, so their energy levels are hardly relevant."

He shook his head. "But you are no ordinary commonborn. You must understand energy even more acutely than a mage-born. All mages have the same finite levels of energy, and all of us use it when we compose. Nothing can prevent the use of power consuming energy. Yes, we can train to increase the amount and control of the power we can access, but we cannot increase our energy levels. Which means there will always be a limit to how far we can push ourselves. Efficiency and strength can only be increased so far. And we are each bound by our natural range. Some are born with greater natural strength and with greater propensity for control."

I opened my mouth to remind him that I knew all of this, but the irate expression on his face made me close it again without speaking. Perhaps being addressed like a first year was part of my punishment.

"You are fortunate in that you are naturally stronger than any trainee mage I have ever encountered," he continued. "But you are limited as well. You cannot store compositions. And I do not believe you take your limits seriously enough. Here at the Academy we teach many lessons. But two of them are more important than any others: how to prevent the uncontrolled release of power—such as occurred in your recent class—and how to access controlled power in such a way that you do not burn out and kill yourselves."

He bent a disapproving eye on me. "The instructors must bear the blame of the recent accident, but no one but you carries responsibility for your own energy."

"But if I hadn't acted, someone might have been killed," I said, struggling to remember my earlier resolve to stay silent. At least I managed to keep the heat out of my voice.

"You cannot be censured for shielding yourself and others from deadly danger," Thornton said.

I stared at him. "But...you just said—"

"I said," he interrupted, "that your energy levels are your own responsibility. You, of all trainees, should know that danger may lurk anywhere, anytime. You must not allow anything less important than protecting your life drain you to the point where you cannot act to shield yourself."

I wanted to snap that I had drained myself in *his* class, but somehow I held my tongue. He must already know that. And he had said the responsibility was mine alone, so I doubted the excuse would carry much weight.

I shifted in my seat. Thornton took his role as combat instructor seriously. He had never liked me, but he had also been one of my first instructors to actually go out of his way to teach me something, rather than simply enduring my presence. And he had done it because nothing was more important to him than equipping his students to stay alive. I could hardly fault him for that.

"So," I said slowly, "you're saying, as my instructor, that I should hold back in classes—fail at tasks, even—if it means preserving my energy reserves?"

"Being top of your year will do you no good if you're dead."

I nodded and cracked a small smile. "I can hardly argue with that."

He regarded me for a moment, either disapproving of my humorous tone or surprised I didn't intend to dispute with him.

"I would recommend you not forget it again," he said. "You have unique challenges that your year mates do not, but you also have unique strength. Don't let it go to waste due to foolishness."

"I'll do my best," I said.

He gave me a long look, his expression suggesting that he wasn't entirely convinced my best would be enough. But he said nothing more than a farewell. Only when he had crossed back out into the corridor did he pause to say, "Lorcan has given me a positive account of your shielding expertise. It is fortunate you were present at the accident." And then he closed the door.

"Well, I suppose that was a congratulations after all," I muttered to myself, getting up and striding across the room. But I had no sooner reached the window than I turned back again. I needed to get out of the Academy altogether. To clear my head.

And there was only one place—or rather one person—I felt any interest in visiting. My brother wouldn't be happy to hear why I had the day off, but his scolds would be worth it for the chance to see him.

No sooner had the idea occurred to me than my arms were already reaching for my cloak. The heavy, expensive material settled around me with the weight of memories and complicated emotions. As complicated as the prince who had given it to me.

I had considered leaving the garment back in Kingslee with my parents, but I hadn't been able to bring myself to part with it in the end. And whatever bittersweet memories it evoked, it certainly performed its primary function admirably. I wouldn't be cold in my walk to the University.

Stepping down into the Academy courtyard, I took a deep breath of the cool, crisp air. Winter was basically upon us, and the bite of the breeze proclaimed it. This was exactly what I needed.

I struggled to open the heavy Academy gate, my weak arms reminding me that I was officially still an invalid. A groaning protest sounded from the metal, and then the weight lifted, the gate sliding smoothly the rest of the way open.

"Thank you."

I turned to whoever had arrived at the perfect moment to assist me, and my voice died in my throat.

I swallowed. "Lucas."

"Elena."

His cool eyes were hard to read, but they certainly held none of the heat of the last time we had spoken.

"Shouldn't you be in bed resting?" he asked.

I bristled. "I rested all yesterday. I'm forbidden from classes and study, so I'm going for a walk."

"You're visiting Jasper." It wasn't a question.

I looked away, the reminder of how well he knew me stinging more than I wanted him to see.

"It's a good idea," he added.

I looked quickly back at him, my mouth falling slightly open. I snapped it shut, a flush driving away the cool of the air.

"Maybe he can talk some sense into you. Tell you to stop stretching yourself so thin."

I almost laughed at that, although he appeared serious. Jasper would say that the prince clearly didn't know me as well as I thought.

The ghost of a smile crept across Lucas's face. "I really don't know why I even try at this point. You'd probably die of boredom

83

if you didn't teeter on the brink of ultimate disaster several times a year."

I tested out the feel of a smile. It twitched slightly before growing more solid.

"I live to keep life interesting for everyone else."

Lucas snorted. "Well, you certainly do that. And then some." He stepped closer to me and then seemed to think better of it and quickly stepped away again. "Thank you for what you did. Saving us all in class, I mean."

I shrugged. "I really can't claim any credit. I acted on instinct."

One side of his mouth tugged up, and a softness crept into his eyes that nearly undid me.

"Ah, but not everyone's instincts are as altruistic as yours, I promise you."

I looked away, scrambling to regain my composure.

"Why aren't you in class?" The question came out more abruptly than I had intended, and I flushed again.

"Royal business. I'm on my way to the palace."

I nodded, and silence fell between us. It happened from time to time that he was called away from classes, sometimes for as much as a day at a time.

He stepped through the gate and gestured for me to follow before pulling it closed again behind us. He turned toward the palace, but I suddenly found I couldn't bear to let him go on such an awkward note.

"You're welcome," I blurted out.

He looked back at me, surprise on his face.

"For what I did in composition class." I grinned at him. "Perhaps you could mention it to General Thaddeus while you're up at the palace? I may well have saved a royal life. As Head of the Royal Guard, he'll no doubt be eager to give me an award."

A startled laugh burst out of Lucas, and he shook his head.

"I'm sure you're right. He is your biggest advocate, after all."

"You can tell him I'd be willing to accept a statue in my honor instead, if he'd prefer. A small one would do."

"I'm sure he'll have the creators get right on that," said Lucas. "Make sure you invite me to its unveiling."

A wagon rolled past on its way up to the palace, and I jumped out of the way to avoid getting splattered with mud. My movement took me away from Lucas and toward the University, so I waved my hand, not bothering to call out over the sounds of the street.

He waved back before striding off up the road, two royal guards in neat red and gold uniforms falling in beside him. I hadn't seen them appear, but they must have been waiting for him outside the Academy grounds. Had they heard us laughing and joking about their general? I hoped not.

Although, then again, they were commonborn guards rather than gold-robed mage officers. I could imagine the jokes they must have among themselves about their mage seniors.

The wide gates to the University gave me less trouble than the Academy ones had done. Perhaps due to the greater daily traffic, they had been designed with a regular size door cut out of one gate, and I easily pulled it open and closed behind me. The fountains, elegant buildings, and arched walkways of the University spread before me, giving an utterly different impression from the utilitarian Academy, despite making use of the same white marble.

The morning was moving toward lunchtime, and several people hurried between the buildings, some dressed as students and some wearing the black robes of University academics. A blue-robed wind worker and a green-robed grower passed, their heads close together in whispered conversation. Harvest must be finished for the year which meant the number of blue and green robes in the capital would be on the increase.

I moved toward a side door in the northern building, but a silver-robed mage officer appeared out of the main building, his path crossing mine. I halted, straightening my spine and pulling my hand up in a hasty salute.

The officer gave me an odd look as he hurried past, clearly unsure why he was receiving a salute from a random civilian. I wondered belatedly if I should have been wearing the untouched gray army uniform from my wardrobe. I didn't bother usually since I wore my white trainee robe instead, but I had no idea if it was expected dress for privates out and about on personal business.

The officer didn't stop, continuing on toward the gate, so I shrugged the thought aside and hurried inside. I was knocking on Jasper's door before it occurred to me that he might have changed rooms for his final year.

But a second later the door opened, revealing a familiar face.

"Elena!" Clara blushed prettily and stepped back for me to enter. "Did you know she was coming, Jasper?"

My brother, looking only slightly more composed than his petite friend, protested that he hadn't known and came over to give me a hug.

"I hope I'm not interrupting," I said in a loaded voice, and he hurried to assure me that they had merely been quizzing each other. But he wouldn't meet my eyes as he said it.

I showed great sisterly restraint and refrained from asking why two geniuses with perfect recall needed to quiz each other. I liked Clara, having spent some time with her in Abalene the year before, and I was perfectly ready to accept her as a sister-in-law. And I hoped my family would feel the same, especially now that Clemmy had been healed.

Our immediate need for a vast sum of money had disappeared. Hopefully any serious dreams they might have held that Jasper would marry into a rich commonborn merchant family had died with it.

"You're lucky to find us here," Jasper said, rushing to change the topic. "We have a free period before lunch. But what are you doing out of the Academy? It's not a rest day."

I glanced at Clara.

"Don't hold back on her account," he said. "I've told her all about our family, including you and your powers."

I smiled at the other girl, but it felt tight on my face. He had told her everything about me? For all I liked her, I didn't know quite how I felt about that. I glanced around the room, trying to regain my balance.

A crumb-filled plate and a half-full cup of tea sat on the desk, and a hat and cloak had been crumpled heedlessly on the single storage trunk. The bed covers looked rumpled as if someone had been sitting there recently, and the shutters on the window were thrown open, letting in a cool breeze. Someone had sprinkled more crumbs across the windowsill, and a tiny brown bird pecked at them.

The whole thing had a homey feel. It should, since it had been Jasper's small home for almost four years now. And the truth was that Clara looked far more at home here than I did. Time had passed, our lives had changed, and Jasper had found a family in her when his true one was out of reach.

I nodded once, to myself rather than to them. If Jasper said I could speak freely in front of her, then I would trust that. I briefly explained what had happened, and my current enforced rest.

"But as you can see, I'm fine," I said, holding out my arms to display my intact body.

To my surprise Jasper refrained from lecturing me, or even exclaiming. Instead he merely sighed.

"Is it a bad sign that I've gotten used to you having near death experiences?"

"Um, maybe?" I grimaced. "But you try mastering an unheard-of new power while surrounded all day by extremely important people. It's not as easy as it sounds."

Clara laughed. "It doesn't sound easy at all."

"Thank you!" I said with a dramatic hand gesture. "You should listen to her, Jasper."

A strangely guilty expression passed over Clara's face, and Jasper gave her a weighted look instead of replying to me. Something in my joking words had crashed the mood of the room, but I couldn't read whatever his face was conveying.

Clara apparently could, though. She bit her lip and turned away, her shoulders slumping as she crossed over to the window, causing the little bird to abandon its perch and take off into the sky.

Another small wave of jealousy washed over me that she could read my brother when I could not. But I pushed the unfair thought aside. Jasper had left Kingslee for the sake of our family. He had never asked for any of this.

Clara didn't turn back to us, but I saw her give the tiniest nod of her head. I tried to decide if I should say something, but Jasper placed his hands on my shoulders, distracting me.

"Easy or not, you're my little sister. I just want you to be safe. Promise me you'll at least try."

I slipped my arms around his waist and gave him a squeeze.

"You know I do. Every day. For all of us."

He nodded. "That's what family does."

The words were no more than I would expect from Jasper, no more than he had always displayed in his actions. But something about them stayed with me as I strolled back to the Academy after my visit. I couldn't shake the feeling that there had been a second conversation going on in Jasper's room. One that I had missed entirely.

CHAPTER 9

When I entered the dining hall that night, my usual table companions crowded around me to congratulate me on my recovery. Clarence and Araminta, the other trainees from minor mage families, hadn't seen me since I collapsed, and they both thanked me profusely for my actions. Clarence, in particular, apologized and thanked me so many times that I began to lose patience with him.

"Redmond was furious with our instructors," said Saffron. "Finnian and I heard him railing at Lorcan about it in the corridor the other day."

"I heard he wouldn't let them bring in a creator to fix the classroom," said Araminta.

"No, he insisted on doing it himself." Finnian rolled his eyes. "Foolish if you ask me. Better to leave such things to the experts."

"Don't let Redmond catch you suggesting he's not an expert at any type of composition." I rolled my eyes while ladling soup into my bowl as quickly as I could. I had missed eating in the dining hall. Room service didn't seem to be conducive to hot food.

"It was very romantic, though," said Araminta with a hesitant smile. "The way the prince caught you just as you collapsed and carried you out of the room."

I tensed at the casual mention of me, Lucas, and romance. "Was it? I wouldn't know." My words came out caustic, and Araminta almost visibly shrank into herself.

"Sorry," I said quickly, rubbing at the side of my head. "I'm still a bit tired." I tried to inject as much sincerity into my smile as I could. "Just don't let Natalya hear you making comments like that, or I'll really be in for it."

"Oh, goodness, no." Araminta's eyes widened. "But then I generally try to avoid Natalya hearing me say anything at all."

I blinked at her. Had that been a joke? Belatedly I smiled, and she smiled back which only made me feel worse about snapping at her.

"Next time I'll make an effort to be conscious so I can enjoy the experience." I looked across the table at Finnian. "Perhaps you can be my knight in shining armor on the next occasion."

"While I am always willing to assist a damsel in distress," Finnian said, cheerfully buttering his roll, "if there's a next time, I will kill you myself. Although I might have to settle for killing one of your less important body parts because I imagine there would be a few people in line before me. Friends don't let friends burn out, you know."

"That makes literally no sense at all," said Saffron.

"Don't bother me with the details," said Finnian, "I'm trying to make a point."

"Point received," I said. "I love you all too."

"And now I'm blushing," said Finnian, calmly starting on his roll. "Are we all proclaiming our love now? Because I'm perfectly willing to get involved."

"I love you, Elena, oh most troublesome of friends." He turned slightly to face Coralie who sat beside me. "I love you, Coralie—"

"Oh hush, you idiot," she said, cutting him off. She kept her voice level, the only detectable emotion exasperation, but I noticed a faint pink tinge in her cheeks, and beneath the table-cloth, one of her hands trembled slightly.

"No one appreciates me, Saffron," said Finnian. "It's a sad, sad world."

"It could be sadder," said Saffron. "Elena could have been absent from class two days ago, and you could have been the one to die."

Finnian paused, an arrested expression on his face, his first spoonful of soup half way to his mouth.

"Now there is a truly terrifying thought. Imagine! An Academy without me. How would you all survive? I'm going to write to my aunt and tell her you're giving me nightmares."

"Please do," said Saffron, calmly slurping her own soup. "Maybe Mother will send us more cookies."

"But would they be to console Finnian or congratulate you?" I asked.

She looked up at me and grinned. "Does it matter?"

But her smile fell away, replaced by a look of mild confusion as she gazed at something over my shoulder. Frowning, I turned to look and found Calix paused behind me. Weston stood several steps further on toward their usual table, looking back at his friend with the same confusion as Saffron.

"My father sends his thanks, private. Apparently he wasn't too keen on the idea of his children ending up speared by their own classroom."

I tried to weigh up his meaning, but his humorous tone threw me. When Natalya called me private, the mocking disdain was clear, but Calix almost sounded as if he were attempting to laugh with me rather than at me, however poor a job he was doing at it.

"Um...thank you?"

He nodded, apparently satisfied with my lackluster response, and continued on to Weston. The Stantorn gave his friend a confused look, but Calix merely shrugged, as if there was nothing particularly noteworthy in his thanking me.

I turned slowly back to my own table.

"Someone please tell me that was as odd as I thought it was?"

"Odder." Coralie nodded vigorously and stared across at where the fair-haired Calix was taking his seat across from his dark-haired twin.

"I don't know," said Finnian, also eyeing General Griffith's son. "Maybe not so odd."

I raised both eyebrows at him. "Have you met the twins before?"

"I grew up with them, remember? And they're dissimilar in more ways than just their looks. Natalya can hold a grudge like no one I've ever met." He shook his head. "None of us children would cross her if we could avoid it. At the end of the day she's not thinking about anyone but herself. But Calix? Calix is a much more dutiful son. Rivalry with his talented older brother, Julian, probably."

I frowned down into my soup. It might have been two years ago, but I could still feel Calix's foot connecting with my ribs. He had felt nothing but contempt, disdain, and anger toward me then.

But I also remembered what Coralie had told me when I first arrived. How the other students—the ones from the great families—were waiting to see what position their families took regarding my presence at the Academy. And the winds of opinion among the members of Devoras had shifted. I had gone from dangerous risk to powerful potential tool.

"Ugh." I glowered at my poor unoffending bowl. "I almost prefer Natalya. At least she has dedication."

"Watch your tongue, Elena," Coralie scolded me. "You have quite enough enemies without going begging for more."

"Thank you, Coralie," I said, a smile returning to my face. "You are, as always, a source of comfort and inspiration."

She just rolled her eyes and pushed aside her empty bowl, reaching for a platter of meat.

"I speak nothing but the truth. What else are friends for?"

Finnian stared across at her with widened eyes. "Definitely not for that! My fragile ego might not survive."

"What a horrible blow that would be for us all," Saffron murmured into her soup, and Coralie and I both broke into giggles.

Two days banished to my room had been quite enough. It was good to be back with my friends.

My good humor lasted all through the next day, and the day after. But Lucas returned from the palace the day after that, and my mood plummeted, along with the rest of the Academy's.

He had been away for an unusually long time, and along with his return came rumors from the front lines. The Kallorwegians had become ghosts, impossible to catch, their raids increasing in frequency. And there had been another young mage death. Only one this time, and no one who had been close to any of my friends, but Coralie seemed unusually upset about it.

"Hardly the furor there was last time, is there?" she whispered angrily to me as we passed a group of trainees discussing it in the corridor.

"Well, there were five deaths last year," I pointed out tentatively, unsure what had raised her ire. I had already checked twice, and she had only ever met the mage in question once since he had been three years above us at the Academy, serving his second year at the front.

"And you don't think they'd be equally devastated this time if a Devoras or a Callinos had died?" She gave me a pointed look. "Instead of some poor member of a minor family."

Ah. I hadn't known which family the casualty belonged to. It hadn't occurred to me to ask, and my friends must have already known.

The year before I had been in her shoes—the only one mourning the commonborn who had died alongside the mages. But I didn't comment on that now. We all had our people—and could we really be blamed for that?

"I'm sorry, Coralie," I said instead, unsure what else I could say.

"Mage deaths do happen, you know," she said. "From time to time. Not like last year. I'll admit that was a lot all at once. But when they do happen, they're more often from the minor families. It makes sense because we lack the strength of the others. We're less able to defend ourselves."

"Coralie." I gripped her arm. "I'm sure the officers—those who've actually chosen the armed forces discipline—take everyone's strength into account when assigning duties."

"I suppose." Her hands balled into fists before slowly relaxing as she looked up at me. "Listen to me! As if you, out of all of us, need reminding that the world's not fair."

I pressed my lips together and looked away. I hated seeing my usually bubbly friend so depressed, and I wished I could reassure her that I would keep her safe when our time at the front came. But I knew I couldn't make promises like that. Because members of the army didn't belong to themselves. They had officers and orders in place of their own decisions.

Coralie had no more outbursts, but she remained subdued over the following days, and her mood infected me. When I tried to study in the library during discipline studies, I couldn't concentrate. I couldn't shake the thought that those from minor families —like Coralie and Araminta—were more at risk at the front.

"That's it. Out. Get out." Jocasta's irritated voice snapped me back into the present.

She glared at my fingers, and I realized I had been tapping my pen against the table.

"Sorry, I'll—"

"Out. Go study in your suite. You've been up and down twenty times and I, for one, could do without your presence here."

I sighed and gathered up my things. Jocasta had never been my biggest supporter or the most cheerful of people, even without the current tone of the Academy.

But my feet didn't take me back to my rooms. Instead I somehow found myself in the waiting room outside Lorcan's office.

I didn't remember deciding to come here, or even what I intended to say, but somehow I needed reassurance. I needed to remember that there were still months before we would be visiting the front, and even then, only as observers. Our own terms wouldn't come until after fourth year.

But the Academy Head wasn't alone. Heated voices from inside his office made me pause just outside his door. Whoever was visiting him must have been too angry to close the door properly behind them, because it stood the slightest bit ajar, making it even easier to hear the slightly raised voices inside.

"You pulled a neat trick with the girl, Lorcan, and you know it," said the other voice. It only took me a moment to place it as General Griffith.

An unpleasant creeping feeling spread from my scalp down my body. I hadn't known the Head of the Armed Forces—a Devoras with far too much control over my life, thanks to my enlistment—was in Corrin.

"I had the support of the royal family," said Lorcan, sounding considerably calmer than the general.

"Ha!" barked Griffith. "As if I didn't know that. You always land on your feet, Lorcan."

"I endeavor to do so, certainly."

The general muttered something I couldn't hear.

"Do not tell me there has been another major offensive like

the surprise attack last year," said Lorcan. "I have heard no reports of one."

"Not a major offensive as such." The general's voice had dropped slightly, and I leaned forward closer to the crack in the door. He sounded almost weary now, and I somehow grew even more afraid.

"It's more of a constant pressure. There's no doubt they've increased their numbers. Despite the losses we gave them when we drove them back last year." He sighed. "But then we took some losses of our own then."

"Yes, that was most unfortunate," said Lorcan.

"We need this, Lorcan. Ardann needs this. We need something new at the front line."

"I am not bringing untrained children to fight." Lorcan sounded sharp for the first time.

"They're hardly children, are they? Eighteen-year-olds the lot of them."

Lorcan made an outraged sound, and the general rushed on.

"I'm not planning to set them to fighting. My own children are among them, may I remind you! But the girl. You should hear how the soldiers speak of her." He paused, and a chair creaked as if he had just sat down. "They need hope, Lorcan. They need to see that Ardann has strength. And if you will not release her from the Academy, then you must bring the Academy to us. It will do your trainees good, too. Let them see the reality of what they'll be coming to after they graduate. They'll only train all the harder when you get them back here."

A moment of silence sounded, and then he heaved himself back to his feet with a groan. "You know the Stantorns agree with me about where she belongs. They understand the importance of the war efforts. And if things turn bad at the front again, as they did twenty years ago, we might end up having to recall a great many mages to active service. Such an exercise isn't cheap, as you must know."

He gave a dry chuckle. "And if the crown is forced to look to the Ellingtons for finances, you know the only ones who will hate that more than the king are the Ellingtons themselves. A messy eventuality when we have a much less disruptive option within our reach."

"Messy indeed," said Lorcan. "But I can't imagine we need to trouble the Ellingtons with such a disconcerting idea. Now that I know the importance you place on our visit, I am more than willing to bring it forward."

"I thought you might feel that way," said the general with grim humor in his voice. "That's why I wanted to come have a little chat with you myself. So we'll see you at the front in...a week, shall we say?"

"A week?" I could almost hear Lorcan's raised eyebrows. "I wouldn't look for us before two at the earliest. Surely the Head of the Armed Forces understands the complexities of logistics."

There was a pause.

"Very well, then. Two it is."

My frozen limbs twitched, and I almost tripped over myself as I hurried back out into the corridor, desperate to get out of sight before the general emerged. I flung open the closest door I could find and huddled inside the empty workroom on the other side.

But when the general had safely passed, my heart rate refused to slow down. I continued to stand there, unmoving. Coralie and all my year mates would be in danger even sooner than we had thought. And it was all because of me.

CHAPTER 10

The rumor had been that both third and fourth years were to visit the front, but only the third years stood huddled together on a chilly morning a week and a half later. The official word was that the third years would visit first and the fourth years take their turn after the third years returned. Unofficially it only confirmed what I had overheard outside Lorcan's office. This wasn't really about the trainees at all. I wondered if the fourth years would ever even make it to the front.

In some ways the scene felt reminiscent of when we left for Abalene to observe the green fever epidemic. And the appearance of the purple-robed Beatrice and Reese only confirmed the impression. I pushed through the throng to greet them both as soon as they appeared.

"Don't tell me you're to accompany us," I said with a smile.

Reese narrowed his eyes at me. "Unfortunately, yes. I begin to ask myself if I will ever be free of you."

I just grinned back at him. Reese was not exactly my favorite person, but you didn't save countless lives together without developing something of a fellow feeling. And after seeing his dedication to the task, his barbs no longer did anything but amuse me.

Beatrice, on the other hand, was as kind and gracious as she had ever been. And I was pleased to see she looked more rested than I had ever seen her as well.

"Elena, what a delight." She pulled me into an affectionate hug. "I've been hearing some wild stories about you. Some of which make me think I'm not going crazy with the things I half-remember you doing in Abalene." She gave me a knowing look.

"I admit nothing." I chuckled. "Not with Reese around anyway."

Reese sighed loudly and turned away to direct the storage of their baggage. When we had worked together in Abalene, both of them had been too absorbed in their tasks to notice me deviating from their instructions as I used it as an opportunity to hone my abilities. Well, almost too absorbed, as it turned out.

"I thought they didn't want you at the front lines," I said, forgetting for a moment that Beatrice was both an extremely senior healer and a Stantorn, albeit the only kind one I had ever met.

Reese wheeled around to glare at me.

"Hey! You were the one always saying she should be resting," I said, and he stomped off.

"Sorry, I didn't mean to be rude," I said to Beatrice. "I'm just surprised to see you."

"It has been well over a year since I returned to Corrin, and my strength has been sufficiently restored." She glanced to one side, and I followed her gaze before looking quickly away again when I saw the object of her study.

"One of the royal family traveling to the front gave me just the opportunity I needed," she said. "It was a simple matter to convince the king that the prince would do best with a skilled and experienced healer at his side."

Her eyes twinkled mischievously, and I smiled back at her.

She had been sent away because she cared too much—expended too much of herself—and I was willing to bet not just toward the mages. The need at the front was too great, and she ran the risk of bleeding herself dry. And yet, here she was taking the first opportunity to get back.

Even the nicest and most caring mage I had ever met played *the game*, as Lucas called it, but at least she played it in order to help others. So perhaps it wasn't such a terrible thing to learn to play myself.

Two major differences separated the scene from the one the year before, however. Jasper did not come striding through the gate to accompany us, something I could only be thankful for. The thought of my brother near Kallorway was almost as unsettling as the idea of Clemmy at the front lines.

The other difference was that it seemed the entire Academy had come out to see us off. Lorcan was to accompany us, a fact that had brought me considerable relief since no one else could stand up to the general. And apparently the departure of the Academy Head in such circumstances warranted a great deal of interest and farewell.

Thornton had decreed he would also travel with us, and no one had attempted to gainsay him. He seemed outraged that trainees of his would be sent out into the world before his training was complete, and so our combat training was to continue despite our change in location. And not one of the trainees had grumbled about it. Not with the war staring us in the face so much sooner than expected.

I caught a glimpse of Acacia, come to wave us off, but she hung back near the Academy entrance and responded to my calls of farewell with only a small smile. When I saw her eyes dwelling on Beatrice and Reese, I didn't push the matter.

If strength were awarded on the basis of personality and virtue, it would be Acacia accompanying Beatrice in Reese's place, as she so obviously longed to do. She had wanted to be of use at the front lines for as long as I had known her. Reese on the other hand was almost certainly going merely because he always stuck to Beatrice like a shadow. The healers had used their connection as cousins to assign him as a sort of minder over her. At least that was how they both talked of it, and he certainly made efforts, mostly futile, to curtail her expenditure of strength.

But seeing them work together more than once now, I suspected it was as much an apprenticeship of sorts. Reese had strength for all his poor temper, and his older cousin had great skill and experience. It was unfortunate her empathy and kindness didn't seem to be transferring to him along with her knowledge. If Reese was intended as her replacement, it would be a sad day for Ardann when Beatrice retired.

Most of the other trainees milled around giving extravagant farewells to younger or older siblings, cousins, or friends. Even Coralie had abandoned me for her younger brother. Anyone would think we were being sent to fight and not just observe.

But an instant shaft of guilt made me repent of the ungenerous thought. We were going to a war, and anything could happen. Perhaps I was just jealous that I had no one to farewell.

"It seems a sad day for the Academy," said a voice behind me, "to see ourselves thus divided for a chunk of the year."

I turned around and nodded at Walden. The library head had come out of his book-filled retreat, no doubt forced to do so since Lorcan had decreed the Ellington in temporary charge of the Academy. From his look of ill ease, the responsibility didn't sit entirely well, but I could understand why Lorcan would find him a more desirable person for the role than Redmond. Although Redmond's foul mood since the news had been announced suggested he didn't see things the same way.

"We can only hope we'll be back before long," I said. I certainly hoped so at least.

"Yes, indeed." He hesitated, opening his mouth to speak,

closing it, and then opening it again. "I do hope you'll be careful, Elena," he said at last.

"I certainly intend to be," I said.

He nodded, something clearly still bothering him.

"Yes, I imagine you will be, of course. And Lorcan will no doubt keep you under careful watch. All of you, naturally," he hastened to add.

He glanced around, and then lowered his voice, although no one stood near us. "Not everyone thinks as he does, sadly. The general, in particular—" He cut himself off, quickly smiling and even forcing out a small chuckle. "A good thing, at times, no doubt. Each of the great families have their own strengths. Only...some of us are stronger than others."

He gave me a significant look, reminding me that while Callinos currently held the most seats on the Mage Council, traditionally Devoras and Stantorn had been the strongest of the families. He didn't continue the thought, however, his voice instead returning to normal volume as he gestured expansively around.

"But here I am blathering on when an adventure lies before you all. If nothing else, this trip will expand all of your knowledge, and since that is the task to which I have dedicated my life, I can hardly object too loudly. Even if I could wish every place you might travel was as safe as my library."

He gave me a final smile before moving through the groups of trainees, wishing the rest of my year mates farewell as he encountered them. I watched him go, unsettled.

For all his cryptic manner, it didn't take much to interpret his words—a warning to take care, that I approached a place of danger. And a reminder that the strongest of the great families might not have my best interests at heart.

Hardly news to me, any of it. But it unsettled me that Walden had felt the need to issue a warning. And he had slipped with a direct reference to the general. What had he heard, buried in his library, to give him such concern?

My main suspicions had centered on the Stantorns ever since I saw my attacker in their company. But by all accounts, the Stantorn and Devoras families had always been close allies. Was it possible my attacker had been placed with the Stantorns by one of their friends—a Devoras, perhaps?

My eyes roved over the busy courtyard without seeing, until they caught unintentionally on someone looking back toward me. Even at the distance, I could see the calculating gleam in the green depths of Lucas's eyes as he looked between me and the retreating librarian. What would he have made of Walden's warning?

In a different world, I might have asked him. But I didn't live in a different world. So I would have to puzzle through its significance on my own.

Perhaps it was for the best anyway. Lucas hadn't taken kindly to my previous efforts to point out attempts by the Devoras and Stantorn families to have me murdered. Even the evidence of my own eyes when I saw my attacker with the Stantorns had been discounted.

The memory of Lucas's words then made me shiver. He had reminded me that I accused relatives of his—important members of the Mage Council—of treason. He had seemed to think such a thing impossible.

And yet somehow Kallorway had mounted a major surprise offensive. And now the reports suggested they were eluding us at every turn. Was it really so impossible to imagine we had traitors in our midst?

Walden's warnings took on a whole new light. I would certainly do well not to overlook Devoras—especially when one of their number controlled the Armed Forces. The insistence of General Griffith that I attend the front as soon as possible became even more sinister. I was walking into a situation I didn't understand, and it seemed increasingly clear that the results could be deadly. I only wished I knew for who.

~

It took a long time for our cavalcade to make it out of the city. As well as the carriages which carried us trainees and our instructors, we had a number of wagons bearing additional supplies for the front lines, and a squad of royal guard rode in formation around Lucas's carriage, although I noted they were all common-born with no gold-robed officers among them.

Progress down South Road was necessarily slow as all other traffic had to make way for us. The sight of the red and gold uniforms of the royal guard sent most people scurrying, but some moved more slowly than others.

Our group grew even larger when we made it as far as the central training barracks. I had spent a brief day inside its walls during second year, so when we stopped outside it, my friends directed their questions at me. But I had been there for too short a time to have much insight into its internal workings.

Peering out the carriage window, I noted an older woman in crisp silver robes that matched her silver hair. She delivered a series of orders to a younger man beside her, also wearing a silver robe, and he turned to bark them to the squads of soldiers pouring out of the building.

Someone brought forward a chestnut horse with elegant lines despite his enormous size, and the woman swung herself into the saddle. From her new height, she observed the soldiers forming themselves into columns.

Some of the youngest looking among them fumbled their way into position, casting nervous glances up at the woman's no-nonsense face. But even so, the chaos around our collection of vehicles gradually gave way to two ordered platoons—one ahead of us and one behind.

The woman guided her mount to the front of the procession, and I exchanged a loaded glance with Finnian who sat across from me, peering out the same window.

"I count two full platoons," said Clarence, in a manner that suggested he was attempting to take an academic approach to a situation that made him uncomfortable. "Eighty soldiers. Plus Lucas's squad of royal guard. That's a full nine squads. They're taking our safety seriously, at least."

"That's old Jennica riding out the front there," said Finnian. "That's what tells us they're taking this seriously." He shook his head. "I can't remember the last time she left the training barracks for the front lines, although she was a star officer there when we were young."

"I think they're using the opportunity to ship across some new recruits," I said.

Saffron nodded. "No member of the royal family is permitted to travel west without at least a full squad of royal guard and a full platoon of experienced soldiers. So they would have had to bring a platoon back from the front to collect us. It looks like they've taken that platoon and mixed its veterans with the recruits to form two new ones."

That explained the disparate appearance of some of the soldiers. A clever strategy and much more effective than sending out a platoon made entirely of inexperienced youngsters. Colonel Jennica might be a Stantorn, and the training for new recruits might be insufficient, but she clearly understood something of both command and war.

Our numbers had grown significantly, and we now had to move no faster than a sustained marching pace, but our progress didn't noticeably slow. We had attained enough bulk that other traffic no longer bothered us now. Perhaps the citizens of Corrin had grown accustomed to clearing the streets for marching platoons of soldiers.

Once we had collected our entourage, we veered off South

Road, taking West Road through the western gate. I had only seen this side of the city once before. But since I had been bouncing along upside down over someone's shoulder, still groggy after being knocked unconscious, I didn't have many clear recollections of it.

We had hardly escaped the confines of the city before we hit the Overon River where it curved around the western side of the city on its passage south. Our pace had to slow once again to file across the narrow but sturdy bridge. No more than a single vehicle could fit across at a time, but at least all the traffic heading east toward Corrin stood aside, deferring to our train.

"My father told me this bridge used to be as broad as the one where South Road crosses the Overon," said Araminta, regarding the swiftly flowing waters of the river when our turn came to cross. "But they replaced it with this one before we were born."

"Easier to defend." Clarence kept his eyes focused out of the window as well. "And easier to destroy, if it ever comes to that."

I shivered. Such a necessity would indicate a very bleak day indeed, given the capital's presence a mere stone's throw away.

"The whole thing is laced with power," said Finnian cheerfully, craning his neck to look at the bridge itself rather than the river. "They say only the two generals and the king himself have the composition keys to set it off."

He sounded fascinated and a little delighted, but my stomach immediately began to churn and didn't stop until we were back on solid ground and a safe distance away.

CHAPTER 11

$\mathcal{I}$n the open ground we moved a little faster, but not by much. I had been comparing this journey to the longer trip to Abalene, but I hadn't accounted for the difference in pace. With so many of our number on foot, and inexperienced marchers at that, we seemed to inch along. None of us complained, however. That would have suggested an eagerness to reach our destination.

We traveled through farmlands, field after field lying fallow, with the occasional hardy winter crop starting to sprout. The sun had risen high, burning the frost from the fields, but it remained cold enough to require cloaks.

Rumors of the legendary northern fields of the Sekali Empire —where the temperature remained warm enough all year for a full rotation of summer and winter crops—had always existed. And Lucas's delegation three years ago had reported traveling through such winter fields on their way out of the Empire. Unfortunately that sort of warmer climate existed only in the northernmost parts of Ardann—where forests covered the land— and in the small northeastern pocket between the southern forests and the Grayback Mountains where Abalene sat beside the Overon delta.

We broke our journey over two days, the group from the Academy and the mage officers spending the night spread across two inns in a western village. I didn't notice the colonel at the inn I had been assigned to and assumed she was at the other one, until I heard someone mention that she always slept with her troops. Reluctantly, my respect for the Stantorn officer increased.

Fields continued to line the road on our second day of travel, but the further we got from the capital, the fewer farmhouses and hamlets could be seen from the road. After three decades of war, only the hardiest chose to live this close to the hub of the conflict.

More depressing than the empty stretches and fallow fields, however, were the occasional blackened stretches of earth, or burned ruins of a building. Stark reminders of why so many of the locals had long since fled.

I had seen enough maps to know that the coastal cliffs protected the eastern border of Ardann from invasion by sea, and the southern forests that stretched across a large part of our border with Kallorway grew too thickly for any significant troop movement. But that still left a long section in the middle of the kingdom where only the Abneris River—our western border—stood between us and our enemies.

Smaller fortifications existed along the border, but our goal now was the fortress town of Bronton, set a short way back from the river. And when we approached it, I observed for myself why so much of the fighting centered on this one small section of the border.

Once again our procession slowed, passing through a second artificial bottleneck. This one was created by a wide stretch of jagged rocks that pressed against the road on both sides, too large and sharp to permit either horses or vehicles to cross.

I stared in fascination at the unnatural looking phenomenon.

"Twenty-five years those rocks have been there," said

Clarence, reciting the facts in the same voice he had used earlier. "Colloquially known by members of the Armed Forces as the Wall. It took a team of a hundred creator mages to set it into place, and every mage officer of the Armed Forces since has added compositions to its layers of protection. The whole length of it is a death trap, and the only safe passage to and from the border is the West Road."

None of us replied to his unnecessary history lesson. We had all learned the same thing in our armed forces discipline studies. But somehow seeing the reality was altogether different from reading about it in a book.

"Do you feel safer, seeing it in person?" Saffron asked the quiet carriage.

I bit my lip as we left the rocks behind us. "I did when we were on the other side of it."

The barrier was necessary, I could understand that. It was the only reason the rest of the kingdom could function almost normally despite the protracted conflict. Its protection allowed us to secure the border with a far smaller force than would otherwise have been necessary. But it didn't escape me now that the same bottleneck would hamper any evacuation, if it ever came to such an eventuality.

I had grown up with an awareness of the human cost of this war, but I had never experienced the destruction it had also wrought on our physical land. If King Osborne ever broke through the Wall and brought Ardann to its knees, what would be left for him to claim? What good was the ancient birthright he claimed gave him overlordship of both kingdoms if his prize was a dangerous ruin?

I ground my teeth. Osborne's greed had already consumed too much of Ardann. Had it not done the same in Kallorway? When would the madness end? When would his own people say *enough*, if he would not do so himself?

The possibility brought me no comfort. Kallorway had

continued to harry us for thirty years with occasional major incursions. I had no reason to believe our western neighbors were likely to see reason any time soon.

Bronton came into view long before we reached it, the ground in every direction around the border town cleared for miles. High, sturdy walls surrounded the buildings, blocking them completely from view. Instead my attention was caught and held by a tent city that surrounded Bronton to the north and west.

Canvas walls and flags filled my vision, and the sound of barked orders, shouts, marching boots, protesting livestock, and clanging metal nearly drowned out the background roar of the river. The smell of too many people and animals living in close proximity hit us as we approached closer and set everyone in the carriage coughing.

"They say you get used to it," said Coralie weakly, but no one looked impressed at the idea.

I risked leaning my head slightly out of the carriage window to see Colonel Jennica at the head of the columns directing the soldiers behind her on where to disperse. The wagons also trundled away from our procession into various parts of the huge camp city. The carriages, however, along with Jennica herself, proceeded into Bronton.

The town's western-facing gates stood wide, although as we passed through them, I noted they were thick and built of solid wood treated in a special flame-resistant pulp. No doubt they were soaked in invisible protective compositions as well. The entire town certainly pulsed with a stronger sensation of power than even Corrin.

A number of the intelligencer compositions we had studied in discipline studies began to make more sense. I had always wondered why the Kallorwegian mages didn't sense the power involved in their use. But if their border towns were soaked in as much power as Bronton, almost any working could be conducted undetected.

An uncomfortable sensation wiggled down my spine. Yet another reminder that for all its protections, the front was not a safe place to be.

The town itself was an ordered grouping of low stone houses. Two considerably larger houses of red sandstone had apparently once belonged to branches of the Ellington and Stantorn families, but the original owners had long since relocated elsewhere. Instead the Armed Forces used them as headquarters and lodging for senior officers, with a steady stream of local townsfolk and soldiers coming in and out.

General Griffith emerged just as we rode up to the front of the larger of the two buildings. He greeted Colonel Jennica, Lorcan, Beatrice, and Lucas, ignoring the rest of us. Except for me. Several times I caught his eyes straying in my direction despite my attempts to bury myself in the midst of the cluster of trainees.

But thankfully he didn't call me out to join the group of senior mages, and he made no attempt to issue me any orders. We could hear enough of their conversation to learn that there was no room for us in the town itself. While the prince, Lorcan, and Beatrice could be accommodated in the mansion being used for the general's quarters, the rest of us would be housed out in the tent city.

Only Beatrice took him up on the offer, Reese also being offered a place once Lorcan and Lucas had turned the general down, asserting their intention to remain with the rest of us from the Academy. I couldn't help a feeling of relief. I didn't like the idea of Lucas separated and alone, although logically it made sense that he would be safer behind Bronton's walls.

And with Lorcan it was a purely selfish sensation. I wanted to shelter behind his presence before I was consumed by the enormous and ravening beast that was the war effort.

Back outside the town walls, several soldiers appeared with orders to show us to our assigned tents. The girls were to share one tent, the boys another, with the exception of Lucas who had his own tent along with his squad of the royal guard.

I expected a protest from Natalya and Lavinia at being forced to share, but neither of them said a word. When Coralie caught me eyeing them both suspiciously, she leaned over to whisper to me.

"They may not like us, but in some ways they're not so different from us."

I gave her an incredulous look.

"They're scared," she said. "And they like being alive just as much as the next person. More, probably." She snorted.

When I still looked unconvinced, she shook her head at me.

"They might not have ever thanked you, but I guarantee you they haven't forgotten you protected us all back at the Academy. No one can react to an unexpected crisis as quickly as you can. You just became everybody's favorite bunk mate."

"No pressure." A sick feeling settled in my stomach like it had no intention of leaving any time soon.

But perhaps she was right about the reason for their silence over our sleeping arrangements. They certainly seemed to feel no such reticence when they discovered we were to eat in the mess tent along with the regular soldiers. Apparently the Devoras and Stantorn trainees had finally become accustomed to my proximity. Commonborn soldiers, on the other hand? The general's children didn't expect to find themselves eating shoulder to shoulder with the common rabble.

"This is life at the front, children," said a commanding voice from behind where our group stood huddled together, just inside the enormous tent used as the mess hall. The words broke through Natalya's torrent of complaint.

She spun around, an icy look aimed at whoever had dared to interrupt her, but the expression disappeared and she made no retort when she saw the identity of the speaker. Colonel Jennica.

"She's about as senior as they come among the Stantorns," Coralie whispered in my ear. "With the exception of Duke Casimir and General Thaddeus."

"Even your father eats here when he's not up at headquarters," the colonel continued, directing her words at Natalya. "We don't have the resources to be wasting time and energy carting food to individual tents. You'll learn that soon enough."

She eyed us all, the faint traces of a smile curving her lips. "And I warrant you'll see the value of eating the food where it's hot once you've been on your first winter patrol."

"Evening, Jennica," said Lorcan who had approached during the colonel's comments. "Naturally we will eat here, as is your way." He eyed the Stantorn. "But please don't forget these are Academy trainees and not new recruits. They will not be doing patrol duty."

The slightest rise in her eyebrows suggested surprise, and the sick feeling in my stomach renewed its churning. At the Academy Lorcan had seemed a solid rock, able to shield and protect us all. But we were on the general's turf now, and it didn't give me a good feeling that the second highest ranking officer at the front seemed to have the impression we were here to do more than observe.

I stumbled blearily into line for breakfast the next morning desperate to get some food into my still-unsettled stomach. I hadn't slept well, and from the rustling blankets around me all night, I hadn't been the only one.

With a full tray, I turned to find a spot to sit. Everywhere I looked was a seething mass of gray with only the occasional flash of silver robes. Was I supposed to find the other trainees? Or

Lorcan? I looked around for white robes but couldn't see any in the press of people.

"What are Academy trainees doing here?"

Several other voices quickly shushed the curious soldier.

"Wait a minute..." said the first voice. "I recognize her!"

I gave up pretending I wasn't listening to their conversation and swung around. Her voice did sound vaguely familiar. Perhaps it was someone from Kingslee.

"Elena?"

My eyes latched onto a face that looked far too young to be wearing a soldier's uniform. Her startled expression gave way to a friendly smile when our eyes met.

"Over here!" She gestured for me to join them with one hand, while with the other, she shoved the young soldier beside her. With a grumble, he shuffled down the long bench, making room next to the girl.

I walked over, hesitating before sitting down.

"Leila?"

"Yes, it's me. Do sit. Your porridge will get cold, and it's not the most edible stuff to begin with." Her nose wrinkled.

"I thought you were posted to the training barracks in Corrin?" I climbed over the seat and sat down.

"That was last year. This is this year," said an unimpressed young man on the other side of the table who also looked familiar.

I tried to remember his name. John? Jack? Jason. It had been Jason. The boy from the front desk when I arrived to enlist.

"Never mind us," said Leila, still examining me with wide eyes. "There's nothing astonishing about us being here. But you..." She shook her head. "I don't know where to start!"

"Not Elena as in Elena of Kingslee?" A soldier I hadn't seen before leaned around Jason to get a better look at me. "The Spoken Mage?"

"Um, yes. That's me."

He stared at me in awe, and I quickly spooned in a mouthful of lukewarm porridge.

"She enlisted, you know," said Leila. "And I was her mentor." She winked at me, and I grinned weakly back.

Another young man pushed in to sit beside Jason, grinning at Leila before his gaze moved on to me. For a moment he focused on my white robe before he latched onto my face, his eyes widening. This face I recognized.

"Tobias, right?" I asked, my voice flat.

"Uh..." He glanced down the table. "I didn't know who you were. None of us did. I—"

"Oh, stow it, Tobias," said Leila. "That doesn't make it all right, and you know it."

She grinned at the other soldiers. "Tobe here tried the moves on Elena when she arrived, and she showed him his place quick as anything. Most beautiful thing I've ever seen." She turned to me. "But I'll admit, he wasn't the only one who had no idea who was gracing our humble barracks. I wish you'd told me." Her face dropped into a slight frown. "I just about had a heart attack when old silver robe came to collect you that day."

"Sorry. I wasn't expecting that. I guess...I guess I just didn't know what to say."

Jason quirked an eyebrow at me across the table. "Next time feel free to start with, 'I'm actually a mage.'"

"Not that you had to tell us anything, really. I mean it's none of our business." Leila glared at Jason as if he had been the one to bring up my previous reticence.

"Elena?" Coralie sounded at least half asleep.

I turned and grimaced apologetically at the soldier beside me, and with a sigh, he shuffled even further down, creating space for my friend. She barely managed to make it over the seat without tripping and landing with her face in her bowl, and as soon as she was seated, she began to inhale her food.

"Whoa, slow down there," I said.

She groaned. "I had the worst sleep. Those cots are—"

"The worst, right?" Leila interjected. "But you get used to them. Everyone does eventually. Or just gets too tired to notice."

Coralie blinked and looked around at our table mates as if only noticing them for the first time.

"Uh, hi. I'm Coralie."

"I'm Leila. And that's Jason." She proceeded to name everyone else around us, although most of the names went in one of my ears and out the other. "And next to you is Matthis."

While I had been distracted, the young soldier beside us had left, revealing a mage at least two decades our senior.

"He's a captain and a very important person," Leila continued, "but don't expect to get anything out of him until he's finished his breakfast. He doesn't do mornings."

Coralie peered at the man sitting next to her. "Wait, Matthis? As in, of Callinos?"

He grunted and nodded but didn't take his attention away from his food.

"I told you, he doesn't do pre-breakfast. Nothing but a full-scale attack could rouse him, I swear." Leila seemed to find it amusing and showed no discomfort at sitting beside a senior mage officer.

"He was one of my mother's year mates," said Coralie. "I'm pretty sure we've met several times."

"Well, if you run into him in the afternoon, I dare say he'll recognize you," said Leila. "He's particularly bad this morning because he was out on patrol half the night."

"Do you know everything that goes on in camp, Leila?" asked Jason, shaking his head.

"Of course not, there are thousands of troops here." She grinned. "But I like to know as much as I can."

Turning to us, she added, "It helps that I had that year at the training barracks. A lot of recruits came through, and even officers. Like Matthis, for example. He was in and out all the time. So when I arrived here, I already knew a few helpful tidbits." She winked at us. "Like that I don't have to worry about formality with him until at least an hour after he's consumed his morning meal."

"The training barracks?" Coralie looked between Leila and me. "So is that how you know each other? You're the girl from the barracks?"

"The girl from the barracks?" Leila crowed triumphantly. "Did you hear that boys? The Spoken Mage told her friends about me."

"Spoken Mage?" Matthis frowned at me around Coralie. "You're the Spoken Mage?" His eyes narrowed as he examined Coralie and me as if seeing us for the first time.

"Trainees." He made a disgusted face, picked up his half-eaten breakfast, and left the table.

Coralie and I blinked at each other in astonishment.

"Don't worry about him, he's probably just sour because he found out last night that he's being assigned to babysit one of your teams," said Leila.

"One of our teams?"

"Elena? Coralie?" Finnian stopped behind us, directing a nod at the soldiers sitting with us. "Apparently we're all wanted at the command tent."

The large square command tent was the hub of the entire camp. General Griffith's personal flag flew from it, despite his spending most of his time in the main headquarters in Bronton. But the officers who spent their days in this tent ensured that his orders were carried out regardless of his physical presence.

On first arrival, the sprawling mass of tents had overwhelmed me with chaos. But walking among them, I could see the organization that underlay the busy hubbub. Everyone moved with purpose, and the neat rows made it easy to identify the various sections.

The smell and sound of the livestock might permeate the entire area, but the animals themselves were confined to the support and supply quadrant. And silver stars marked the mages' tents, the same symbol that had identified the officers' rooms back at the training barracks.

When we arrived at the command tent with Finnian, we found two royal guards stationed outside the entrance. One at least of our year mates had arrived, then. But when we entered, we discovered all nine of them had beaten us there and now stood clumped to one side. Officers came and went around them, some giving them curious glances, others resentful ones.

Lucas stood a little apart from the others, another two royal guards standing two steps behind him, and each passing officer nodded respectfully in his direction. His face was closed off, letting the watchers know nothing of his inner feelings. I didn't let my gaze dwell on his features long enough to even attempt a guess.

Colonel Jennica approached as soon as we joined our year mates, and I sincerely hoped it was my imagination that her attention seemed focused on me. "There's no time to be wasted at the front, as you'll soon learn. And only one way to gain experience. You've been divided into three teams, and you will operate in these groups throughout your time here. I have assigned an experienced officer to lead each team. You will obey his commands as if your life depends on it—because it very well might."

I thought I felt the weight of Lucas's gaze, but when I risked a glance in his direction, he was focused on the colonel, his expression cool.

"I understood we were only here to observe."

Jennica faced him down unflinching. "Certainly, Your Highness. But I would prefer that you observe under the protection of an experienced officer." She nodded at the guards behind him. "Meaning no disrespect, but there's a big difference between Corrin and the front lines of a war."

Lucas narrowed his eyes at her but made no further protest.

The colonel wasted no more time on explanations, dividing us into the three teams. And whatever she might know or not know about our visit, she clearly knew something of us. We had been divided into three teams of somewhat balanced strength.

Coralie gave me a pained look when we were separated, and then a look of part relief, part frustration to find herself with Finnian. I didn't envy them the rest of their team—Weston and Lavinia—but at least they were together.

The general's children had been placed with Dariela and Saffron, and I felt almost as sorry for Saffron as I did for myself. Normally I would have rejoiced to avoid both of the Stantorns as well as the Devoras twins, but that meant I had been placed with the prince. There would be no careful avoidance of him now.

At least I wouldn't have to worry about our finding ourselves alone. Not from the way Araminta was clinging to my side at any rate. And Clarence looked almost as relieved to be on our team as she did. Their expressions reminded me of Coralie's earlier words, and even worse of the overheard conversation between General Griffith and Lorcan. Everyone seemed to be expecting great things from me, but I had no idea how to win a war.

I had no idea how to fight in a war.

Two other figures in silver robes stepped forward, and to my surprise I recognized them both. Captain Matthis looked only slightly less irritated than he had at breakfast, his demeanor making his companion look stiff and detached in comparison. I didn't remember Captain Carson being particularly stiff when he saved me in Kingslee, however. Merely capable. Perhaps why he had been chosen.

Carson introduced himself and gestured for Coralie and Finnian's team to follow him out of the tent. Coralie waved at me as they left, and I felt a slight release of the tension in my chest to know that she would be in the hands of an officer I had seen in action.

Matthis didn't bother with introductions, merely signaling for

Saffron's team to follow him. Her glance back at me as they left was a look of desperation, but I could do nothing but smile encouragingly.

The four of us who remained looked around expectantly, but no further officers appeared.

"And you four are with me," said Colonel Jennica after a moment of silence had passed. "It's time to move out."

CHAPTER 12

"You're going to lead our team yourself?" Lucas made no move to leave the tent.

"Certainly. Your Highness could not be trusted to anyone less senior."

"You have time for that?"

"I can't afford not to." She paused, a considering look in her eye as she examined him. "You are not just another soldier, Your Highness. But at the same time, while at the front lines, you must respect the hierarchy. Lives depend on a clear chain of command."

"I have no wish to cause problems."

I could hear the faintest off note in his voice as if he didn't quite believe his own words, but Jennica didn't seem to hear anything amiss. Nodding, she directed us out of the tent. Walking briskly, she expected us to keep up, pointing out various places around the camp as we passed.

"The sooner you learn your way around, the better," she said. "My soldiers have better things to do with their time than direct lost trainees."

Araminta made a stifled squeaking sound and took a step

closer to me. I nearly tripped over her and couldn't resist shooting her an irritated look.

"Sorry, Elena," she whispered, giving me more space.

When we reached the edge of the tents, Lucas stopped abruptly. His four guards closed in around him, their heads whipping around as they looked for what had startled him. His eyes were on Jennica, however.

"Where exactly are we going, Colonel?"

She looked for a moment as if she didn't intend to answer, but I saw her eyes flick to the red and gold uniforms in formation around Lucas. "We're catching up with our patrol."

"Excuse me?"

"We're running behind schedule, so they will have already departed camp."

"Patrol." Lucas sounded beyond unimpressed.

"Yes. We're going to observe a patrol."

"And Lorcan approved this?"

"I received the orders from General Griffith himself. Your Head is with the general at headquarters now."

Lucas's gaze shifted to the open land beyond the tents before he nodded once and made no further protest. I had no doubt he had noticed the same thing I had, though—Jennica hadn't actually said Lorcan was in agreement with our little outing. Or that he even knew about it.

I wanted nothing more than to crawl back into my firm cot, but Lucas was made of sterner stuff. I didn't need to read it in his face to know that he wanted this. The chance to see what life was really like on the front. He was willing to give up love for the war effort, and yet he had never had the chance to see it for himself until now.

We didn't have to go far to find a squad of ten soldiers with a silver-robed mage officer leading them. All of them, including the officer, greeted the colonel with a swift salute.

"As you were," she said, nodding at the mage. "Remember we

are here purely in an observational role. Please proceed as if you were alone."

The mage nodded once, but I snorted quietly. Yes, ignore the fact that three Academy trainees, the second highest ranking officer at the front, four royal guards, and the prince himself had joined them. Our numbers alone almost doubled their small group.

To my surprise, however, Jennica pulled our group behind and had us group together far enough back that we could observe and hear them, but not close enough to be easily engaged in conversation ourselves. And after half an hour or so, the patrol began to relax and operate normally—or at least what I assumed was normal.

The longer I watched them, the more certain I became that the young mage leading the patrol looked vaguely familiar.

"He was a fourth year when we were first years," Araminta whispered to me when I risked asking her about him while Jennica spoke to Lucas.

So he was serving the second year of his two year term with the Armed Forces, then. At first he had seemed hesitant, throwing glances back at us every time he spoke or withdrew a composition. But as time passed without comment or intervention from us, he settled into a rhythm and no longer paid us any particular attention.

The patrol moved south along the bank of the Abneris, a mere stone's throw from the rushing waters. Here the ground sloped gently down to meet the river, providing easy access for someone brave enough to attempt to ford the fast-moving water.

The commonborn soldiers—a mix of youngsters around my own age and older veterans who had chosen to remain in the Armed Forces after their original three-year terms, presumably because no better opportunity awaited them at home—walked in two columns. At first glance they appeared to be disorganized, with no unity to their focus. But as I watched a pattern emerged.

Their attention was scattered in all directions because between them they scoured the environment around them for something, although I didn't know what. Some soldiers watched the near bank and the water itself, others studied the far bank, while still others devoted their attention inland.

"They're looking for signs of anything amiss. For any change that doesn't seem natural," Jennica said when she saw me watching them intently. "Compositions can only take us so far since we must spread our power thinly across a great many needs. The human eyes can see more than you might think."

"And the mage?" I asked, watching him.

He walked in the center of his squad, his eyes gliding loosely over the landscape without the focus of theirs. Almost as if his attention were somewhere else entirely.

"He searches for any sensation of power," she said.

Lucas, who was walking a few steps ahead of us, slowed, joining the conversation although he kept his gaze on Jennica.

"But there's power everywhere here. I can sense it in the water, in the ground, in the sky. It even lingers around many of the plants."

I nodded my agreement. "I assumed those were compositions of ours, like the ones that seem to coat every inch of Bronton."

"They are. Or most of them. Some are the residual compositions of the enemy, ones we have already dismantled. The job of the patrol mage is to look for any changes in the tapestry of power this battlefield has become. When mages first arrive, they are required to walk the patrol routes many times until they can recognize the feel of the existing power."

"Couldn't a composition achieve the same task?" I asked.

"It could," she said. "But it would be a significant drain on our power resources. Many years ago that was how we did it. But then the enemy started sending workings across the river with inbuilt triggers that would blow on contact with a search composition. The general was a young man in those days—a rising star in the Armed Forces—and he was the one to come up with this system. It has served us well since."

I looked away from them both, mulling over her words. How many of the systems currently in place had been established by the general? I had been casting my suspicion on entire families, but here was a single man with enough knowledge and access that—if he turned traitor—he could single-handedly change the course of the war. In first year Lucas had assured me that none of the great families would act against the crown. But the attacks on me were no longer the only suspicious happening. Something had changed at the front, and my certainty that Ardann harbored a traitor had only grown.

I wished now I had seized the moment and questioned Walden when he mentioned the general's name. The librarian might spend his life sequestered in the Academy, but a lot of important people came and went inside its halls. What had he heard to make him so ill at ease? Did I have reason to fear a defense system that had been entirely formulated by the general? And should I mention my fears to Lorcan or Lucas?

I shook my head. Supposition would do no good against a general. If there was treachery at play, I needed proof. Hard evidence that Lucas could not gainsay as he had done last time. And I could not trust him to find it for himself. Lucas would not be able to see treachery among the great families because he did not want to see it.

"Sir." One of the soldiers spoke in a tight, low voice, and the entire squad, including the mage, stopped instantly.

The man who had spoken pointed at a small group of trees and bushes a short way from the river. Most of his squad mates trained their eyes on the patch, but at least three of them kept their suspicious gazes roving over the river on their other side.

"Might be something, might be nothing," said another of the soldiers, a veteran like the one who had spoken.

I looked to Jennica, but she made no move to intervene, watching the squad with a calm expression.

"What do they see?" I asked quietly.

"I don't know. I haven't been at the front in some time and am unfamiliar with the specific patrol routes. Something different I can only imagine."

The mage moved forward, drawing a small roll of parchment from inside his silver robe. When he ripped it and flicked his fingers toward the area in question, new power surged out, rushing toward the indicated spot. It settled over the area, doing nothing that I could see or sense.

I blinked. And blinked again. Now that I looked more closely…

At first it had seemed like a trick of the light, but both the land and the greenery now glowed in a faint overlay of color. Filmy red, green, yellow, and blue washed over the natural landscape, twining through each other in some places while leaving others entirely bare.

A composition to visually reveal power.

I had only ever seen one in the classroom before, and it had looked different inside in an enclosed environment. Plus it had only been revealing two previous compositions, not the hodge-podge that had saturated this area.

The colors the composition created meant little to me, but the mage officer looked alarmed.

"Saunders. Thompson," he barked, and two soldiers—one young and one an older veteran—stood to attention. "Go back to camp. We need a suppression team out here as soon as possible."

Both soldiers saluted him before jogging past on their way back toward the tent city. Neither broke stride to pass us, but they both saluted again as they drew in line with the colonel.

The young officer surveyed his remaining soldiers. Two young girls—perhaps eighteen or nineteen—looked nervous as his gaze passed over them, but his eyes settled on an older woman. When he ordered her to remain at the spot to observe the trouble area until the arrival of the suppression team, I understood the younger soldiers' nerves. I wouldn't want to be left here alone with a potential enemy composition either, and I had the ability to protect myself at least.

The chosen solider expressed no concerns, however, merely saluting and stepping away from the rest of the group. From her look of long-suffering, I guessed this wasn't her first time being assigned such a role.

The patrol soon resumed their progress. The officer looked twitchier than before, whether because they had actually located something, or because he only had two veterans remaining among his reduced squad, I couldn't tell. He certainly cast a few concerned glances at the seven soldiers. But he also sent one surreptitious glance back at us, and the sight of his shadows seemed to buoy him.

We continued on for some way with no further unsettling incidents. Twice the mage stopped to retrieve compositions from his robe, ripping the parchment, and then staring intently at the water. I watched it closely for the same wash of color as earlier but could see only the blue-green of the water, interspersed with the occasional patch of white foam where it rushed around submerged rocks.

If the mage saw something I missed, it didn't appear to concern him, and the patrol moved on quickly after both incidents.

"What is he looking for?" Lucas asked.

"Any kind of interference with the water quality," Jennica replied.

"We're downstream from camp, though. Shouldn't the tests be run upstream?" asked Clarence, speaking for the first time since the command tent.

"Naturally we run the same tests upstream," said the colonel.

"But parts of northwestern Ardann use this river as their sole water source. We have a responsibility to them as well."

Clarence nodded quickly before drawing back slightly behind Araminta and hunching his tall frame. Even so, Araminta's short stature did little to obscure him.

I tried to think of something to say that might set him back at ease but hadn't come up with anything when the grizzled soldier at the lead of the squad eased to a stop. The rest of his comrades halted behind him except for the mage who continued forward to stand beside the veteran. The two of them faced into a gully that veered away to our left, ancient evidence that the river had once run a different course.

"What do you see?" asked the mage.

The soldier grunted. "Nothing I can exactly put my finger on, sir."

The mage looked away from the gully to frown at him. "And what exactly does that mean?"

"I've walked this patrol more times than you can imagine, meaning no disrespect. Something's off, even if I can't point at exactly what."

The mage sighed, his face twisting into a frustrated grimace. For a moment he stood in silence, and then with a subtle glance back at our group, he pulled out a parchment. Ripping it, he flicked his fingers toward the gully, focusing his full attention on the power that rushed along them and out to cover the surrounding area.

I stared forward as intently as he did, although my view was more obstructed, and caught faint glimpses of color, although fewer than last time. We all stood in frozen silence until the mage made a disgusted sound in his throat.

"Nothing. As you can see as well as me. I don't like wasting my compositions because you're jumping at shadows."

"I ain't the jumping type," said the soldier, not backing down despite his superior's displeasure.

The other remaining veteran, the one who had pointed out the previous anomaly, nodded in agreement, although he didn't say anything.

"Well, there's nothing there. You saw for yourself."

"There ain't nothing that composition of yours can see, you mean. That don't mean there's no danger to be had."

"Our patrol leads us through this gully. Would you have us shirk our duty?" The mage asked sharply, trying to stare the man down.

"I'm no shirker, but I didn't survive this long by rushing heedless into danger either," the soldier said, refusing to budge.

"I am your senior officer," the mage snapped. "And for a reason. I have worked a composition; the area is clear. Do you refuse to obey your orders?"

The soldier growled quietly in his throat but stepped back to join his fellows, reluctance in every line of his body. A flash of movement to my right drew my eye, and I turned slightly, just in time to see Lucas step away from one of his royal guards. He looked at me as he did so, but his gaze quickly jumped away when he caught me watching him.

The guard immediately stepped forward, clearing his throat. The mage officer looked at him in surprise before raising an inquiring eyebrow.

"Our orders come direct from General Thaddeus, Lieutenant. The prince is not to be exposed to any undue risk."

Jennica looked between the guard and Lucas, frowning. The prince gave no acknowledgment of her regard, his face impassive and his attention focused on the mage officer.

The uneasiness on the young man's face grew, as he looked between his squad, the colonel, and the prince. I could easily read the indecision on his face and the moment he made up his mind.

Straightening, he nodded at the royal guard. Apparently his desire not to be responsible for putting a member of the royal family in potential danger overrode his desire not to appear weak in front of either his inferiors or his superiors.

"The end of this gully marks the end of our patrol route. We will turn around here and return to camp. When we pass the suppression team, we will leave word for them to continue on here once they have dealt with the other incursion. Lannis, you will remain here to explain your concerns to them and assist as necessary."

I got the impression the mage would be perfectly happy if the suppression team requested Lannis throw himself into the ravine as part of their investigations. Certainly his expression promised punishment for the soldier who had put him in an untenable position in front of both the colonel and royalty.

No one said anything, so he stalked between his squad members, leading them back away from the gully. Lannis remained behind without comment, leaving the squad reduced to six. Did every patrol go like this, or was this one unusually eventful?

As we trailed along behind, I glanced back over my shoulder at Lannis's lonely figure. He was already scaling a tree, and I could see he would soon be hidden out of sight. He at least seemed to take his own warning seriously. Was he right? Was there danger there? I hoped Jennica would tell us what the suppression team found when they examined the spot.

She had made no comment on the situation, perhaps determined to back up her assertion that we were present merely to observe. She did watch Lucas, though, with a look of calculation that I didn't like. Lucas himself seemed to be absorbed with carefully avoiding any chance he might accidentally lock eyes with me again.

His efforts allowed me the surreptitious chance to observe him as we moved further away from the gully. What had motivated him to intervene as he had so clearly done?

I hadn't made up my mind on the issue when racing feet

behind us made first the rearmost royal guard slow and then Jennica and Lucas with them. The rest of us stopped, the squad in front several beats behind the Academy group.

The guards turned but had barely raised their spears and shields when Lannis came into view, racing toward us.

"Attack!" he yelled without waiting to reach us. "An attack in the gully!"

An enormous explosion rocked the ground a second after his words. Bright light blossomed a moment later, and a low, ongoing rumble sent him staggering to a stop.

"Back up," he panted, still some distance from us. "They need back up."

CHAPTER 13

ennica took a step toward him, any question of remaining an observer gone.

"Who has been attacked? We were there only minutes ago, and the gully was empty."

Lannis struggled to pull himself up straight, but she waved a dismissive hand, and he leaned down again, bracing his hands on his knees as he fought to regain his breath.

"Another patrol," he said. "One of ours. No idea what they were doing there. But there was an ambush waiting." To his credit he didn't so much as look at the young mage officer who had earlier dismissed his warning. His whole focus was on delivering the news.

"They're hard pressed," he said. "I'm fairly certain their officer managed to send a distress signal, but I couldn't guarantee that was the purpose of the composition."

"Even if a communication has been received back at command, it will take some time for a relief force to arrive," said Jennica. "We must go at once."

The young mage officer looked relieved to have the colonel take charge, and only the royal guards hung back, one of them murmuring to Lucas in an undertone. The prince gave them a cold look and replied in more audible tones.

"You may stay here if you wish. I shall certainly not be doing so."

The man stepped back, giving a slight bow, but didn't entirely manage to hide the frustration from his face. I certainly didn't envy him the task of keeping a royal safe in the middle of a war zone.

Somehow Lannis found a second wind and joined us as we all sprinted back in the direction we had come. As he ran, he panted out further information to the colonel.

"A full platoon of Kallorwegians it looked like. At least."

She threw him a sharp glance, not breaking stride.

"I didn't stay for a good look—every second could count," he said. "But that's my rough estimate. And at least five mages."

"Five?" This time she did falter. "Five mages and over forty soldiers?" She regained her pace, adding some extra speed that my shorter legs struggled to match. We spent half our days in physical training and were several decades younger, but you wouldn't guess it to see her move.

I could see in the grim lines of her face that she didn't hold out much hope for our people. We were close, but not that close. One squad couldn't hold out against so many for any length of time.

Lannis glanced sideways at me and the other trainees.

"There's a chance for them, sir. They had an observation team with them, like us."

"What?" The word slipped out before I realized I had spoken. "Who?"

He gave me a helpless expression, and my mind conjured up a horrifying picture of Coralie lying dead at the bottom of the gully. When I reminded myself it might not be her and Finnian's team, the image in my mind only changed to Saffron. Somehow my feet discovered they could fly across the uneven ground even faster.

Jennica didn't seem to share my concerns. Instead the news had lightened her eyes. "They've got more troops, then, but we have more mages."

"Trainees," snapped Lucas. "Four of them are trainees."

She didn't bother to reply, perhaps because the gully had at last come into view. Signaling with her hand, she had us all drop our pace, making the final approach more quietly. I itched to sprint forward but forced myself to fall in with the rest of the group.

"Lieutenant," she whispered, "you're with me. The rest of you, wait on my command."

The mental image of Coralie's lifeless body hit me again. I pushed forward.

"I'm coming too," I whispered.

The colonel turned furious eyes on me. "You will do as you're ordered, private."

When I opened my mouth to speak, she cut me off. "Or you will face the consequences."

Lucas's hand on my arm pulled me back toward the others. I bit my lip, hating myself for giving way before his warning. But her talk of consequences scared me—particularly since I didn't trust that I fully understood what they might be.

The loud rumble of falling rocks made us all shift, exchanging uneasy glances. I immediately regretted my cowardice, but the colonel had already gone.

Thankfully she didn't stay away long, racing silently back to us while the lieutenant remained in place, observing the gully from behind several large rocks.

"The enemy are facing away from us. Our people must have been coming from the other end of the gully. It looks like there have been several casualties, and they're barely holding their ground. We can't afford to wait, so we're going in now to surprise the attackers from the rear."

She bent a stern look on the four of us. "We need you in this battle, but I don't want anyone taking unnecessary risks." Her eyes dwelt on both Lucas and me, her explanation of the situation more than I would have expected her to give to those under her command. Perhaps my earlier insubordination had reminded her we weren't truly soldiers. Yet.

No one protested this time, however, and she led us back to the lieutenant. Her next orders came fast, leaving no one time to think them through.

"Soldiers, at my mark, charge down into the gully." As she spoke, her hands flashed, pulling parchment after parchment out of her robe. She barely glanced at them, her eyes on us, as she unrolled them and arranged them in a neat pile.

"Lieutenant, you two," she pointed at Clarence and Araminta, "throw any shield compositions you have between the attackers and our people. Don't hold anything in reserve. The rest of us will shield you if it comes to that."

Clarence swallowed, but Araminta nodded, a look of determination on her face. It didn't escape me that she took several steps in my direction, however.

"Your Highness, Elena, we need to capture some of those mages alive, if we can. I'll handle them. Which means the two of you need to help our soldiers take on their platoon. Can you do it?"

Lucas nodded once, and she didn't wait for similar agreement from me before turning back to look down into the gully. I barely registered her orders, too distracted by the scene unfolding before us as she spoke.

Some way down the gully stood a formation of soldiers. Unlike our commonborn, they wore black uniforms that looked as if the hems had been dipped in blood. The mages arrayed behind them wore similarly colored black and red robes. Kallor-wegian Armed Forces mages.

The colonel's assurance that she would handle the mages, despite the unknown number and power of their stored compositions, made more sense now that I had absorbed the state of the battlefield. Sometime before our arrival, the beleaguered squad had evened the numbers a little.

Two enemy mages lay still, and a third knelt over one of them, frantically pulling compositions from his robe. Whether she searched for a healing composition or merely wished to harvest the downed mage's unused workings, I couldn't tell.

Further down the gully, at least three sprawled bodies of our own wore gray uniforms. The white-robed figures all still appeared to be upright, but my darting eyes could find no sign of Coralie. When I made out the tall, distinctive figure of Dariela, I realized why. This was Saffron's group.

A low, ragged smoke screen hung between them and their attackers, but even as I watched four enemy arrows flew through it. Three smashed harmlessly against the ground, but one found its mark, one of our soldiers screaming, a horrible sound that gurgled into silence. One of the enemy mages ripped a parchment, and a strong wind blew down the gully, sending robes and hair flapping and driving away the lingering barrier.

Captain Matthis shouted something, and a boy in a white robe—Calix presumably—pulled out a parchment and immediately ripped it in half. Smoke billowed impossibly from the rocky ground, shielding them all once more.

The moment of visibility had been enough for the enemy, however. From where we stood, we could see they had marked the various positions of our people, and one of the mages issued an order I couldn't hear.

A group of ten soldiers broke off from the main group, making their way down the side of the gully. They sheltered behind a string of large rocks which appeared to have recently broken from the gully wall. Their path would lead them straight to where three white robes sheltered behind a particularly large boulder.

I sucked in my breath at the sight of this attempt to flank my friends, but before I could take action, Jennica shouted, "Now!" in a loud voice.

Our seven soldiers took off without hesitation, sending themselves hurtling dangerously fast down into the ravine. They looked pitifully small in number compared to the thirty or so men and women who still remained grouped below us.

But they had barely begun to move when a particularly loud tearing sounded near my ear. I glanced over in time to see the colonel rip the entire small stack of parchments she had assembled. Power rushed past me in such force that I staggered backward a step.

A roar sounded, echoing from both sides of the gully, and for a moment, I thought she had triggered another landslide. But a moment later I recognized the battle cry of a large force, and the pounding of countless feet. Behind our small band of seven, more soldiers sprang into existence, their weapons glinting in the sun.

For half a breath, I stared in confusion, wondering if the colonel had the power to call people from the air. But even as I exhaled, understanding dawned. This was a simpler but more sophisticated version of the illusions we had used to battle within the Academy arena.

The enemy wheeled to confront the avalanche bearing down on them, their mages screaming orders that were lost in the chaos. Their soldiers responded, however, springing into formation and surging forward to surround the remaining Kallorwegian officers.

Despite their protection, one of the mages—a woman— screamed, flailing around as if fighting an invisible foe. The other two mages ignored her, their focus on the horde that appeared to bear down on them.

The ten soldiers who had been sent to flank our forces hesitated, turning back toward the head of the gully in confusion. Their movement alerted my year mates to their presence, only feet away from them. Dariela drew her sword, her movement swift and graceful, and a moment later the other two with her followed suit. Together the three of them charged the flanking soldiers, several gray uniforms racing to join them.

Nothing prevented the trainee swords meeting those of their attackers with a clang that could be heard all the way where we stood. Whatever shields Clarence and Araminta had activated must only be protecting our people against the main enemy force.

The sound of the swords galvanized me into action, shattering my frozen state. What orders had Jennica given me? The soldiers. The enemy soldiers.

Dariela neatly ran one of her attackers through, pulling her sword free of his chest. She didn't appear to notice that a man and woman approached her from the other direction, spears lowered.

My mind raced, throwing up words in front of my eyes that I had only ever read in books and never had the chance to practice.

The colonel, busy withdrawing yet more pieces of parchment from her robe, looked up at the sound of my voice racing through the binding words.

My eyes hadn't left the fight on the other side of the gully. One of the gray uniforms tried to call a warning to Dariela but was cut off by a blow that sent her sprawling to the ground. Her attacker raised his weapon, preparing to run her through.

With a jolt, I recognized her. Leila. Words poured out of me, barely recognizable I spoke so fast.

"Stop the heart of every black-uniformed soldier in the gully." It was the only wording I could think of that wouldn't touch either our forces or the enemy mages. Jennica had ordered them left alive, and I retained enough sense to know they might have personal protections in place that would drain me. I hadn't had time to set proper limits to my composition.

Darts of my power shot into the air and down with unerring precision toward each of the soldiers below. I staggered as they hit resistance—a wall between my position and the enemy. But whatever shield the Kallorwegian mages had erected failed beneath the strength of my working.

The darts flew forward again, spreading out to spear into each commonborn Kallorwegian soldier. I felt them slow as they neared their internal targets. Each soldier below fought a battle they knew nothing about—their bodies throwing up a natural defensive mechanism I had read about but never experienced. There was a reason this composition wasn't more popular, but I had lacked the time to come up with other options.

More strength poured from me, and I dropped to my knees. Gritting my teeth, I closed my eyes and strained, forcing my power onward. I felt the moment thirty-nine hearts stopped beating, and my own body hit the ground at the same moment as all of theirs.

Lucas swore and dropped to a knee beside me, but I weakly waved away his supportive hand. He stayed in place, however, so I forced myself to crawl several steps away before emptying the contents of my stomach into a nearby bush. Repeatedly.

A soft hand brushed against my forehead, pulling back my hair. I stayed in place, panting, my stomach heaving and aching from the spasms. But as soon as it subsided, I scrambled back onto my feet, pushing past Lucas as he tried to grab at my arm.

Racing to the edge of the gully, I looked down at the battleground below. I swayed and felt Lucas's hand against my arm again. I let myself lean into his support, afraid that my exhaustion would send me tumbling down the steep slope.

The smoke had dissipated, and the remaining upright figures picked their way among the dead. So many of them. They lay where they had fallen, unmarked, although the red edges of their uniforms gave the impression of wounds from this distance.

A third enemy mage lay among them, cut down while I wasn't looking, but the other two knelt amid the wreckage of the battle, their hands on their heads. Their robes had been removed and lay in two crumpled piles. Underneath they wore plain leather outfits, and both the lieutenant in charge of our patrol and the one who had led Leila's patrol searched them for hidden compositions.

Captain Matthis watched on, directing them, his expression ugly as he glowered at the two prisoners. The trainees under his protection ranged behind him, three of them with their attention on the search underway. The fourth, however, looked straight up at us.

I met Dariela's eyes across the distance, and she slowly nodded before turning to look back toward the area where she had been fighting when I worked my composition. I picked out the bodies of her two fallen attackers before looking back at her. Apparently she had seen the danger after all.

This is why you did it, I reminded myself as my stomach roiled once more, threatening to dry retch. *If you hadn't, it would be Dariela dead, and Leila—*

I looked around quickly, trying to pick out the gray-clad girl. I found her sitting with her back to a rock, red staining her uniform. But as I watched, Saffron approached her and withdrew a parchment from her sleeve.

Leila gave a pained grimace which melted into a look of relief as Saffron ripped the composition, flicking her fingers at the injured soldier. They exchanged several inaudible words, and then Leila's searching eyes found me on top of the gully. I stepped swiftly back, out of sight.

Dariela's gratitude I could take, but I did not want Leila's awe. Not for something like this.

"Spoken Mage."

I turned slowly to face Colonel Jennica. Her eyes held the awe I had been trying to avoid, but with an edge of greedy calculation that made the shock on Leila's face pale by comparison.

"I had heard stories," she said. "But I didn't realize..." She shook her head. "It's different to see it for myself."

Her words drove back the horror that had been making everything around me hazy, turning it instead into unreasoning anger.

"Yes," I snapped. "And I counted five of our own dead down there. Perhaps some of them would be alive now if you had listened to me and let me approach from the beginning."

The colonel stared me down, her expression cool and unflustered.

"If I had comprehended your strength, I might have chosen differently, it is true. But perhaps not. We did not know the situation when we arrived." She looked me up and down. "It is the job of an officer to do more than consider individual lives. It is our job to see the broader picture. This gully has no strategic value. It lies far from our troops, our headquarters..." She glanced back toward it with narrowed eyes. "It is not even near any farming land."

"That was no raiding party," said Lucas quietly, referencing the small squads of soldiers who regularly attempted to break through our line of defense to wreak havoc on the kingdom beyond.

"No indeed," said the colonel. "Too large and well-equipped for a raiding party, too small for an invading force. An officer must consider what their purpose could be in preparing an ambush in such a place."

Her eyes lingered on me for a moment before looking over my shoulder where I could feel Lucas's presence.

"Perhaps it has not occurred to you, Spoken Mage, but I can assure you it has occurred to me that ours was the patrol intended to traverse that gully. And it just so happens that our patrol contains a number of persons of very great interest indeed. Perhaps you can say with any certainty that it was me the enemy was after, and not you or the prince. But I cannot. And since you are both in my care, I hardly intended to let you any closer to danger than absolutely necessary."

She gave me a disgusted look. "I hope you will ponder on that before questioning me again. I am not new to war, youngster."

Shock had dissipated my anger, and I could think of nothing to say. Turning, she strode to the edge of the ravine and called for the prisoners to be brought up.

I swallowed and turned to face Lucas, swaying again. It was hard to think clearly through the fog that filled my mind, and I had no idea how I would manage to walk back to camp. I intended to ask him if he thought it possible one of us had been the target, but my words died in my throat at the burning anger in his expression.

"All of them, Elena? At once? Really?"

I winced and tried to think how to explain there had been no time for subtleties. He leaned closer to me, gripping one of my shoulders. A spark jumped between us, clearing my brain slightly.

He dropped his voice low. "Do you have any idea how many compositions I'm carrying on my person? Of the stored strength I currently possess?"

When I did nothing but blink at him, his expression darkened.

"Stored power, Elena. The kind that won't exhaust me. That carries no risk to me whatsoever. We were both instructed to deal with the soldiers. You didn't need to target them all at once."

One of the royal guards called for him, and he let me go abruptly, striding away before I could point out that the pre-prepared compositions he carried were, by necessity, broad. The time it might have taken him to come up with a strategy and choose the best ones to use was time Dariela and Leila hadn't had.

Only once we had begun the slow trek back to camp, prisoners in tow, did it occur to me that I hadn't had the chance to ask either Lucas or Jennica the most important question.

If that had been an ambush lying in wait for one of us...how had the enemy known which patrol we had joined or what our route was to be? For that matter, how had they known we were to be away from Bronton today at all?

How long before someone acknowledged out loud that we had a traitor at work among us?

CHAPTER 14

$\mathcal{I}$ was stumbling before we made it more than a few minutes. The ground ahead of us stretched out agonizingly far, a seemingly insurmountable distance. But when I tripped over a small stone, sturdy hands steadied me, surprising me with their strength.

"Here, lean on me," Leila offered, slinging my arm across her shoulders.

I considered protesting but didn't have the energy. She nodded at another soldier I didn't recognize, and the older woman moved forward to prop up my other side. Together we moved faster, my whole concentration focused on putting one foot in front of the other.

At some point we passed Saunders, Thompson, and our female soldier with the suppression team. Vaguely I heard them reporting that the working they had investigated had been harmless.

"A decoy, perhaps," the distant voice of Jennica said. "To reduce our squad's numbers by the time we made it to the gully."

I didn't hear any more, and I couldn't bring myself to care enough to try. Not until I had some sleep.

As we approached camp, however, I finally put my finger on an off feeling that had been niggling at the back of my mind.

Leila. She was so quiet. Had battle finally done what army conscription had not and quashed her bubbly positivity? A worse idea occurred to me. Had Saffron done only a partial healing?

As we reached the first of the tents, I stopped, lurching forward when my two supporters took an extra step to halt themselves. Separating from them, I peered at Leila.

"You're awfully quiet. Are you injured still?"

Leila shook her head, unshed tears shining in her eyes.

"I suppose...I suppose you didn't have a chance to look at the..." She swallowed. "At the bodies. You never came down into the gully."

"I'm sorry," I said quickly, but she jumped over me.

"No, that's not a criticism. What you did—" She exchanged a look with the other soldier. "You saved us all." She looked back at me. "I just mean that you probably didn't see..."

She drew a shuddering breath, making an effort to pull herself together.

"They got Jason. An arrow to the throat. None of the mages even had a chance to try to..." She looked away, her face deathly pale. "We enlisted in the same batch and both got our first posting to the training barracks. I know this is a war, and soldiers die, but..."

"Your first friend to die is always the hardest. Nothing can prepare you for it, not really," the other soldier said in a quiet voice. "We'll drink to him tonight at dinner, but it doesn't do much to heal the ache."

She glanced over at me. "Our small version of an ashes ceremony. His family back home will have the real one, of course."

"Oh. His family." A stifled sob shook Leila.

We all stood in awkward silence, unsure what to do to help until she looked up with a martial light in her eye.

"It's all the fault of that—"

"Hush!" The older soldier jumped in quickly, silencing whatever insults Leila had been about to utter. Her face dropped into sympathetic lines. "Some truths can't be safely spoken," she said more softly.

I looked back and forth between them, noting the rebellious light still in Leila's eyes.

"Whose fault?" I asked.

The woman looked at me warily, and I tried to look as approachable as possible.

"I may wear one of these," I plucked at my white robes, "but I'm as commonborn as you, remember. I've cursed the mages myself, often enough. I'll carry no tales."

The soldier didn't look entirely convinced.

"We need them, Leila, just remember that," she said. "We'd all have been dead back there without Captain Matthis. He kept us together when the attack hit." She nodded at me. "The trainees, too. I almost enjoyed watching that Lady Dariela at work. Never seen death look so elegant."

She nodded again once and strode away into the camp.

Leila sighed. "She's right about Captain Matthis. For all his early morning humors, he's as solid as they come. I'd heard as much, and now I've seen it for myself." Her expression soured. "It was that lieutenant."

I stepped closer, encouraging her to drop her voice. I wanted to hear what had happened—the real account—but I didn't want her getting in trouble for it.

"What happened?"

"He's new. Only graduated from your Academy last year and only just got posted to doing patrol. Our previous lieutenant was capable enough, but he got promoted, thus how we ended up with a fresh one."

She paused and ran a hand over her eyes.

"Jason tried to tell him we were off our route. And that—" She broke off and looked around before modifying whatever she had been going to say. "That lieutenant gave him latrine duty for a week for questioning orders. Even so, when we reached the gully, Williams tried again. Tried to tell him something didn't feel right, that we shouldn't go in. Only made the officer angrier, and he insisted we increase our pace."

Her color still hadn't returned, and I could see her reliving it in her mind.

"They sprang out from nowhere. They'd concealed themselves behind boulders and trees using blankets covered in dirt and branches."

So that's how they had evaded our lieutenant's composition. They hadn't been using power to disguise their presence at all.

"Jason tried to tell him, and so did Williams." Leila's voice hitched. "And now they're both dead. But that lieutenant's still alive. When that attack hit, the first thing he did was pull out a personal shielding composition."

I frowned. Cowardly, of course. But I couldn't help thinking of Clarence or Araminta. That could be them in two years' time. For all I knew, it was the first time the mage had ever even seen a Kallorwegian, let alone battle. It didn't change the fact that things should have gone differently, of course. That they could have gone differently if he'd recognized his inexperience and listened to his squad.

"Williams was the oldest veteran on the team," Leila said. "He'd been doing this longer than some of us have been alive. Knew the ground, knew the squad."

She didn't say any more, but she didn't need to. Williams should have been in charge. Everyone would still be alive right now if he had been. He should have been the lieutenant, and the mage the private. She knew it, I knew it. But nothing could be gained by saying it.

"Go get checked out properly at one of the healing tents," I said. "I'm sure Saffron did her best, but she's not exactly a trained healer."

Leila nodded a little absently and insisted on seeing me to my own tent before she would obey my instruction. I didn't stop to watch her go, too eager to talk to Saffron and Coralie and reassure myself that both my friends had returned unharmed. Who knew what dangers Coralie's group might have run into?

But their patrol had been uneventful, as it turned out. Coralie and Lavinia sat on their cots, listening with wide eyes to Natalya tell the story of the attack. Araminta, Dariela, and Saffron made small additions, but no one tried to correct a narrative that gave Natalya far more of a central role than in reality. In fact, for a moment I couldn't remember seeing her there at all. Only when I thought back did I realize she had been the third trainee fighting off the breakaway group with Saffron and Dariela. Calix had been on the other side of the gully with Matthis.

When it came to my involvement, Natalya attempted to gloss over it. But Dariela looked up and saw me. Immediately she cut in on the tale.

"Elena saved us all. She certainly saved my life, at any rate. Worked a composition that killed every one of the attacking soldiers. Every one."

She crossed over to me and raised her hand in the air in front of her, its back toward me. Hesitantly, I twined my arm around hers so I could grip her hand. Squeezing it, she thumped the back of my hand once against her chest.

"I, for one, am grateful. That's twice now. I don't intend to forget it."

Natalya humphed, sticking her nose into the air. "There's one thing, for sure," she said, "my father isn't going to be pleased to hear that Calix and I were put in such a dangerous situation. That fool Jackson had no idea what he was doing and could have gotten us all killed. He was always useless, even back at the Academy. Matthis should have stepped in. At least the captain seemed competent."

Dariela stepped away from me and looked back at the Devoras girl. She raised an eyebrow but didn't actually disagree.

"If the general sees fit to reassign Lieutenant Jackson, it would no doubt be better for everyone. Perhaps the Armed Forces has other roles that would better suit his strengths." Her tone made it clear she rather doubted that.

Coralie rushed over to me, ignoring their discussion of Jackson. I dragged her into a corner and gave her the real story. Saffron and Araminta quickly followed, backing up my less varnished version.

"Honestly, though," said Saffron, "when it came to it, I was glad to have Calix and Natalya there. I mean, not as glad as I was to have Dariela—or you, Elena, when you arrived—but they fought well. And it took all of us to hold them off. I don't know how much longer we would have lasted without your assistance."

She looked pale and shaken, and on impulse I pulled her into a big hug. She returned it, looking a little teary when I pulled away.

"Thank goodness for Captain Matthis. He moved faster than I would have thought humanly possible when they sprung the ambush. He had a shield up, all of us hiding behind boulders, and had cut down one of the enemy mages while the rest of us were still trying to absorb what was going on."

"I get the impression they've assigned the best to watching over us, at least," I said.

Coralie nodded slowly, still looking shocked at the news of our eventful patrols. She met my eyes across Araminta's head.

"Lorcan's going to be furious, though, isn't he? I mean, our first day, and this happens. One of you could easily have been killed or captured."

I nodded. I needed to sleep. But once I had, I intended to give that possibility a great deal more thought. It seemed to me vitally important to know which of us the enemy had tried to capture or kill. Second only to the need to discover how they had known so much.

~

I slept for the rest of the day, waking only once dark had fallen. The sleep had finally settled my stomach, and it growled at me, complaining at being so empty.

I slipped out of bed, whispering to Coralie that I was off to find some food. She made a half-hearted attempt to get up, but I told her to stay put. From the looks of it, most of my year mates were just falling asleep, so it must still be evening. I didn't need company.

I made it only two steps from the tent when a shadowy figure fell into step beside me. I flinched.

"Sorry, I didn't mean to scare you," said Lucas.

I didn't reply. He hadn't scared me—his presence was too familiar for that. But I still didn't trust myself to be alone in the dark with him.

We walked in silence between the tents until I finally spoke.

"What were you doing there?"

This time it was his turn not to reply. Had he been waiting for me to emerge? It must have been a long wait.

"I'm sorry I spoke to you like that back there," he said after another pause. "What you did was incredible, and I should have..." He sighed and ran a hand through his hair, the dark locks falling back into perfect place afterward. "You scared me. When I heard your composition, I feared..."

"You're right, it was reckless." I spoke quietly. "I've never been in a situation like that before. Dariela and Leila were both about to be killed. I just..." I spread my arms helplessly. "I reacted. Like I always do. And then I did it again with Colonel Jennica."

"No one can predict how they'll respond the first time they

see battle," he said. "There are worse ways you could respond."
My mind flew to Lieutenant Jackson and then to Lucas himself.

"I suppose so…" I thought of the way the prince had inter-
vened to prevent our own patrol walking into what had turned
out to be a trap. Somehow his responses always possessed a
subtlety mine lacked.

"I'm still afraid for you, Elena," he said.

I glanced sideways at him. Was it the darkness hiding our
faces that made him so open all of a sudden?

"For me or of me?" I asked, the memory of all those motionless bodies making me shiver.

He turned slightly, reaching out a hand that he quickly let
drop.

"For you. Always for you." He paused while a soldier passed in
the other direction. "I've been thinking on what Colonel Jennica
said. They were coming for you, Elena, I'm sure of it. And now
they've seen what you're capable of. Next time they'll bring two
platoons and a dozen mages."

"We can't know that," I said quickly, trying to hide the shiver
that ran through me. "They could just as easily have been after
you. How long has it been since a member of the royal family was
within striking distance of the front lines? Perhaps they hoped to
hold you to ransom, to force your family to cede something."

"Perhaps…"

The darkness hid his eyes, but I didn't like what I heard in his
voice. Was he thinking of his delegation to the Sekali Empire?
Thinking that his family would not sacrifice any part of their
kingdom for him?

"But," he continued, "only one of us has been the victim of an
attempted Kallorwegian abduction before." He gave me a pointed
look.

I said nothing, unable to dispute his point.

"But that's not the only thing I've been thinking," he said, except his words cut off as the mess tent loomed out of the darkness. We slipped inside, and he didn't finish his thought.

Had he been intending to point out how perfectly the gully attack had proved his point about my value to the war effort? If so, I was glad our arrival at the mess had cut him off. My stomach had finally settled enough to eat, and thinking about ever repeating my performance would be enough to set it off again.

And the feeling of nausea was only exacerbated by the memory of Leila's wound, and her tears for her friend. Was I being inexcusably selfish? Had Lucas been right all along? I thrust the thought away. He had said nothing on the topic, so I didn't have to think of my answer now.

My stomach growled audibly, and Lucas chuckled. Lights still burned inside, no doubt for those returning from night duty. Simple, cold food had been left out on a long bench, and I took an apple, closing my eyes as I bit into it. Had apples always been this delicious?

When I opened them again, Lucas was looking at me with an expression that made my cheeks warm. Amusement, affection, and perhaps something else. Something he had whispered in a library, that I didn't dare name even in my own head.

I looked away quickly.

"You two." The voice sounded long-suffering and a little weary. "I should have known the two of you wouldn't be anywhere as sensible as in your beds."

I turned to confront the Academy Head.

"Where have you been all day?"

I had thought the question, but it wasn't my mouth which uttered it.

Lorcan frowned at Lucas. "Bronton, of course. I was with General Griffith when news of the attack came. Naturally I wished to be present at the interrogation of the prisoners."

"And?" I asked. "What did you find? Who...what were they after?"

He ran a tired hand over his face. "We don't know."

I frowned at him. Not that I had ever been at an interrogation before, but in Corrin they had been able to compel the truth from my attackers.

"They're dead. Both of them."

"What?" Lucas didn't raise his voice, but he didn't need to.

"Dead the moment the truth composition hit them."

"How is that possible?" I asked. "We saw them searched and stripped of all compositions."

"That is what I have spent my day attempting to determine."

"And?" asked Lucas.

Lorcan spread his hands slightly. "Inconclusive. They were felled by a composition, certainly. Our best guess is that it was placed on them before they left Kallorway. Triggered to spring into action if a truth composition was applied. Who knows if they even knew it was there?"

Or the deadly composition had been worked by a traitor in our midst.

"Who was there?" I asked. "Who knew the prisoners were there?"

Lorcan frowned at me. "Half the town knew they were there, I imagine, since they walked through the streets to the headquarters. As for who actually had access to them..." He paused, his face considering. "They were in my or the general's sight from when they were brought in until their deaths."

I swallowed, the apple suddenly sitting heavy in my stomach. Lorcan or the general. I knew who I'd put my money on as the traitor. The Head of the Armed Forces had access to every report, every plan, every building, every tent. I looked from Lorcan to Lucas. I didn't need to speak to know how quickly they would both reject the idea.

"How very convenient," I said instead. "Dead. Just like my attackers from first year. Both sets. Except for the one who brought down the balcony. We never found him."

The general had been there that night too. It was the first time I had met him.

"What are you doing here now?" asked Lucas.

"I was getting some food," said Lorcan. "And then I was coming to find you."

Lucas raised a quizzical eyebrow.

"With such momentous happenings, I have not had a suitable moment to have a word with General Griffith," said Lorcan. "A word alone. And I suspect I might need back up." His face twisted a little as if he hated having to admit it. "And since there are no other members of the Mage Council at the front, I will have to make use of the only member of the royal family in reach."

"Sending us out on patrol," said Lucas, catching on more quickly than me.

At his words I realized why Lorcan might want a private word with Griffith. Discipline heads did not battle it out in public.

CHAPTER 15

*L*orcan wanted to send me back to bed, but Lucas insisted I accompany them. And Lorcan had already admitted he wasn't in much of a position to be issuing orders. Not to the only member of the royal family in reach.

And so we approached the main headquarters building together, although I had the good sense to stay a step behind the other two. Griffith didn't have the same vested interest in my presence, so it was best if I didn't draw too much attention to it.

We found him in what had once been a ballroom. The room now held far too many desks and one enormous central table. Parchment was scattered everywhere. This wasn't a room for commonborn soldiers.

"Ah, Lorcan, back already." The general's face tightened as he took in Lorcan's face and Lucas's presence.

"I would like a word with you, General," Lorcan said. "A private word."

Griffith heaved a sigh, like a long-suffering parent forced to take time out of his busy schedule to try to explain something to a small child.

"Very well, if you insist."

He didn't have to issue any orders. The few remaining officers in the room filed out without question. I recognized both Captain Carson and Captain Matthis, and even one of the lieutenants looked familiar. It had been months since Martin had helped save me in Kingslee, and I almost didn't recognize him without the darker summer skin tone.

But he smiled at me in a friendly manner as he left, trailing behind Captain Carson as he had done then. Perhaps I shouldn't be surprised to find them both here at the front. I should have known the general would assign two of his top men to watch me when he received Lorcan's request for officers for the role. I just no longer knew what his purpose had been. Lorcan had said it was a test. But whose test? Who exactly was playing who here?

"What exactly are you playing at?" Lorcan snapped, as if he could read my thoughts. It took me a moment to remember he was speaking of our inclusion in the patrols.

"I really don't know what—"

"Griffith, please," Lorcan suddenly sounded old and tired, although I wasn't sure if this was another act. "We've known each other for a long time. Can we cut out the protestations? I said my trainees were here only to observe."

"And they were. They went out on an observational capacity only. You can hardly blame them for fighting for their lives." He placed both hands on the table and leaned forward. "This is a war, remember. You might forget it back in your tidy little Academy, but it is harder to escape out here."

"I never forget," said Lorcan, drawing himself up. Something hard entered his eyes, and neither of them spoke for a moment, something passing between them that I couldn't understand. A sideways glance at Lucas told me he was as clueless as me. Whatever this was about, I was guessing it was something long before Lucas or my time.

The general drew a long breath and relaxed slightly, and the moment passed.

"You sent them out on purpose when I was occupied here," Lorcan said. "Patrols on their first day? Really Griffith, I expected a more subtle hand from you."

The general grinned a tight-lipped smile. "Sometimes bold gestures are needed." He glanced over at Lucas and me. "We wished them to see the reality of war. They will not find it in camp. The battle is out there." He pointed in the direction of the distant river.

"See it, not conduct it," Lorcan said. "There is an important distinction."

"Lorcan," said Griffith with a sigh. "You are an excellent academic, but you sometimes lack imagination. You were there. You heard the report from Jennica. You know what she's capable of."

His eyes focused on me, and a chill ran through me when I realized the *she* he referred to wasn't Jennica.

"Incredible," he breathed, still looking at me. "The power. The flexibility." He shook his head. "Jennica said she used less than a dozen words. On a composition she can never have performed before in her life!" He looked back at Lorcan. "Don't you see the possibilities?"

"Yes," said Lorcan, his voice cold. "I do. You accuse me of lacking imagination, but it is you who does so, Griffith. You see only this war. I see far beyond it."

Lucas cleared his throat, and both of them looked at him, a sliver of uncertainty on their faces for the first time. Lucas might be much younger than these men, but the throne he represented was far older.

How exhausting it must be for them. Each with their own agenda, and no one entirely sure who shared it with them.

"I believe we were discussing my and the other trainees' duties during our stay in Bronton," Lucas said.

Lorcan nodded. "As you say, Your Highness." He directed a piercing look at the general. "We might be in the middle of a war,

Griffith, but they are still my trainees. All of them. And they will not be accompanying any more patrols."

"Very well," said Griffith, collecting several papers in front of him as if bored of the discussion. "I will inform Jennica that all further orders regarding their movements must be counter-signed by both of us. They can take up training within the camp, at least." He glanced up. "I assume that meets with your approval."

Lorcan hesitated, as if looking for some unseen trap. "Of course," he said at last. "I would not wish them to fall out of practice."

"No indeed." The general looked at us with raised eyebrows. "Is there anything more?" The long-suffering parent—eager only for his bed but kept up by the pesky questions of his children—had returned.

Lorcan turned to leave, ushering Lucas and me out of the room ahead of him. As we crossed into the corridor, Lucas muttered, "That was easy."

Lorcan froze at his words, still inside the room. For a moment he regarded Lucas's raised eyebrows, and then he turned slowly back to the general, his manner exaggeratedly casual.

"You wanted us here to see what she can do, I know that well enough. And for morale, you said." He paused, but no one said anything. "I'm already hearing the talk around camp. I walked past a fire where someone was assuring his fellow soldiers there were a hundred enemies in that gully." He paused again. "Big gestures, you said, Griffith. I find myself wondering just how big a gesture you would be willing to make."

The following silence was charged in a way the earlier ones hadn't been. I could feel the shock coursing through my body. Was it possible the whole thing had been a set up by the general? Was it? I thought of all those dead soldiers and nearly threw up again.

"Don't be a fool, Lorcan," the general's voice sounded low and angry. "Two of my own children were in that patrol. My own children."

Lorcan examined him for a moment before dipping his head in a partial bow.

"I apologize. I overstepped."

The general growled something I couldn't distinguish, and Lorcan took it as a signal to leave. Griffith had sounded sincere, but I had been out in the corridor. I hadn't seen his eyes.

Lucas walked me all the way back to our tent, and only when we reached it did either of us speak.

"I could feel them, Lucas," I whispered, glad the darkness hid my expression. "I could feel each one of their hearts stop beating."

He sucked in an audible breath. For a moment we both stood motionless, and then he stepped closer, gripping both my arms in his hands.

"I've known the general my whole life, Elena. He loves his children. He would never…That was a real attack. Those were our enemies. You saved lives today, perhaps a great many."

I drew in a breath. "I suppose Griffith does love them, but there's one thing I can't stop thinking of." I looked up at him, although I could barely make out the gleam of his eyes in the gloom. "It was supposed to be our patrol in that gully, not theirs."

Lucas might not be open to the idea that the general could be a traitor, but he seemed more receptive to the suggestion that he might have staged a demonstration of my power. At least that was how I interpreted the discomfort I saw lurking in his eyes whenever they rested on the general.

Confined within the camp, our lives took on a routine almost like life at the Academy. Except instead of a comfortable suite, we returned each evening to a shared tent. In the mornings we still had combat practice, and in the afternoons we studied compositions with a variety of instructors, although the most common were Beatrice and Reese.

In the healing tent we had the opportunity to see real healings at work, although I overheard enough conversations between soldiers to know the number of injured was unusually low. Patrols made contact with the enemy, but they were small, isolated battles. The ambush in the gully had been the largest, and the only one involving more than one squad.

But the relative quiet seemed to do nothing to reassure Lucas that I wasn't in any imminent danger of Kallorwegian abduction. At least I assumed that accounted for his becoming my shadow. Not that we found ourselves alone again—the camp was too busy for that, and Coralie rarely left my side, plus Lucas himself was always accompanied by two guards. He must have slipped away from them the night after the attack, and they must have increased their vigilance after that since he didn't do so again.

But though we found no opportunities to speak, still he was there every time I turned around. As if he feared that if he let me out of his sight, the Kallorwegians would somehow spirit me away. It was actually sweet, if a little misguided.

The morning training was overseen by Thornton, as it had been at the Academy, and he seemed entirely undismayed by our new surroundings. In fact he greeted us after the attack at the gully in an almost cheery tone. Perhaps because his trainees had seen battle and emerged unscathed. But I got no opportunity to enjoy the improvement in his mood. On our first day training, Captain Matthis approached the practice yard Thornton had chosen before we even had time to begin.

"Private Elena, you're to come with me," he announced.

Thornton stepped forward, but Matthis stared him down.

"Orders from the general. She's to train as one of ours."

Thornton looked from him to me to Lucas, indecision reflected in his eyes.

"Relax," Matthis said, sounding bored. "We'll only be two

yards down." He pointed to where a group of nervous, youthful recruits stood, clearly waiting for his return.

I glanced over at Lucas myself, but he gave me the smallest shrug. I wasn't leaving camp. I was even training. We had ourselves heard Lorcan give his approval for training, and neither head had specified who was to give it.

Reluctantly I followed Matthis. If this was a power play, and I was truly to train with fresh recruits, I would lose my conditioning and my edge against my teammates in weeks. But somehow I didn't think I was going to get off that lightly.

I was right.

As soon as we had finished running laps, General Griffith himself appeared.

"I've come to observe my new soldiers," he said, with a jovial smile that didn't sit entirely naturally on his face. "Pretend I'm not here."

From the terrified looks the newcomers cast him, it was clear they would not be capable of ignoring his presence. I refrained from looking in his direction, but I was just as aware of his observation as they were. And all too soon, he called for me.

A lieutenant, almost as young looking as the commonborn recruits, appeared to take over their instruction, leaving Matthis free to join the general and me.

"Captain Matthis is going to run some exercises with you, Elena," Griffith said. "Nothing too onerous, of course, but it is my job to understand the capabilities of all my soldiers."

I mistrusted his assurance regarding the ease of the exercises so was surprised when his words proved true. I had no difficulty fending off the stones Matthis threw in my direction. Even when he graduated to using compositions to send heavier stones at a faster pace, I still had no trouble. I had practiced shielding compositions until I could do them in my sleep. Boredom would be my biggest problem if these were the exercises the general had in mind.

Two hours in, I began to feel differently. At three hours, I dropped to my knees. My shield flickered, only partially slowing the next stone. I dodged it by tipping forward onto the ground and not getting up again.

Familiar hands helped me up, and I groaned at Coralie and Saffron. "Are you sure none of those boulders hit me? I feel like they might have hit me."

My friends tried to smile, but I could see anger beneath their gazes. And when I looked up and met Lucas's eyes, his held the same anger, although he hid it better.

"What exactly is the meaning of this, Griffith?" he barked.

"You seem to have a great deal of interest in her," said the general, a note in his voice I didn't like.

Lucas's own voice turned cold. "My family has a great deal of interest in the Spoken Mage, General. I thought you were already aware of that. Now, please explain."

I knew why he said them, but his words hurt anyway. And I didn't even get to hear the general's explanation since my friends were already half-carrying me toward my tent.

As we passed the trainees' practice yard, Thornton caught my eye. Our Academy instructor watched our progress, having made no move to approach the yard where I had spent the last few hours training or to intervene with the general. When I met his gaze, his eyes tightened slightly, his face hardening. And as my friends helped me limp past him, he quietly spoke.

"Remember, Elena."

I looked up sharply, but he said nothing more, merely giving me a significant look. I lowered my eyes, embarrassment mingling with my exhaustion. We might be in a new environment, but that didn't excuse my forgetting his warning. Here on the front lines of a war, I had more need than ever to guard my energy levels.

It was almost as if he had foreseen this eventuality, and he had already told me what I must do. Even if it meant deceiving

Captain Matthis or the general about my true exhaustion levels, I couldn't allow myself to be driven to collapse again.

Over breakfast the next morning, Finnian confirmed my fear that my testing wasn't over.

"The general has realized your main limitation." He shook his head at me. "Almost your only limitation, in truth. Energy. Your strength and control are remarkable, but you cannot store your compositions, so you will always be limited by your energy levels. He's testing them. And perhaps trying to train them. To work out a way around them, if he can."

I imagined for a moment the freedom of being able to access unlimited energy. And then I imagined the feel of a million hearts ceasing to beat at once, and the dream burst into flames. No one should have access to that sort of power, and certainly not the general.

The following weeks proved that he certainly intended to try, however. Captains Carson and Matthis were my most common instructors, but others came and went. Some had me try different techniques to increase my efficiency, minimizing the power I used to achieve various compositions. More often they simply drove me to the point of exhaustion.

At least they never questioned my eventual collapse, and after that first day I carefully hoarded my power, collapsing before I truly needed to. I would let them push me so far, but no farther. The exercises were always tiring enough even so, and it was easy to drag my feet and drop my head as I shuffled off to the midday meal.

On one occasion Matthis led me a short way out of camp and instead of throwing rocks at me, had me throw rocks at a number of small trees until the stones smashed their way through the trunks and sent the trees hurtling to the ground. There was something cathartic about the exercise, and I threw more of myself into it than I should have. True exhaustion made it hard to walk as we made our way back.

I didn't have to worry about a repeat, however. Lorcan met us at the edge of camp, his expression dark.

"I've spoken to Griffith," he said, not bothering with a greeting. "You stay inside the camp in the future."

Matthis's eyes narrowed, but he nodded a begrudging acquiescence. The next day we were back in the training yard, but he had a particularly nasty concoction of compositions for me. He had apparently decided that I was to be tested with each of the elements, in case one came more easily to me than another. And day one consisted of my producing waterfalls from the air to douse the balls of flame he threw at me.

It was hard to be precise with the amount of water I needed, and the unfamiliar exercise threw me off stride enough that I failed to properly monitor my energy. When a final torrent of liquid doused a steady stream of fire, I collapsed for real and didn't get back up.

"Endurance training," said Finnian grimly, as he carried me to my tent. "They're just going to keep trying anything they can think of. If they can't increase your energy levels, they can at least increase the amount of strength you can access. And the worst of it is you're already improving, Elena."

I sighed and rested my head against his chest, too tired to hold it up. He exchanged a look over my head with someone I couldn't see, his hands tightening around me, but he said nothing.

When we turned the next corner, my line of sight changed, and I saw Lucas watching us, both hands balled into fists. For a moment our eyes locked, and then a tent came between us.

He hadn't said more than two words to me since the general's comment.

You seem to have a great deal of interest in her.

~

I slept poorly as the weather grew colder, and Coralie even fetched me an extra blanket from the supply tent. But I could tell from the look in her eyes when she handed it to me that she didn't really expect it to help. She just didn't know what else to do.

It wasn't the cold disrupting my sleep, it was the nightmares. I knew I woke in the night gasping, sweating, and yelling. But not one of the girls in my tent commented or complained about my noise. Most of them had been at the ambush in the gully. Maybe some of them had nightmares of their own.

Between the nightmares and the general's training, my friends seemed to have reached an agreement that I needed cheering up. I always had at least one of them with me, and at mealtimes our table rang with laughter.

Leila joined us sometimes, her bright chatter having returned. But sometimes, when others were talking, she would fall silent for a moment, and I would see it in her eyes. Some things you never forgot. Some things you never fully recovered from. You just learned to live with them, to push them to the back of your mind. The epidemic had been like that, but at least then I had not been directly responsible for any of the deaths.

I carried the feel of death with me now, and it ate away at me. With each day that passed, I knew that I couldn't turn my back on the war and go back to living as if it wasn't happening. But neither could I repeat my performance in the gully. I felt myself caught in the middle, compelled to act, but repulsed by the thought of it at the same time.

And yet every time I looked at Leila, or thought of the missing Jason, I wondered what they could have achieved for Ardann if their lives hadn't needed to be squandered here. Could this be the change I needed to make to help the commonborn after all?

"You know Midwinter is in two days, right?" Coralie asked me as we walked to breakfast one morning.

I frowned. "Is it? I lose track of the days here."

"The general always hosts a party at one of the headquarter buildings in the town, apparently," said Coralie.

I raised both eyebrows. "And we're invited? That surprises me. Surely that will be Natalya's affair."

"Maybe it's her way of saying thank you? For the gully?" Coralie glanced at me sideways. "She invited the whole year during composition yesterday afternoon. I think you must have dozed off mid class."

I groaned. "I go straight to bed after the evening meal. Some days I'm sure I do nothing but sleep. I cannot be blamed for my constant state of exhaustion. Natalya probably picked her moment on purpose. Maybe she doesn't want my commonborn self polluting her event."

"Actually she specifically mentioned to me to make sure you'd heard the invitation."

I snorted. "Of course she did, since she couldn't possibly repeat the invitation to me herself. It's not as if we sleep in the same tent, eat our meals in the same place, have the occasional class—"

"Well, I guess she's not *that* thankful," said Coralie, glancing at me again before we burst into giggles.

"It's nice to see you both so cheerful this morning," said Finnian from the entrance to the mess tent. He grinned at us both, but I noticed his eyes lingered on Coralie.

"We were just discussing this Midwinter party we're all invited to," I said.

"Ah," he said, assuming a knowing tone. "Nothing like a party to get the girls giggling."

"Well, actually it was Natalya...never mind." I rolled my eyes and pushed past him, my nose twitching at the smell and my stomach grumbling. Captain Matthis had pushed me particularly hard the day before, and I had slept through dinner.

"You know," I said, as we sat down, my mouth already full of roll, "I thought the food here would be worse. But it's actually quite nice. Except for the porridge. Or is it just that I'm always hungry?"

"It all depends on who's posted to the kitchens," said Leila with an air of experienced wisdom. She slid in beside me on the bench seat. "But it's true we're kept well supplied with food stuffs."

"Least the rest of the kingdom can do, if you ask me," said Tobias.

"Ignore him," said Leila. "He was on night patrol."

I didn't like Tobias, but I still winced. It had rained for more than half the night.

"So are you going to those fancy festivities up at headquarters?" asked Leila. "It's almost a pity because us regular soldiers throw a little celebration of our own down here." She winked at me.

"Some poor souls will be on patrol, of course." She grinned. "But not me, thank goodness. We hear about Midwinter and Midsummer at the front all the way back at the training barracks. Nothing like certain danger to put everyone in the mood to kick up a storm."

One of Leila's friends whose name I could never recall joined in.

"They have giant bonfires scattered around, and any soldier who can play an instrument brings it out so there's playing and dancing everywhere. No one eats in the mess, of course, so the whole tent is set up with a full feast and plates we can take back to the bonfires."

"Probably not as much fun as your event, though," said Leila quickly. "I used to dream about attending a ball when I was little."

"Actually, I much prefer the sound of your celebrations," I said. "It doesn't matter how nicely everyone is dressed if they don't really want you there."

Leila stared at me. "Not want you?" She shook her head and

laughed. "You're joking, of course. You're the Spoken Mage. I'm sure everyone wants you at their parties."

I glanced sideways at Coralie who just shrugged. I didn't quite know how to explain the reality of my situation to Leila.

The soldiers had taken to coming past my training sessions, hanging around to watch until the officers moved them along. Everywhere I walked now, soldiers stepped aside for me, nodding their heads and murmuring, "Spoken Mage," respectfully.

And then to each other, after I had passed:

"Have you seen her training? I've never seen anything like it."

"I heard she took out a hundred soldiers in that gully. With one composition."

"And five mages, don't forget them."

And then the worst of all:

"Just you wait until she graduates. We're finally going to see an end to this war. Show those Kallorwegians what we're made of."

Followed by the wet slap of their spit hitting the ground as everyone present gave the traditional commonborn Ardannian response to the mention of our enemies.

It would be impossible to explain to these soldiers how the mageborn saw me. An oddity. An opportunity. A threat. And—worst of all—a commonborn.

No, they didn't fall over themselves to host me at their parties. *And yet*, an inner voice said, *Natalya of all people just invited you to hers.*

CHAPTER 16

*I*certainly hadn't packed any ballgowns, and I couldn't imagine my year mates had done so either. But my assumption that the day would proceed much like any other and the ball would be a simple affair where we would wear our robes was shattered when Coralie pounced on me Midwinter morning.

"Finnian says you're not to touch your presents until we're all together. He says he'll be desolate if we leave him to open gifts with no better company than Calix and Weston." She rolled her eyes.

"He has Clarence," I muttered, pulling my pillow over my head.

"Elena! It's Midwinter. Get up!"

Grumbling, still half asleep, I hauled myself out of bed. The sight of the small pile of presents Coralie had dumped on my bed quickly woke me, however.

"Those aren't for me, are they?" I asked.

"Yes, of course they are."

"Oh no. No, no, no."

"Elena! They're presents not poisonous snakes. What is wrong with you?"

I grimaced and ran a hand through my hair. "You know I didn't get anything for anyone, right? I've been too tired to think at all. I didn't even realize it was Midwinter until two days ago." I didn't mention that unlike my mageborn friends I also had no money with which to purchase gifts. Usually I relied on having the time and opportunity to make something.

"Relax." Coralie laughed. "Your friends will still love you with or without a present. Although I'm disappointed you didn't compose one for me."

"Very funny." I shot her an unimpressed morning face glare, and she started laughing again.

Coralie knew that any physical item composed from nothing would last only as long as power continued to pour into it. But she thought it hilarious to tease me about how under the general's tutelage, I would soon be enjoying limitless power.

The day was crisp but clear, so we all took our breakfast out to a small patch of grass that had somehow survived between the two trainee tents and opened our gifts there.

Coralie repeated her joke, and they all had an excellent time laughing at me and making more and more extravagant requests as to what they would each like for their gift. I responded by throwing lumps of grass at them and muttering darkly that I no longer felt sorry for not getting them a gift.

"The only thing I feel sorry about is that I ever got any of you a gift in past years," I said. But in truth, I didn't mind. I knew they were only trying to make me feel at ease in an otherwise awkward situation.

I couldn't joke when I opened Finnian's present, though.

"Finnian!" I breathed, my mouth falling open.

He shrugged, a falsely modest expression on his face. "It was nothing."

"Whatever this is, it's not nothing," I replied.

He grinned. "Well, you know me. I can't stand to be outdone. And all this talk of the Spoken Mage...I had to remind myself I have a few things to offer too. You know, other than my charm and rugged manliness." He winked at me.

I shook my head and glanced over at Coralie.

She had also just opened her present from Finnian, and the contents seemed to have robbed her of words.

"Wow! Coralie, that's…" She looked up at me. "Perfect for you," I finished while she nodded in silent agreement.

I glanced over at Finnian who was now accepting thanks from Saffron and Araminta without even the pretense of modesty. He had outdone himself, somehow procuring four beautiful ballgowns. But Coralie's gown…

It wasn't so much that it was more expensive than any of the others. Or even more beautiful. It was just so exactly fitted to her. Her face, her figure, even her style. I had never seen a material that matched the shade of her eyes so perfectly.

But it was more than that, too. The soft layers evoked a sweetness that reflected her essence as much as it did her looks, but when she turned it over—holding it up to show me the other side —I saw that it plunged into a daring v, coming to a point only at the small of her back. For all its soft sweetness, the dress had a daring edge to it.

It had never quite struck me before, but Coralie did have the hint of the rebel around her. Of all my year mates, she had been the only one to approach me when I arrived at the Academy. The only one not to care what anyone else thought.

I couldn't help but think that Finnian might have tipped his hand more than he realized. Or perhaps, he had revealed exactly what he wanted to reveal.

The same thought gripped me when I saw Coralie in the floating tulle that evening. It shimmered when she moved, changing color in the flash of firelight. Not that I envied her the dress—my own surpassed anything I could have imagined wearing in the circumstances.

The red dress fitted tightly in the bodice, with the softest, fullest skirt I had ever worn and long sleeves tapering into points over my wrists. The wide dip of the neckline showed off the smooth skin of my neck and collarbones. I'd been self-conscious about having no jewelry to wear until Coralie produced a small mirror from somewhere. As I gazed at my reflection, I realized that the simplicity only enhanced the effect. Something stirred inside me.

I had caught Finnian alone for a moment as we all dispersed after the gift exchange.

"Really, Finnian? Red?" The color of blood, the color of royalty.

He had looked down at me, something more serious than his usual joking manner lurking in his eyes. "You're the Spoken Mage, Elena. It's time to be bold."

And standing here in the middle of a battle camp, looking at myself in a striking, blood-red gown, I felt bold. It hadn't been by chance that red had been chosen as a royal color. And it wasn't by chance I wore it now. Some battles weren't fought with compositions, and in the world of politics, some weapons were more powerful than words.

So, no, I didn't envy Coralie her gown. But a small, foolish part of me envied her something else. I had received no Midwinter gift from Lucas. I always felt him near me these days, and yet so much distance separated us. An impossible distance of watching eyes, expectation, history, family, and differing views.

You seem to have a great deal of interest in her.

My family has a great deal of interest in the Spoken Mage, General.

If only I could untangle the horrible knot of his family's interests and his own feelings for me. Because the longer I spent among these soldiers the more my certainty grew that I could not turn my back on them. Not on the hope and expectation that I saw in their eyes, nor the quiet grief I saw in Leila's.

You'll see that I'm right, Elena, Lucas had promised. And now that we were here, part of me did.

But the other part woke up screaming and sweating at the feeling of thirty-nine hearts ceasing to beat. I could not be General Griffith's weapon, and I could not be Lucas's either. No matter how much our kingdom needed one.

No fancy carriages carried us through the tents to the town, but I enjoyed the walk and the glimpse of the soldiers' celebration that it afforded us. Already the bonfires had been lit, and the first of the musicians had begun.

A carefree air hung over the camp, unlike its usual tones. I knew Beatrice and Reese had been hard at work to ensure the healing tents sat empty today, and we hadn't had a raid or attack to refill it in two days. Even the Kallorwegians celebrated Midwinter.

I heard hardly any murmurs of, "Spoken Mage," as I walked, few of the soldiers recognizing me in my new attire. I didn't mind, though. I was dressed for a different audience tonight.

Torches lined the front steps of the Bronton mansion-turned-headquarters, and I got a glimpse of what the house must have been like when a Stantorn family lived here. Not that I would ever have been invited inside in those days.

A footman announced Coralie, Saffron, Araminta, and me, and we joined the throng inside. It looked like every mage officer not on active duty must have been invited. I spotted Colonel Jennica, Captain Carson, and Lieutenant Martin. Even unfortunate Lieutenant Jackson, who had indeed been reassigned. The only familiar face I couldn't see was Captain Matthis. But then he seemed the type to have little patience for these sorts of events—perhaps he had requested to be on duty for the night.

The general held court half way across the room, but he looked up at our arrival. Turning away from his companions, he made his way straight to us, the crowd parting before him.

He nodded a general sort of welcome to us all, but his attention was on me. I had seen the brief hesitation in his step when he got a good look at my gown, and he actually gave a ponderous bow over my hand now.

"Spoken Mage."

It did not escape my notice that he used my popular title instead of my name as he usually did.

"General." I nodded back at him.

"I wasn't sure if we'd be seeing you here tonight."

I raised my eyebrows in subtle surprise.

"I hear you've been extremely busy training," he added before glancing at my dress again.

His message was clear. To the Devoras family I had proved my value as a weapon. But that didn't mean they were ready to see me as one of them.

My eyes strayed across the rest of the room. They fell first on Lorcan who was watching us with a small smile on his lips. When I met his eyes, he dipped his head in a brief nod, raising his glass slightly in my direction.

Lorcan and Jessamine had made it clear the previous year. To Callinos, I had earned my place among the ranks of the mages. But he looked just a little too pleased to see that Devoras had not yet come so far. Seeing his desire for my loyalty only made me want to pull away from him.

But another figure caught my attention, and I watched him out of the corner of my eye as I pretended to listen to the general extricating himself and moving on to other guests.

Lucas.

He stood alone in the middle of the floor, his eyes on me. Instead of his usual formal red uniform, this year he wore black. Black uniform, black boots—only the gold sash across his chest alleviated the effect.

I swallowed and moved toward him through the crowd without breaking eye contact. Dimly, I thought I heard Coralie say something behind me, but I didn't catch the words. Lucas drew me magnetically forward until I stood in front of him, just within arm's reach.

Had Finnian known what the prince planned to wear? I didn't need a mirror to know the picture we would create together. Black for death and mourning. Red and gold for blood and power and royalty. We were dressed to match—a royal couple in the midst of war—and the audacity of it made me tremble.

"Elena," Lucas breathed.

"Lucas." Somehow my voice remained steady.

He put out a hand, and I put mine into it, letting him sweep me into the dance as the musicians began to play. He moved smoothly, and in his arms I could almost forget I didn't really know how to dance.

"You look..."

"I'm sorry," I said quickly. "Finnian—"

His hand at my waist tightened at my friend's name, and I fell silent. After a breath he relaxed, loosening his hold.

"Ah yes. I should have guessed. The duke's son has a dangerous mix of mischief and perception."

I stifled a laugh. That about summed Finnian up.

"Maybe I shouldn't have come tonight. The general certainly didn't seem overjoyed to see me."

His hand at my waist tightened again, sending little currents of warmth shooting through my middle.

"I'm glad you did."

The warmth turned into a raging fire.

Lucas had never held me so close for so long. And it was all too easy to forget we were only dancing. To forget the many reasons we couldn't be together. To forget he wasn't willing to fight to change the laws that would truly allow us to be together. And, worst of all, to forget that the eyes of the mageborn surrounded us.

After a pause that was far too loaded, Lucas spoke,

commenting on the party, and the training we had been doing in class. As we conversed, our light words coasting over the charged moment between us, I remembered a time when we couldn't speak without clashing. How angry I had been with him then. It seemed a lifetime ago.

When the music ended, it took a moment for me to even notice. But as soon as I did, I stepped hurriedly back, giving the prince a small curtsy. He gave me a half bow in return, thanking me formally for the dance. But his eyes held a smile that was just for me.

I hurried over to the refreshment table and downed a glass of cool juice. I hoped I didn't look as flushed as I felt. I gave myself a moment to stand there, my back to the room, before turning back to face the sea of mages.

My eyes immediately picked Lucas from the crowd. I couldn't help myself. He was dancing now with Natalya, and my hand tightened so hard around my empty glass that I made myself put it carefully down.

Of course he's dancing with Natalya, I reminded myself. She's the general's daughter, her family is hosting the event. But I still hated the way she clung to him, pressing closer than the dance required. He said something quietly, and she laughed loudly in response. I made myself turn away.

"Elena." Dariela's greeting startled me, and I hoped my thoughts hadn't just been visible on my face.

I nodded at her. "You look lovely." Even without Finnian's assistance, the Ellington girl had managed to produce an elegant looking gown with simple, slim lines.

"Thank you," she said before glancing away. When she looked back at me, guilt tinged her features.

"We had this conversation once before, or near enough," she said.

My brow creased as I tried to think what she could be talking about.

"Our first Midwinter at the Academy. And after I thanked you, I just walked away."

Now that she said it, I remembered. The sting of the rejection came rushing back to me, although the subsequent events of the evening had far eclipsed it. But that had been a long time ago, and a different Elena. I had no desire to hold onto that humiliation.

"I didn't know what to think of you then," Dariela continued. "But I resented you." She looked down at me, an apology on her face. "Not for being a commonborn, but for being a distraction. I don't have time for distractions."

She took a deep breath. "But I am not above admitting my mistakes. Or apologizing for them. So you have my apology, Elena."

"Please don't think of it," I said. "We've all changed since then."

"You most of all." She didn't look at me as she spoke.

I tracked the direction of her eyes, but she was watching Lucas and Natalya dance, so I looked quickly away again.

"Yes, perhaps," I said. "But then you were already brilliant from the beginning. You didn't need to change."

She sighed. "My parents expect it, you know."

I gave her a confused look, but she still didn't meet my eyes.

"To be top of my year, better than everyone. They've been training me for it ever since the first hints of what my power might grow into. When Lucas joined our year, it was something of a blow. He's a year older and has had even more extensive training than me." She shook her head. "My parents seemed pleased about it, though, so I assumed they wouldn't expect me to beat him in everything. But I didn't appreciate your arriving and bringing even more chaos to my careful plans."

"That makes two of us," I muttered. "Attendance at the Academy didn't exactly fit in with my plans, either."

She chuckled. "I can imagine. I just...I wanted you to know. Friendship certainly never occurred to me. It was a distraction I could never afford. Even among my true peers." She winced. "Sorry, I didn't mean—"

I waved her apology away.

"Well, you aren't my peer, really," she said. "You're something set apart, something entirely new. My mistake was in thinking that put you below me. That you were an obstacle, instead of someone I could learn from."

I made a soft sound of protest, but this time she was the one waving me to silence.

"I fought creditably in that gully," she said, and I respected her for not bothering with false modesty. "I was proud of myself even, to fight so well as only a third year trainee. But then you came along and ended the battle. And just in time for me, as it turned out. I owe you, and I'm not one to forget my debts."

"I don't want your sense of obligation," I said slowly. "But I would appreciate your friendship."

She raised both eyebrows.

"Friendship." She said the word slowly, as if it were entirely new to her. "I suppose that would be an acceptable alternative. Are you sure, though? Credit with me might be worth something one day."

I froze awkwardly and then laughed when I saw the joking glint in her eye. Her sense of humor was drier than I had expected.

Clarence wandered over to us. "Hi Dariela. Hi Elena."

We both greeted him back.

"Would you like to dance, Dariela?"

The other girl hesitated, and Clarence smiled.

"Don't worry, I'm not getting any ideas. It would just be nice to dance with a partner a little more my height for once."

A reluctant smile nudged its way across Dariela's face.

"Go on," I whispered to her. "It is a dance, after all. No one's grading us on this."

She rolled her eyes at me, clearly not quite comfortable with being teased yet, but offered her hand to Clarence. They disappeared into the dancers, and I watched them go with a smile. Until my eyes fell on Lucas, now dancing with Lavinia.

When I looked quickly away, I realized I wasn't the only one watching them. Colonel Jennica stood chatting with Reese, both with a glass in hand. They watched the prince dancing with Lavinia, smiles on their faces, and I remembered that they were both Stantorns, like her.

Stantorns like my attacker from first year who had apparently died in prison—except for the fact that I had seen him alive and well among the Stantorns. Lucas hadn't believed me. His mother's precious family would never be involved in treason.

And yet here we were, with treason stalking us again. My party mood soured. Devoras might have come some way toward changing their view of me, but I couldn't imagine Stantorn would ever see me as anything but an invading commonborn. The question was how far their disgust might drive them.

I was considering leaving the party completely when Coralie searched me out. She looked stunning, and I could tell she knew it. Her cheeks glowed, and her eyes kept creeping to Finnian, who had barely left her side all evening. But she insisted I join them.

Together they drew me back into laughter and the spirit of Midwinter. And I remembered that I was allowed to put the war and treason and death and training away for a single evening. All I had to do was pretend it didn't hurt to see the glances Finnian and Coralie stole when they thought I wasn't watching. The sort of glances I wished I could share with someone who hadn't spoken to me since our one dance.

Finnian broke away from Coralie long enough to dance with me. And Clarence invited me, too, despite my diminutive size. I danced with them both but rejected all other offers. Because being on the dance floor only brought me pain from the magnetic pull still connecting me to my first partner.

As I spun around, occasionally our steps brought us close together, my heart beating hard every time our eyes swept past each other or his sleeve brushed against me, the skirt of my dress sliding along his leg.

It was an exquisite torture, and I could only endure so much. When midnight chimed, I slipped away from Coralie and Finnian. A backward glance told me they were too distracted by each other to notice as I left the building.

CHAPTER 17

J stopped in the neglected garden of the mansion, enjoying the feel of the cold night air on my face. I hadn't realized how hot it had grown inside.

"You look stunning," said a voice behind me, and I didn't startle.

Only now, as his voice surrounded me in a warmth all its own, could I acknowledge even to myself that this was why I had left. When midnight sounded, his birthday began, and I had hoped to speak to him alone. Had hoped he would come after me.

It scared me to admit it, even in the silence of my own mind.

"Shouldn't you be inside receiving birthday congratulations?" I asked, without turning to look at him.

The crunch of his boots on the cold ground sounded, and then he came into my line of sight. The moonlight outlined his dark hair, shining off the circlet of gold and the gold at his chest. My heart squeezed painfully.

"There's only one birthday congratulation I want," he said, his eyes steady on my face.

"Happy Birthday," I whispered.

"Elena, I—"

He broke off, and I wanted to tell him not to bother. That we had been here before.

But the words wouldn't form. Because whatever my head said, my heart refused to accept it. And because I wasn't so sure even my head agreed anymore.

He stepped close. Too close. One hand reached out and gently cupped my cheek before tracing down my neck, across my shoulder and down my arm to my hand.

My whole body trembled at his touch. But I forced myself to sway away from him.

"Lucas—" My dry mouth struggled to say his name. I swallowed and tried again. "Lucas, what are we doing?"

"It's so busy at the camp," he said, his voice low. "I can't get you alone there."

"Why...why do you want me alone?" I asked.

"I wanted to finish saying to you what I tried to start saying after the attack. When we were interrupted." He gripped my hand in his, his thumb tracing circles on my palm, and the touch made it hard to think.

"I told you that when we came to the front, you would realize I was right," he said, but his voice didn't turn the words into an I told you so. I tried to untangle the expression in his eyes.

"But the truth is," he continued, "I was the one to learn *you* were right."

"Me?" I shivered, wondering if the moonlight was infecting my mind or his. "But I can see it now—what you meant, what's been driving you all this time. I can see how important winning this war is, how many lives are being lost. Only...I can't do it." Unshed tears gathered in my eyes. "I can't be your weapon, Lucas."

He sucked in a breath. "I don't see you as a weapon, Elena. I don't want to send you out to kill."

I peered into his face, trying to read the truth of his words there. He pulled me closer to him.

"I could never want that for you. But there are lots of ways you could help the war, lots of ways your strength could be used to our advantage. And there is always the possibility that you might unlock some further secret regarding how we access power. One that all of us could then apply. When it comes to you, the possibilities seem endless."

He shook his head. "Ending the war has been my focus for so long. I couldn't let anything else in to distract me. And yet suddenly there you were, filling my heart and mind. It exhilarated and terrified me at the same time. I thought if I agreed to try to bring change to our laws, to our mindsets, to everything about the way we run our kingdom, I would be leading all of Ardann down the same path of madness that had swallowed me."

"You were trying to do what you believed was right," I said softly, shaken by the intensity of his expression. "And I can finally see why the war has been so important to you. How important it is to all of us. Just think if all these young lives could be used elsewhere instead of needlessly lost."

"Yes." His eyes were hard. "We must stop the war. But being here has helped me to see that the war isn't separate to the rest of the kingdom's issues. They're entwined together."

"What do you mean?"

Another gentle tug pulled me closer still. We now stood as near as possible without fully touching. Each time he breathed, his gold sash brushed against my dress. My own breathing hitched.

"You want change," he whispered. "Change in the way we see the commonborns. And you're right."

"I...I am?" I wished his nearness didn't scramble my brain so completely.

"That attack in the gully would never have happened if an

incompetent child hadn't been placed in command over experienced soldiers."

I refrained from pointing out that the child in question was older than both of us.

"With only mages acting as officers, we spread ourselves thin, unable to work together because we must each lead a squad. No one asks the commonborn for ideas, no one listens when they speak. Who knows what ideas, what military genius might be lying out there untapped?"

He gestured toward the tents around the town.

"Perhaps if we truly used all of the kingdom's resources, we could win this war without even needing our Spoken Mage. You were right when you said we can't afford to wait for change. We need it now."

The inferno of hope that burst into life inside my chest hurt me with its fury. I struggled to hold it in bounds.

"Are you saying...are you saying you're ready to fight for change now?"

He leaned down until our faces were as far apart as our bodies —a mere breath.

"I'm saying that for the kingdom you were right—we need to bring change." He paused, and for a moment the garden was still, except for our ragged breaths. "And I'm saying that for me, you were even more right. I need us to be together—truly together no matter what laws I have to overturn to achieve it. I cannot bear to be always so close to you, and yet so far away. I cannot keep on like this. I will fight for us. I have to fight for us."

The inferno leaped from my control, burning everything in its path. I didn't wait to hear any more. Pushing myself forward and up, I closed that last agonizing space between us and pressed my lips to his.

He responded instantly, sweeping his arms around me and crushing me tightly against him. Our lips molded together, as our hearts had already done, and I never wanted it to end.

When he pulled away, panting, a tiny groan escaped me, and he pulled me back in for another kiss. The next time he came up for air, he gripped my arms and took a full step away from me.

He trembled a little, even as he chuckled.

"Don't look at me like that, Elena. I have some things I need to say to you, and all I want to do is kiss you when you look at me like that."

"Is that so bad?" I asked, but I maintained the distance he had set between us. Because he was right. There were things that needed to be said, and I was as distracted by his nearness as he apparently was by mine.

"I want you to know that I mean every word of what I just said," he told me.

My heart sank. There was a but coming. And sure enough...

"But this news." He gestured between us. "You and me. That's the sort of thing I need to tell my parents in person. I owe that much to them. And even if I didn't, we need them to hear it directly from me. If someone else gets in their ear first, if we return to find them already turned against you..." He looked genuinely afraid. "Then I don't know how much I'll be able to do."

"What does that mean?" I asked slowly.

"It means this has to remain a secret for now. Our secret." He looked into my eyes. "From everybody.

"But just for now," he hurried to add. "As soon as we get back to Corrin, I'll talk to my parents. And no matter what they say, I'm not giving you up. I'll make them see how strong you are. How there couldn't be anyone better for the royal family."

I flushed as the reality of what he was saying sank in. The royal family. Lucas intended to fight for the right to become betrothed to me. Elena of Kingslee. He wanted to make me a princess.

It didn't feel real. Until I looked into his eyes and remembered this was Lucas. And then it was all too incredibly, wonderfully, deliriously real. I tried to make my mind focus.

"Does that mean…should you be returning to the party now?" I tried not to let the disappointment sound in my voice.

"No." He tugged at my hand again, but this time he pulled me behind him rather than drawing me close, leading me through the garden. "Tomorrow I will return to thinking about what my duties as a prince require from me. But I must have one night. Just a few hours with you before I keep my distance again. Just a few hours of my birthday to be spent as I wish. Tomorrow we go back to normal. Tonight there is a celebration going on, and I think no one will miss us until dawn." He looked back at me, his eyes flashing in the moonlight, and I realized what he intended. My steps quickened.

When we reached our tents, he pulled me close and whispered in my ear.

"As utterly delicious as you look in that dress, I'm afraid it stands out a little too much. Meet back here in two minutes?"

I nodded before tumbling into my tent and overturning my small storage trunk in search of something more subtle. My hands found the plain gray uniform I had only ever worn once before. I hesitated for a moment and then thrust it on.

As fast as I had been, Lucas still beat me back out. He wore a plain leather outfit, the kind he probably wore daily beneath his white robe. He still looked commanding, though, and too handsome to be real. But at least he'd lost the circlet.

His eyes widened slightly when he saw my uniform, but I shrugged, and he said nothing. His intention had been to blend in, after all.

Tucking my arm into his, Lucas pulled me into the flickering darkness. The bonfires sent dancing shadows everywhere between the tents, and the music and laughter filled every crack. When we found a group of dancers, Lucas wrapped me in his arms. We didn't try to talk, instead just soaking in the other's nearness. We danced until our ragged breath demanded we search out a drink, and then we found one in the mess tent, along with the leftovers of what had clearly been a bountiful feast.

When we stepped back out into the night, Lucas pulled me into the dark shadows around the side of the tent and pressed a kiss against my lips. I stood up on my tiptoes, stretching to meet him, only to pull back at a burst of raucous laughter.

Three soldiers emerged from between the tents, calling good-natured insults at us. None of them gave any indication of recognizing us, though, so we merely laughed along with them and took off for a different bonfire.

The rest of the night passed that way, with dancing and heady, stolen kisses in dark corners. Dawn was beginning to lighten the darkness the tiniest fraction when Lucas gave me one final kiss, holding me tight and long, all his emotions in the embrace. The night was ending, and somehow we had to return to normal. At least for a little while.

I was the one to finally pull away.

"This is already the best birthday I've ever had," he whispered into my hair. "I don't want the dawn to come."

"It's not as if one of us is going away forever," I said. "It won't be long, and we'll be back in Corrin."

He took a long breath, giving me a final squeeze. "Back in Corrin."

When I sneaked into my tent, even breathing echoed throughout it, much to my relief. I hesitated beside Coralie's bed, mourning that I wouldn't be able to talk over the night with my friend.

"Back in Corrin," I whispered to myself.

I hurried out of my gray uniform, shoving it down to the bottom of my trunk, and climbing underneath the blankets. Sleep claimed me almost instantly, but not before it occurred to me that although Natalya lay still in her cot, from her alone I hadn't heard the heavy breathing of sleep.

～

We all slept late the next morning, and when we stumbled into the mess tent at lunchtime, we were relieved to find them serving breakfast food.

"Don't think you were the only ones having a good time last night," one of the soldiers behind the serving bench said with a wink.

Natalya turned away in disgust, but I smiled back at him. She crossed the tent to slide in beside Lucas, and I nearly tripped over my own feet. He looked up, and for the briefest instant, our eyes met. Then he was looking at Natalya again, his face calm as if nothing had happened.

My heart raced, and my palms went clammy. Lucas was a prince. He had twenty years of practice at this. But could I do it? Could I look at him as if last night had never happened?

Coralie followed my gaze. "Never mind her. I haven't told you off properly yet for stealing away last night when we weren't looking." She sat down and groaned. "I have *not* had enough sleep. Consider your chastisement completed."

"I didn't think you looked like you had much need of me." I raised both eyebrows at her.

Instead of flushing, as I had expected, she looked away, tearing at her roll with nervous fingers.

"Come on," I said. "Bring your food." We needed to talk—properly—and I needed space from Lucas.

I led her to the grassy patch where we had exchanged presents the morning before. I settled myself comfortably on the ground before turning to her.

"All right, it's time to tell me what's going on with you and Finnian. You told me that you didn't want to get serious while we were still at the Academy. That neither of you did. But I'm starting to wonder if Finnian knows that."

I bent a stern glare on her until she sighed and threw the grass she had been shredding into the air.

"Fine. There might be a little more to it than that." She sighed, looking away, and I ate quietly, letting her find her words in her own time.

"It's not that what I said isn't true," she said at last. "I don't think getting serious at the Academy is the wisest idea."

My guilty mind flashed back to the promises Lucas and I had already exchanged, but I thrust them away. What existed between Lucas and me wasn't a fling, a relationship that might end and make our final year awkward. With every barrier that stood between us, only utter determination had even gotten us this far.

"But..." She swallowed audibly and looked down at the ground. "Maybe I'd be willing to rethink that if it wasn't Finnian."

"What do you mean? Coralie, I know Finnian is a bit of a flirt, but everyone knows he doesn't mean it. It's just his manner. It's different with you. I can tell." I hesitated, watching her face with concern. "To be honest, I don't think his heart has been in it this year. I get the impression that whenever he pays me extravagant compliments, or hugs me, it's just an excuse so he can do the same to you."

She looked up at me quickly, and I knew her expression too well from the other side to misread it. It was hope mixed with a desperate desire not to feel hope.

But when she spoke, her voice didn't sound hopeful. "It's not the way he acts. It's who he is. I know that from the outside we probably look like one big privileged group, but on the inside..." She sighed. "You've been living among us for over two years now, Elena. You know what I mean. It's not just that Finnian is a Callinos. He's the son of a duke. He can flirt with whoever he wants. Dance with them. Kiss them even. But the son of the Head of the

Healers isn't going to marry a Cygnet. And I have no intention of having my heart broken."

I stared at her in dismay. "Any more than it already is," I whispered.

"Any more than it already is."

CHAPTER 18

$\mathcal{S}$everal waves of new conscripts came quickly one after another in the new year. They looked young, scared, and bewildered as they wandered around camp.

"I didn't think we'd be here long enough to feel like old hands," said Coralie, watching a couple of particularly young-looking soldiers gaze around the mess tent in dismay.

Finnian frowned at her and then at them. He hadn't been his usual joking self since Midwinter.

"No," he said, "I can't say I thought we would be either."

Neither of them looked at me, but I looked down into my bowl anyway. I knew why we were still here, but there was nothing I could do about it. It didn't matter how much General Griffith wanted things to be different—my energy had limits, and no amount of training could circumvent them. I wasn't making the progress he wanted.

Even if my friends didn't blame me, others did. Natalya returned to her usual griping, taking swipes at me whenever the opportunity presented itself. I let it roll off me as I had always done, but I couldn't shake the feeling there was an extra edge to her now. That her tone held the smallest note of smug satisfaction, and that her gaze followed me more than usual.

When she was around, I tried even harder than usual not to look at Lucas. It was a battle I frequently lost, and all too often when I gave in and snuck a glance in his direction, I found him looking at me.

When I turned to pass between two tents on the way to composition class one afternoon and smashed into a solid pack of soldiers heading in the other direction—sending me straight to the ground—he was at my side before anyone else could move. I accepted the hand he held out but snatched it away as soon as I was back on my feet, conscious of Natalya and Lavinia's heavy gazes. But the heat of his fingers burned my hand for hours afterward, and we accidentally locked gazes so many times I had to excuse myself from class before one of us did something stupid.

That evening at dinner, I arrived a little late, and my eyes searched him out as I waited in line for food. He stood to one side of the mess, a tray bearing the remains of his meal in his hands. But though his guards followed him, as they always did, they stood several steps away, giving him space for whatever conversation he was conducting.

The older man standing with him held himself in a respectful posture, despite the age gap between them. But his face held none of the surprise or confusion I might have expected a common-born veteran to feel if he found himself approached by royalty. Had they spoken before?

I frowned at the man. He looked familiar. He shifted slightly, coming into better view, and the movement jogged my memory. Lannis. The veteran who had sensed something was off about the gully.

I realized the line ahead of me had moved, leaving a gap, and I shuffled several steps forward. But my eyes remained on the conversation on the other side of the tent. What were they discussing?

Their body language shifted, farewells clearly being exchanged, and I looked away quickly before either of them could notice me watching. But out of the corner of my eye, I tracked Lucas as he disposed of his tray.

His passage through the tent brought him right past the line where I waited, and he shifted slightly as he passed me, brushing lightly against my arm.

"Midnight. Here." He spoke so quietly, I wondered if I had imagined the words.

Hours later, I lay in bed, buzzing with far too much energy to be in danger of falling asleep, counting down the minutes. When it finally approached midnight, I got up, threw on my warmest outfit and hurried for the mess tent.

Hands reached out from the dark and grabbed me before I made it through the entrance, pulling me around the side of the tent instead. My tiny startled squeak was silenced by his lips against mine, and I melted into his embrace.

A sound off to one side made us both jump, leaping apart, but it was only a soldier wending his way through the tents. He disappeared without seeing us, but my heart continued to beat at a frantic pace.

"How much longer is the general going to keep us cooling our heels here?" he growled, frustration in every line of his body.

"I don't know," I said. "But unless you want us to be caught—or me to have a heart attack—we can't meet like this."

Rather than replying, he wrapped me in his arms again and lowered his head for a kiss.

"I think we should be able to push for our departure in the next couple of weeks," said Lorcan's voice from inside the mess.

We leaped apart again as he exited the tent, Thornton beside him. Lucas's startled movement placed him partially in a shaft of moonlight, and Lorcan frowned in our direction.

"Lucas? Is that you?"

I shrank back further into the shadows, turning my face away from them, afraid to move too much in case I called attention to myself. With a single longing look in my direction, Lucas stepped toward our instructors.

"Lorcan. Thornton." He nodded at them both.

"Having trouble sleeping, are you?" asked Lorcan. When Lucas said nothing, he took his silence for acquiescence. "It's these blasted cots. I haven't been sleeping too well either."

Their voices faded as the three of them moved off toward our sleeping tents. I waited a long time, pressed into the canvas, before I dared follow.

We didn't try such a rendezvous again.

I took hope from Lorcan's overheard words, but the following week the weather changed. A sudden spike in temperature caused an explosion of greenery all around us. Returning patrols reported the river was swollen and dangerous.

Two days later a loud clanging rang through the camp. Captain Matthis paused in my training at the sound of the bell, frozen for a single second before he launched back into movement.

"The alarm bell." He gazed at me for one longing moment, and then barked, "Get back to Thornton. I'm needed."

He was gone before I had fully processed his words. But I understood his look. He had considered ordering me to accompany him, had wanted to do so.

I hurried back to the other trainees. No attacks had occurred close enough to camp to warrant the warning bell before this, and they looked just as uncertain as me. Thornton took charge, however, wasting no time getting us straight through the tents and into the walls of Bronton. The huge gates clanged shut behind both us and the final stragglers among the local townsfolk, an enormous crossbeam lowered to keep them in place.

Thornton led us up to headquarters, staring down the two soldiers who tried to deny us entrance. Lieutenant Martin, who happened to be passing through the entryway, waved us in.

"Don't blame them," he said, once we had all been ushered inside. "They have orders not to let anyone below the rank of captain in once the alarm bells sound." He grinned. "You lot don't quite fit into our structure here, you know."

Thornton gave him an icy look. "You will ensure we are not so barred again, I hope."

"I'll pass the word on," Martin promised. As I filed past him, he grinned at me. "That is what us aides are here to do," he said, too quietly for Thornton to hear.

I smiled back, but another pair of lieutenant-aides hurried past, calling to him as they went, and he was off running.

We found Lorcan with Griffith in the old ballroom. The Academy Head greeted Thornton with a tense nod, but when the general looked up, he didn't take our presence so calmly.

"What is this?" he roared. "A circus? Get them out of here."

"They are here to learn," said Lorcan calmly. "And here is an opportunity for them to observe how headquarters command an engagement from afar."

Griffith stared at him for several seconds, but an aide behind him called his title, and he turned abruptly, appearing to lose all memory of our presence.

The alarm bell only rang if signs of a large attack were discovered. And this room was the center of coordinating our defense. Lieutenant-aides ripped composition after composition, holding the resulting balls of power to the general's face so he could bellow his orders into them. Another three sat in a quiet room next door, running back and forth to deliver the messages they received in reply.

The general rolled out a large map of the border region, covering it with small colored stones as reports of soldier movements came in. It was a raiding party—far larger than the usual ones.

Five squads were sent out to intercept the raiders, with three more in reserve to assist if needed. A further two took up positions between the attackers and the river, to mop up any who attempted to retreat.

I had been relieved when Matthis didn't order me to head out with a squad, but it turned out waiting safely in headquarters wasn't too pleasant either. Everyone else in the large room seemed to have a purpose and raced to and fro, while the twelve of us had nothing to do but watch. Lucas was invited to join Lorcan and the general at the table, but the rest of us were edged slowly further and further to the side until we ranged along one wall, out of everyone's way.

It seemed the longest afternoon of my life before the general finally received word that the raiders had been defeated before they made it across the Wall to any of our farms. But the elated mood that followed didn't last long.

A nervous-looking lieutenant appeared from the room next door.

"None of the enemy mages were captured, sir."

"What?" bellowed Griffith. "None! But there were five mages with them. Don't tell me they needed to kill them all! I ordered for as many as possible to be captured alive."

The man shifted uncomfortably. "None were killed either, General. I'm afraid the report is that they escaped back across the river."

"Escaped?" The general's anger radiated off every line of his body. "And the squads I placed before the river to prevent just such an eventuality?"

"There was a small skirmish, but all five mages were together, cloaked in invisibility and strong shielding spells. Our two squads weren't expecting them and couldn't stop them."

Another lieutenant arrived from the reports room.

"The main defensive squads are reporting they left behind illusions of themselves to cover their escape. They must have left as soon as they recognized their troops' imminent defeat, and our forces didn't recognize the deception soon enough to sound an alarm for the squads at the river. It's chance as much as anything that they tried to cross close enough for one of our offices to sense their compositions."

General Griffith turned and smashed his fist onto the table in front of him, muttering curses.

"So they abandoned their men and ran like cowards. I should have seen it coming."

I tried to read his face. I didn't know enough about war to know if he spoke the truth. Should he have seen it coming? And, if so, was his frustration with himself now all an act to cover his purposeful omission?"

"You were right about one thing, General," said Captain Matthis from the doorway. He looked tired and disheveled, his appearance suggesting he had only just arrived at headquarters. "A second, smaller team were sent over the river further south. We caught up to them, but they had already made it across the Wall. Their mage must have carried an arsenal of compositions to get all twelve of them through. They razed two farms to the ground."

The general cursed long and fluently.

"Carson?" he called into the subsequent silence.

The captain appeared from the mass of officers.

"Yes, sir."

"Gather up any lieutenants who haven't seen action today and take them down south with you. I want the section of the Wall where they crossed shored up before nightfall."

"Yes, sir." Carson disappeared from the room.

"Was the larger team just a diversion then?" I asked of no one in particular. Dismay washed over me at the idea. So many soldiers sacrificed for such a purpose. Did the Kallorwegians have so many to spare?

The escape of their mages seemed to confirm the idea, though. The mages, at least, they were unwilling to sacrifice.

Lorcan crossed over to us. "Perhaps. Or they may have

thought it was early enough in the season we wouldn't be expecting it. They may have hoped to break through with the main party and sent the second merely as back up."

"But Captain Matthis said the general predicted the second party." I examined him from my position at the side of the room.

"He has been doing his job for a long time," said Lorcan. "Few understand the Kallorwegians as well as he does."

I bit my lip to keep my further thoughts inside. Shouldn't the general have anticipated the mages' retreat then? Did he hope to avert suspicion from his lapse with this second correct move?

At dinner everyone was quiet and subdued, and drinks were raised to multiple absent comrades. Leila appeared to have taken a batch of new arrivals under her wing at the next table over and was explaining the situation to them. When her squad had been disbanded, the remaining members reassigned after the attack in the gully, she had managed to get herself assigned to headquarters. So, as always, she seemed to know more about what was going on than most soldiers.

"Why was it the smaller attack that got through?" a fresh-faced young man asked.

"They're harder to spot," said Tobias, jumping in. "An obvious answer, really," he muttered.

Leila ignored him. "First the raiding parties have to slip through our patrols, and then the Wall makes it hard for them. Those rocks have been there for so many years, the king himself couldn't compose a working to sort through the layers and tangles of workings attached to them."

"Aye," added a veteran further down the table. "And every section is different. One of the first tasks the new mage recruits are given each year is to ride up and down the full length, adding whatever workings they can think of anywhere they want. It takes them weeks, and no one even tries to keep track of what nasties are hiding in it anymore."

"The old hands do it sometimes just for fun. And when they

discharge?" He gave a bark of laughter. "We soldiers give a drop o' blood, but them mages?" He shook his head. "They leave the nastiest old piece of working they can come up with. Spend their whole two years coming up with it, some of 'em. Try to outdo each other." He chuckled again, as if imagining Kallorwegians falling afoul of whatever horrors the mage recruits conjured.

"What do they mean by a drop of blood? For the common-born soldiers?" I asked my own table.

Captain Matthis, who appeared to have managed a wash at some point, looked down the table at me.

"It's something of a rite of passage for those who survive their conscription," he said. "The mages leave a composition, and the commonborns leave a drop of blood." He paused. "I believe it is partially a celebration that they still live, and partially a mark of respect that only with sacrifice is the war contained behind the Wall. Or something like that."

"Better a drop than a gallon," said an older soldier at the end of our table.

"Aye," said several voices around him, and, "Better a drop than a gallon," echoed from several tables around us.

Someone brushed against me from behind, and I felt a hand trail across my back. I recognized the touch without needing to turn. I longed to throw myself into Lucas's arms and cry out all the tears I was hoarding inside at this wasteful loss of life. But for now, all I could do was feel the sensation of his hand against my back as it lingered long after he had passed on to another table.

I finished my meal more quickly than my friends and hurried to leave, wanting a few moments alone. But my steps faltered as I passed a table of soldiers grimly discussing the day's action.

"At least we got every stinking one of the second party— including their mage," one of them said. "None of this running like rabbits business."

"Aye," agreed another. "I was with the squad that arrived in time to help cut them down. We got every last one of them and pitched them all into the same battleground grave." He looked across the table at a youthful recruit. "Don't matter if they're mageborn or commonborn on the battlefield. Not if they're Kallorwegian filth." He paused to spit on the floor. "I saw all ten bodies go in myself."

I froze. Ten? I distinctly remembered Matthis saying there had been twelve in the smaller raiding party. And yet this soldier sounded certain they had fought and killed only ten. The soldiers for such a mission must have been carefully selected. If they had slipped away before battle was joined, it wouldn't have been from cowardice.

An icy feeling gripped me. If this soldier had noted the number of bodies, there was no way his mage officers had failed to do so. Matthis might not have reported to the whole of headquarters that two of the attackers disappeared some time before the final fight, but he would no doubt have done so to the general more privately.

And if the whole of that second raid—the whole of the entire attack, perhaps—had been a cover to slip two intelligencers past the Wall and into Ardann, what did the general intend to do about it?

I was about to exit the tent when General Griffith walked in. I had never seen him at the mess before, so I lingered, watching him. He walked up and down the rows of tables, speaking quiet words of congratulations and commiseration. The soldiers straightened in his wake, buoyed by his recognition of their efforts and their sacrifices.

My forehead wrinkled and my brain hurt as I tried to understand this complex man. Brilliant general or traitor? It was odd to see him respected by the soldiers here. At home those families who still anticipated their conscriptions, or whose child was already at the front, loved to curse his name. Besides the Kallorwegians themselves, he carried the most hatred, a symbol of the conscription system that swallowed their children.

I felt eyes on me. Lucas's gaze skipped across to the general as soon as I turned toward him, and our eyes didn't meet. But I could still read their expression from across the room. He was trying to hide it, but anger burned beneath the prince's cool exterior. And when the general left the mess, he followed.

And I followed them. Lucas might be a prince, but he was also human. I didn't know what had raised his ire, but I didn't want him making a mistake he might regret. Neither of them paid me the least heed as I trailed along behind them.

"How long do you mean to keep us here?" Lucas asked abruptly.

I winced. It wasn't like Lucas to let his emotion overrule his subtlety.

The general regarded him for a silent moment. "As long as is necessary."

Lucas raised an eyebrow at him. "Necessary for your experiments, or for the war effort?"

"For the war effort, of course," said Griffith smoothly. "That's the only reason I'm conducting any experiments."

Lucas looked away into the darkness. "It strikes me that the war effort might be advantaged by a few more experiments."

The general looked at him in surprise, and Lucas glanced across at the older man.

"Different kinds of experiments, I mean." He looked away again. "Colonel Jennica and Captain Matthis aren't your only soldiers with experience and strategic sense. I find myself wondering what we might achieve if we properly utilized all our strengths."

The general frowned, examining the prince's face.

"Jackson has been reassigned after the debacle at the gully, if that is your concern, Your Highness. I will even admit that I should have known better than to give him a patrol squad."

"My concern," said Lucas, his voice icy, "is for the war as a whole, and for the safety of Ardann. Jackson is hardly our only inexperienced officer."

"And what would you have me do, Your Highness? These are the mages the crown sees fit to give me. Recent graduates, all of them. You no doubt know the arguments the Mage Council made when the policy was put into place. Mages can only be spared to the Armed Forces before they have developed expertise in other disciplines."

He sounded resentful, and I could only imagine he had fought against such a decision. Had a poisonous seed taken root when the crown and his fellow heads overruled him? Had he started to wonder if a change in leadership in Ardann might be called for, after all?

The general gave a humorless bark of laughter. "Look around you, Prince. We've been fighting this war for thirty years. Thirty years. Armed Forces isn't exactly the prestigious choice it once was. I consider myself lucky there are any mages at all left with a backbone strong enough to sign up once their two years are done."

He shook his head, continuing to speak although Lucas said nothing. "I can only assume you don't mean that I should put commonborns in charge of patrols. It's a funny thing, but I don't have a lot of soldiers eager to go patrolling without a mage. Not when the enemy forces always come with mages in tow—or their compositions come across the river without any escort at all."

He narrowed his eyes at Lucas. "And I can only imagine how your father might feel if I started equipping commonborn soldiers with sealed, color-coded compositions like those some of the dead weight mages sell to commonborns back in the capital. Even if I set aside the issue of who was to produce these workings, or the role of a mage in sensing the presence of power, I am not such a fool as to set up an army of commonborn with an arsenal of compositions."

"Who said they needed to go without a mage?" Lucas gave the general a level look.

Griffith's eyebrows shot up almost to his hairline. "Mages subordinate to commonborn officers, you mean? You must be joking if you think such an arrangement would be acceptable to a single mage of your acquaintance. Perhaps you could tell me who these mythical mages might be?"

"I can think of one," said Lucas, his words almost too quiet for me to catch.

The general stopped abruptly, and the prince turned to face him, meeting his eyes without hesitation. I stumbled as I pulled myself to a halt just behind them. Did he mean himself? Surely the prince of Ardann could not mean such a thing?

The shock on the general's face told me I wasn't the only one unable to process Lucas's words.

"We must change our thinking," Lucas said quietly. "Change or be consumed."

"Maybe," said the general. "Or maybe there's another way." He turned and looked straight at me, and I realized he had been aware of my presence the entire time.

I shivered, and out of the corner of my eyes, I saw Lucas stiffen. The general looked from me to the prince.

"Interesting," was all he said, and then he nodded his head respectfully at Lucas. "I will take your words under advisement." And he strode off into Bronton.

My eyes met Lucas's, and the longing in them brought an instant flush to my cheeks. But the two royal guards who had been trailing further back to give the prince and the general privacy stepped forward.

Lucas and I walked back toward the center of the camp, carefully remaining a hand span apart and talking of nothing personal. I burst to ask him about his words, and if he had truly meant them, but the presence of his guards restrained me.

When we reached my tent, Lucas looked the other way as he

murmured a rushed goodbye. But the hand closest to me reached out, his fingers trailing gently down my wrist to the tips of my fingers.

He had disappeared from sight before I reminded myself to breathe. And then I crawled into my bed, put my pillow over my head and cried. Because I had seen the general's face, and he would never change his thinking. Just like he would never let me go.

CHAPTER 19

*S*pring arrived quickly, and while it couldn't compare to the Academy, the front improved significantly. We no longer shivered as we warmed up for training, and flowers bloomed everywhere outside the camp.

We had a string of lessons in the large tent that served as a camp hospital, observing as Beatrice and Reese led the efforts to heal the soldiers injured in the attack. Not all healers were willing to serve at the front lines, and not all had the strength for it. The few who that left rotated through on limited terms. All of which meant Beatrice's team was far too small for the number of soldiers they served.

"Reese is composing today, so you're stuck with me, I'm afraid," Beatrice told us with a smile when we arrived for our second lesson in a row. No one looked disappointed. Even the Devoras and Stantorn trainees liked Beatrice. They might see her sympathy for commonborn as a weakness, but they respected her strength and skill.

I wasn't surprised to see that Reese and a couple of the other healers were missing. On an ordinary day at the healing tents, half of the healing team were absent, using their daily energy to prepare compositions against future need. This store of emergency healings—the ones that did just enough to keep the soldiers alive and in some level of comfort—allowed the team to maintain a slower and more manageable pace as they completed the more complex workings often required for full healings. And their stores meant they didn't have to fear the consequences of an unexpected attack.

The sun shone brightly, and several flaps along the walls had been rolled up and pinned open, letting in light and fresh air. It made the makeshift hospital a much more pleasant place to be than it had been in winter, when the cold temperatures necessitated the flaps remain down.

An older soldier, propped up in bed, grinned at the sight of us and winked at Lavinia. She turned away in disgust, but I smiled back at the man. He had been in the hospital tent since not long after our arrival at the front and must be dying of boredom. What did he think of our lessons and the explanations of how the healings worked?

I took a few steps to stand beside his bed.

"Your leg is looking almost whole!"

His smile grew even broader. "Aye, that it is, Spoken Mage. Only me foot left to grow now. Unless you have a mind to speed it up for me." He gave another wink.

I rolled my eyes. "You've seen me compose in here often enough, Gregor. I might speak my workings, but otherwise the same limitations apply. And I know Beatrice has explained to you why we cannot heal you more quickly."

A healer could use power to speed up the natural healing process of the body, even to perform wonders of healing the body could never achieve on its own. But the same rules regarding physical objects applied. Gregor had lost his leg to an explosion from an enemy mage, and while I could have spoken a new leg into existence for him, it would only last as long as I continued to pour power into it.

Thus why he had been stuck in the healing tent for a whole season. Beatrice was treating him with a complex series of compositions that spurred his leg to regrow itself. In order to fuel the growth, he ate enough rations for two soldiers, despite his inactivity. He had confided to me several weeks ago, that it was the only real perk to his situation.

The process was unnerving to watch, and Saffron had almost lost her lunch after Beatrice first explained his case to us, showing us his exposed stump. The power of her compositions kept the blood from pouring out and infection at bay. It was a masterpiece of healing, really, and I could see why she was so valuable at the front.

At least his service won him the treatment. If he had been a farmer who lost his limb to an accident, he could never have afforded the cost of such a healing.

"Elena!" Coralie's whispered warning sent me hurrying back to the rest of the trainees before someone noticed and reprimanded my absence.

With the aftermath of the attack, Captain Matthis had failed to show for training either of the last two mornings, so I felt unusually full of energy. Beatrice must have noticed because she offered to let me take a turn at healing one of the women still waiting to have a deep burn on her arm treated.

The woman was young—my own age possibly—but she had none of Saffron's squeamishness. While the mage girl hid behind Finnian's tall frame, averting her eyes from the procedure that held the attention of the rest of the trainees, the patient watched with as much interest as any of us.

"Remarkable," she said. "It feels sort of...itchy." She wrinkled her nose as if the word didn't adequately describe the sensation.

I looked at Beatrice. "Should she be able to feel anything? You did say you'd already worked a pain relief composition for her today, didn't you?"

Beatrice nodded. "My compositions don't numb all feeling, just pain. The sensation is perfectly normal."

"Well, look at that!" exclaimed the soldier at the same moment as I felt the drain on my power cut off, the healing complete. "It looks as good as new. Better in fact!" She smiled at me. "I had a scar on that arm from a run in with a tree when I was a girl. And now it looks as smooth as a baby's."

"Sorry!" I smiled back at her. "I hope you weren't fond of the scar."

The woman chuckled, assuring me she had not been, her words partially masking the disgusted sound from behind me. Apparently Lavinia's willingness to overlook her fellow Stantorn's friendly manner with the patients didn't extend to me. Big surprise.

A tall, slender figure stepped up beside me. "You know, I have a scar from a similar childhood accident myself," said Dariela, holding out the underside of her forearm for us to see. A thin ridge, the same color as her skin, extended diagonally across it.

"Must have been a sloppy healer, My Lady," said the soldier, regarding the proffered arm in surprise. No doubt she herself had lacked access to any healer.

Dariela shrugged and smiled. "I think my mother left it on purpose, to remind me not to go climbing any more trees."

I watched her out of the corner of my eye. She didn't seem discomfited by the thought, but it made me a little sad. Had Dariela ever been allowed to be a child, or had she always lived under the pressure to perform?

Beatrice congratulated me on my work and gestured for us all to move on to the next patient. A commonborn nurse assistant came in behind us to see to the healed patient's discharge.

Dariela gave no final glance back at the healed woman, and her cool eyes held only academic interest in the next patient. She hadn't stepped in for the sake of the commonborn, she had done it for me, openly siding with me over Lavinia. When she glanced my way, I smiled in gratitude, and she smiled back before returning her attention to Beatrice.

"Is it just me, or is Dariela being much more friendly to you than usual lately?" Coralie whispered.

"I'll explain later," I whispered back. One of the junior healers was watching us with narrowed eyes, and I didn't want to bring down his ire on my friend.

Coralie gave me an unimpressed look but returned her attention to the lesson. I found it hard to focus after that, though, because in the shuffle of trainees, I had somehow ended up next to Lucas. And though he said nothing, I could read what his face was trying to say. He wished he had been free to step up to my defense instead of having to leave it to Dariela.

I only wished I could tell him that I understood. But I was as constrained to silence as him. And so we stood side by side, not speaking, until the lesson finished, and we all dispersed.

Lorcan had been remarkably absent that day, but he showed up to training the next morning with both Captain Matthis and a lieutenant I didn't recognize in tow. I sighed. It seemed my reprieve had ended.

But Matthis made no effort to call me away. Instead he stayed with our instructors as they gathered us together to one side of the yard.

"During the recent attack, you had the opportunity to see how such engagements are directed from headquarters," Lorcan said. "Today we will analyze the battle itself. Please note the efficacy of the strategies ordered by the general and his officers and be ready to discuss their strengths and weaknesses."

He pulled out a composition and tore it in half. A bright light shot out of the pieces, racing forward to envelop the lieutenant. The brightness obscured his features for a moment and then the light moved past him into the empty yard. Small insubstantial figures moved inside the space, five squads of gray-clad soldiers rushing toward a large group of the enemy.

Araminta gasped quietly, and Clarence twisted backward to try to get a glimpse of the words on the torn parchment, seeming more interested in the working itself than the scene now playing out in front of us.

It had been two and a half years, but I recognized the composition. It was one of the first workings I ever saw. Except on that occasion, Lorcan had reproduced only a small number of people and no more than a minute of my history. And I had received the impression that even that was a working of great strength and skill. I glanced quickly over at him. No wonder no one had seen him yesterday. He must have exhausted himself to produce a working of this size.

The scene centered on the lieutenant, who I now realized must have been chosen because of his participation in the battle. It took me a moment to orient the scene with so many fast-moving transparent forms. It didn't help that the power employed by the mages showed in visible silvery waves, just like on the two previous occasions I had seen the composition worked.

A group of Kallorwegians moved, and I caught a glimpse of a section of the Wall behind them. They had been mostly facing toward it when our troops appeared, but they all spun around at their approach.

With the jagged, dangerous rocks at their backs, they formed into lines, spearmen on one knee, spears pointing outward toward the incoming Ardannians. Their archers stood behind, sending arrow after arrow at our soldiers. Most of them hit a number of interlocking silvery walls in front of our squads, falling harmlessly to the ground, but one of the walls flickered and disappeared, three arrows flying through the now empty air where it had stood.

Two of our soldiers fell, struck by arrows. The image of the lieutenant in front of us now tore a parchment, and a new wall of silver appeared, but already another one had fallen on the far end of the line.

The five enemy mages huddled together in a clump behind the lines of their soldiers. One of them still faced toward the Wall, throwing silver at it from a series of parchments. The other four had turned their attention to the attacking Ardannians. I knew we were supposed to be watching the strategy of the battle, but I kept my focus on the mages.

I wished there was some way to distinguish the purpose of the compositions we could see in visible form. Particularly the ones the lone mage flung at the Wall. How did he plan to break through? Or was it all for show, their plans already laid for a secret escape, their purpose as a diversion already achieved?

One of the enemy mages ripped a composition, and several trees behind our troops caught alight. The flames leaped toward two soldiers, drawing my eye, and I recognized the woman I had healed the day before.

An Ardannian captain stepped forward, a composition already in hand, and a shower of water extinguished the flames. The exchange had drawn the attention of many of the soldiers, causing them to falter, but the squad under our lieutenant had managed to break through the Kallorwegian shields at one end.

The whole scene had an eerie feel, due in large part to the silence. As the Ardannian forces pushed forward, their mouths twisted into silent battle cries, only enhancing the effect.

The two lines of soldiers crashed against each other while my focus returned to the mages. They appeared to have abandoned the shielding around their soldiers, and silver no longer battered at the Wall. Instead so much silver washed around the five of them that for a moment their images were entirely obscured.

Then it faded slightly, and their shadowy figures reappeared. But a new clump of indistinct forms had split away, outlined in silver and surrounded by a further silver glow. They moved away from the action at a hurried pace, disappearing from the yard and fading into nothingness as they did so.

Whatever compositions they had left behind them remained in place for several further minutes as the remaining Kallorwegian soldiers surrendered. The Ardannian mages cautiously approached the grouping of enemy mages only to pull back sharply when their illusions shattered.

The whole scene slowly faded, leaving behind nothing but an empty exercise yard. Lorcan immediately began to throw questions at us.

"Why did the Ardannian defenders choose that moment to attack?"

"They knew the Wall would hold for long enough," said Weston, "and it allowed them to trap the forces against it, giving us an advantage in maneuverability."

Lorcan nodded. "And why didn't they send more mages?"

"What? And risk losing them all?" Lavinia shook her head. "Mages are too valuable for that."

"Indeed." Lorcan didn't sound overly impressed. Clarence jumped in to expand her answer.

"They learned their lesson centuries ago when a series of wars between Kallorway and Ardann decimated the mage populations. There used to be a greater proportion of us compared to commonborns back then, but many of the families died out completely. Peace lasted for two hundred years after that, until King Osborne resumed hostilities thirty years ago. But even he isn't foolish enough to over commit his mages this time. He doesn't have the numbers to do so."

"And neither do we," said Lucas, a grim note in his voice.

"So was it all a diversion, then?" I asked, watching Captain Matthis rather than Lorcan.

"That is a more difficult question to answer," said Lorcan,

drawing my eyes back to him. He didn't look pleased, reminding me that he was supposed to be the one asking the questions.

I wanted to push through and demand answers from him or Matthis about the two missing soldiers from the smaller raiding party, but I swallowed my words. Lucas wouldn't blurt out a question like that in the middle of class, so neither would I. Especially when I didn't think they would give me the answer.

I would have to find answers about the Kallorwegians, and about the general, in some other way.

CHAPTER 20

*a*fter that one raid, the Kallorwegians fell largely quiet again. An even more unusual occurrence for this time of year, Matthis informed me. He seemed to think it cause for concern.

"Better the enemy you know," he said, "than a new enemy. Or an old one with new ideas."

The soldiers didn't seem to share his pessimism, some among them assuring one another that their successful defense of the larger raid had scared the Kallorwegians off. Yet more seemed to think something else had scared them away.

"Heard things have changed over here, they have," I caught one saying, with a significant look in my direction. I pretended I hadn't heard and hurried the other way.

The soldiers didn't seem to have lost their faith in me as the Spoken Mage, but I knew the general was growing increasingly impatient. My energy levels had plateaued and nothing his officers tried seemed able to extend them further. I heard Lorcan arguing with him about it on one of our visits to headquarters.

"You're losing perspective, Griffith." Lorcan sounded tired and out of temper. "She's an eighteen-year-old girl. The

214

progress she has already made is incredible. But there are limits. Strength and endurance can only be trained and extended so far. Compositions cannot store energy. We cannot replenish it. And no one—not even the Spoken Mage—has a limitless supply."

"We don't really know what she's capable of," said the general. "There has never been one like her before."

"She's still human, Griffith. Don't lose sight of that." Lorcan spoke quietly, and his words shocked me. Did he really mean them? Perhaps my nearly three years as his trainee had actually succeeded in doing something to change his thinking.

Lieutenant Martin came past, and I drew back, pretending to be examining a chart on the wall instead of eavesdropping. From the quirk to his lips, I didn't think he bought it. But he didn't say anything to give me away, either.

The weather continued to warm, and I joined the vast majority of the soldiers in railing at the mud. It got everywhere and stuck to everything, and I had to spend far too much time every day cleaning my boots. At least I could do it in the sun, though, and my favorite spot was the patch of grass behind my tent.

My friends found me basking there on my nineteenth birthday, stealing a few moments to myself between classes. Even Dariela was with them, standing a little apart from the others.

"Happy Birthday!" they cried, piling into the small space. Coralie led them with a cake coated in chocolate icing proudly held before her.

I laughed.

"I should have known not even an army would stop you from producing a cake."

"Of course you should have." She placed it carefully in front of me, before plopping down onto the grass. "But no doubt Lorcan will be hounding us to get to lessons at any moment, so hurry up and cut us all a slice."

"I'll do it," said Clarence, rushing to my assistance. "You sit and relax, Elena."

I smiled my thanks, my heart twisting a little. Poor Clarence still hadn't forgotten his accident back at the Academy, or that I had been the one to save everyone.

Leila appeared as the slices were being handed around, starting innocently when she saw us.

"Oh! Is it your birthday, Elena? Happy Birthday!"

I rolled my eyes, handing her a slice with a shake of my head and a smile. "Don't pretend you turned up just in time for cake by accident."

"I may have heard something from one of the cooks," she said with a cheeky twinkle.

"Of course you did," said Coralie. "One day you'll have to teach me your secrets."

Not one of my friends balked at a commonborn soldier joining us, and my heart swelled with happiness. I was lucky to have them. I just wished I could forget the one glaring absence. How perfect this moment would be if Lucas sat at my side.

As if conjured by my thoughts, he appeared, although I noticed he kept his eyes carefully away from me.

"Class is at the healing tent again today," he said. "A few soldiers have come down with influenza, and Beatrice wants us to observe the diagnosis process and learn about measures for preventing the spread of infection in camp."

"Surely you have time for a slice of cake first," said Finnian, holding one out to him.

Lucas hesitated and then took it. "They're expecting us there in five minutes."

Finnian groaned but made no further protest, and everyone slowly got to their feet. A hand appeared in front of me, and I took it, letting Lucas pull me up.

"Happy Birthday, Elena," he said. "Thank you for the cake."

"It was Coralie who arranged for the cake," I said.

"Well, thank you for having such enterprising friends, then."

"Careful Lucas," said Finnian, brushing past us. "That almost sounded like humor. And the spot for the good-looking, humorous one is already filled in this group."

"He means himself," I said.

"Of course he does," said Lucas, "he always does." He chuckled quietly, and I remembered they had all grown up together. Lucas knew most of my friends as well as I did.

I flushed, embarrassed, but the warm look in his eyes erased the feeling.

"I don't have a present for you," he said, under his breath. "But I promise to get you something utterly extravagant when we get back to Corrin."

I forced my eyes to look downward despite the smile creeping up my face.

"Don't worry, I didn't get you anything for your birthday either," I reminded him.

"Didn't you? I could have sworn you gave me just what I wanted."

Warmth raced through me, but Coralie appeared, linking her arm through mine and breaking the moment.

"If Saffron decides to lose her stomach in class again, I'm nominating you to help her. I went to far too much trouble to procure that cake to see it come back up again."

"But I'm the birthday girl," I protested. "Finnian can do it."

"Fine by me," Coralie said promptly, and by the time Finnian had replied, Lucas had drifted away. I joked with my friends and tried to pretend I wasn't acutely aware of his absence.

Dariela sometimes joined me on my patch of grass after that, seeming dedicated to the task of friendship she had set herself. We didn't talk of anything of import while we scrubbed our boots, but she had witty observations about the people around us that always made me laugh. She might not have been making friends for the last two years, but she had certainly been observing.

"I wonder what Natalya would say if we threatened to tell the rest of the trainees back at the Academy that she was making eyes at a commonborn guard," she said with a chuckle in her voice one afternoon.

"A guard?" I stared at her. "Natalya would never be interested in a commonborn."

"Oh, not seriously interested, of course," said Dariela, stretching out her long legs. "But she has eyes in her head just like the rest of us."

When I continued to stare at her in confusion, she groaned and rolled her eyes. "Of course the mighty Spoken Mage is the only one free of such weakness. Surely you've noticed that one of the royal guards in the prince's squad is remarkably good-looking?"

"Umm…" I couldn't actually call to mind the image of a single one of Lucas's guards. I tended to focus on someone else when they were around.

"The tall, dark one," Dariela said, trying to prod my memory.

"Oh, yes," I said vaguely, and she sighed.

"Well, take my word for it, he's extremely good looking, and Natalya has noticed. She thinks she's very subtle about it, but she always rubs her neck when she's self-conscious. She used to do it all the time in first year around Lucas." She smiled. "Nowadays she looks more frustrated around him than anything. Not that she wouldn't still snap him up if she got the chance, of course."

She sat up straighter. "Wait, there he is!" She pointed down the side of our tent, and I had to lean forward to follow her line of sight.

The guard stood with his back to us, but seeing him refreshed my memory. He was the tall one. And objectively speaking, I couldn't deny he had an appealing look. But almost immediately my eyes slid sideways to his companion. Lucas. And this was why I couldn't bring up a clear picture of any of his guards.

While I watched, bent awkwardly to see around the tent, Lucas pointed back toward his own tent. The guard showed visible reluctance to whatever order Lucas was giving, probably because the prince appeared to be ordering him to leave his protective post. But when Lucas straightened slightly, the man nodded and walked away.

As he stepped out of sight, Natalya and Lavinia came into view, walking from the mess tent toward the entrance to our sleeping tent.

"Watch," Dariela said quietly, her own eyes fixed on our year mates.

And, sure enough, although my two year mates appeared to continue their own conversation uninterrupted, Natalya's gaze flicked sideways to the passing guard, and her hand slid up one side of her neck before she tugged at a lock of her hair and let it fall again.

"See!" Dariela sounded amused.

"So what do you do when you're self-conscious around someone?" I asked, trying to hold back my grin.

"Me?" She raised one eyebrow, the opposite side of her mouth quirking up. "I'm never self-conscious."

"Of course not," I murmured, but she maintained her innocent expression.

Lucas looked in our direction, and I pulled back into my original position, out of his sight. But I had already seen his remaining guard take up a station at the side of the tent.

Lucas himself strolled into view a moment later.

"Good afternoon, ladies." He sank down onto the grass beside us.

His hands were empty—even trainee princes didn't scrub their own boots—and he held them out imperiously for my boot and brush. For a moment I hesitated, but when I saw Dariela giving me a curious look, I handed them over, not wanting to cause a scene.

"There's something peaceful about scrubbing boots," he said, after taking a few swipes at mine. "No thought required, just the satisfaction of making something shine."

"Maybe you missed your calling as a boot polisher," said Dariela with a snort.

He grinned up at her, his hand moving rhythmically along the shoe, and she blinked several times before looking sideways at me. I just shrugged, my idle fingers plucking at the grass. She had already proved herself far too observant. I was now dreading a future conversation about the subtle changes in the usually serious and focused prince. Would she believe he had scrubbed my boots out of no more than general chivalry?

I told myself I should move away from him, put some distance between us, but I seemed to have grown roots into the dirt below me. Lucas handed me back the clean boot, holding out his hand for my other one, and I reluctantly handed it over. Our hands connected as he took it, and he lingered in the touch for a moment, completely destroying my train of thought. The warm sun and the domestic scene lulled my previous caution, and I swayed toward him.

The rasp of Dariela's brush made me pull back, my face warming. One hand reached up toward my hair, and then I dropped it quickly, trying to remember if I always did that when I was uncomfortable. No doubt Dariela had noticed if I did.

The sound of a cleared throat made Lucas look up, his own view down the side of the tent clear.

"My guard has returned. Enjoy the sun for me, ladies." He handed me back my boot and stood, nodding at us both before striding away.

Dariela had completed her own cleaning and pulled on her

now shiny boots while she watched him go. Once they were both in place, she turned to me.

"I don't know what's going on between the two of you." She held up her hands, as if to cut short my words, although I hadn't spoken. "And I don't want to know. I won't say anything to anyone." She shrugged. "Friends, right? But you should know that if I have my suspicions, others will too. Do with that as you will, it's none of my business." She stood and gave me a small wave before heading off to put away her cleaning apparatus.

I sat there in shocked silence. If only I could talk it over with Lucas, but that was half the problem. We couldn't find a moment alone together.

I still hadn't moved when Finnian came into view. He slumped down beside me, stretching himself out on the grass.

"Wake me when it's lunchtime. Or better yet, when they tell us it's time to go home."

"Don't overwhelm me with your cheery positivity, or anything," I said.

Finnian, who had thrown an arm across his face to shield his eyes from the sun, just chuckled.

I watched him, giving an internal sigh. He seemed like the same old Finnian, but I couldn't look at him without thinking of Coralie. I had always known he was from an important family, that he was as deeply enmeshed in this game of power as all my year mates. But somewhere along the way I had forgotten it, and I had come to see him as just a friend.

"Why are you looking at me like that, Elena?" he asked without taking his arm off his eyes.

"Like what? You can't even see me."

"I can feel the weight of that stare, though. If I was in water right now, I would sink like a rock."

A recklessness gripped me. If Lucas could change—and he'd already begun, suggesting to the general that he would be willing to serve beneath a commonborn officer—then surely Finnian could, also.

"Some things are more important than strength, Finnian," I said.

He rolled onto his side, propping himself on his elbow, his fist supporting his head. He examined my face with a slight frown although his voice was light.

"A great many things, if you ask me. Now if someone could please just convince the good general of that, perhaps we could all get away from this infernal mud."

I frowned, trying to read the truth in his quizzical eyes.

"Surely love is one of those things," I said, but my voice had become hesitant. Was I missing a puzzle piece somewhere?

He sat up fully, leaning toward me.

"Now that is a very interesting proposition. Naturally I, of all people, think so." He gave a flourishing half bow from his sitting position, neatly capturing his usual charming persona with the gesture. "But are we perhaps talking about…someone else?"

I blinked at him, thinking of Coralie, and then my mind caught up.

"Oh. Oh no. I mean, yes." I growled. "Enough of this. Finnian, I'm talking about Coralie. You and Coralie. Does it really matter to you so much that she's only a Cygnet and her compositions have less strength than yours?"

Every ounce of joking good humor fell from his face. "I thought we were friends, Elena. How can you say such a thing?"

Now I was completely lost. I stared at him wordlessly while he frowned back at me.

"You…don't…feel that way?" I asked slowly.

"Of course I do not. How could you think that of me?"

"I understood it was a common way of thinking." I examined him carefully, trying to work out where I had misstepped.

He relaxed a little, leaning both forearms against his knees and looking away from me.

"I suppose it is." He looked back at me. "But then common thinking back in first year was that the commonborn in our midst should be avoided. I've never bought into common thinking."

I blinked at him, feeling a little foolish. This was the Finnian I knew. A heaviness lifted from my shoulders at the knowledge that I hadn't misjudged my friend so completely.

Sudden comprehension flashed across his face. He leaned forward again.

"Where is this coming from, Elena?" His perceptive gaze pinned me in place. "Coralie told me she didn't want anything serious while we were at the Academy. And thus, behold me." He gestured toward himself. "Entirely unserious. I'm wounded you assumed there was anything else behind it."

But his eyes asked me if perhaps it hadn't been an assumption at all. A sudden fear that I was betraying my best friend gripped me. But if Finnian truly didn't care about her family or her strength…

"Perhaps I'm not the one making the assumptions," I said.

He paused for an endless moment, not a muscle moving, and then he stood to his feet in one liquid movement.

"Please excuse me for a moment. I have someone I need to speak to."

He had nearly made it off the grass when I called his name. He stopped and looked back at me.

"Don't make any promises you're not willing to keep."

"I never do."

I didn't see Coralie until the evening meal. She gave me a look that did not bode well, and all my hopeful excitement withered.

"Did you speak to Finnian?" I asked as we collected our trays of food.

"Funny," she said with a flat look, "I was about to ask you the same thing."

I winced. I guess it had been friend betrayal after all.

"But you said—"

She cut me off. "Not here. We'll talk later."

We sat down and began to eat our meal, but I couldn't enjoy a bite without her usual cheerful conversation. After she caught me watching her from the corner of my eye for the fifth time, she sighed.

"Fine. Let's get out of here and talk."

We took our rolls with us, and I grabbed an apple on the way out as well. Neither of us said anything as she led me to a secluded spot on the outskirts of the tent city. I had barely come to a stop when she whirled on me.

"Why did you say something to Finnian? He's been bothering me all afternoon."

"Bothering you?" My brow creased. "Don't try to pretend you aren't a little in love with him, Coralie. Or a lot. Because I won't believe you."

She threw up her hands. "That's what makes it worse!"

"But you told me he didn't want you because of your family. And it's not true! I thought you would be happy."

"What?" She stared at me. "I never said that."

My mouth dropped open. "Yes, you did! After Midwinter."

"No." She shook her head rapidly from side to side. "That's not what I said. I never said he didn't want me because of my family. I said it would never work because of his family."

"But I thought…"

"Oh Elena." Coralie sighed. "At least you meant well, I suppose."

"Why do you care about his family?" I asked. "What does it matter what they think? If he doesn't care, why should you?"

"Because he does care, of course. You've seen what he's like with Saffron and heard them talk about their mothers. Finnian is his mother's world. He may think he loves me enough to flout them, but he would hate actually having to do it. And that's without even considering the mockery of his peers. The snide looks, the omitted invitations."

"Would you want their invitations?" I asked.

"Not for me. But I would want them for Finnian. I couldn't bear to be the reason he was looked down on, overlooked for positions within his future discipline, even. And then one day he would start to resent me for it. Start to wonder if I was worth it. Maybe not today, or tomorrow, but eventually. Maybe only when our children got to the Academy and couldn't keep up with their year mates among the strongest of the great families. I love Finnian, but I don't want to have to spend the rest of my life proving that I was worth the sacrifice."

An icy sensation started in my scalp and spread slowly through my body. I wanted to shake her, to tell her she was wrong. To tell her love was worth it. But I couldn't seem to move. Her words reverberated in my mind. She was speaking of herself, but she wasn't the only one who had dared to love someone who should have been out of their reach.

Was she right? Would Lucas some day come to resent me? And would I come to resent the pressure to be worth it? What sort of children would a Spoken Mage have? Would they inherit my limitations? A prince or princess cocooned in the middle of court but unable to pen a single word.

I had always mocked and even feared the game. Was I really ready to commit myself to a life ensnared at its very center?

When Lucas kissed me everything in the world seemed clear. But he was nowhere to be seen right now, and suddenly the weight of a crown seemed like a burden far too heavy to bear. I stared silently at my friend. I had no answers for myself—I certainly had none for her.

"What's that?" she asked, looking past me. Slowly, awareness of my surroundings returned. A distant commotion split the evening calm. Raised voices sounded from a growing gathering of soldiers on the fringes of camp not too far from where we stood.

Exchanging glances, we took off toward the hubbub. Others had the same idea, and the crowd continued to grow. We wormed our way through, our white robes keeping the soldiers from shoving us aside.

At the center of the gathering, two soldiers crouched beside a third. The third man—the focus of all the attention—appeared to have collapsed onto his knees where he swayed slightly despite no longer being on his feet. A ragged gash along his hairline slowly seeped blood, and his nondescript clothing was dirty and torn, bloodstained in several places. A rough bandage had been wrapped around his upper right arm, clearly not the work of any reputable healer or healer's assistant.

"The general. I need to see the general," he croaked, his glazed eyes sweeping the crowd.

The watchers across from us bulged and rippled as two men in red and gold elbowed them aside, creating a passage through the crowd. Lucas emerged into the small open space in the middle, his gaze fixed on the man.

"What is this?" he asked.

"The general," the man repeated. "I need the general."

"I am Prince Lucas, you may tell me your news."

The man blinked and attempted unsuccessfully to regain his feet. Lucas knelt swiftly beside him.

"No, do not stand. You are injured. Healers are no doubt on their way, but if your message is urgent, we must hear it without delay."

"An attack." The man stopped to cough before regaining his breath. "An attack is coming."

"Then we will prepare for it," Lucas said calmly. "And drive them back as we have always done."

I tried to read if his confidence was real or assumed for the sake of the soldiers around us. I couldn't tell.

"No!" The man pulled at Lucas's robes, and the two royal guards surged forward. Lucas waved them away.

"No," the man whispered. I leaned forward from my place at the front of the crowd to hear better. "This isn't like the last one. This is a full-scale attack. Their entire force is on its way here. They will arrive within hours."

CHAPTER 21

Only the closest soldiers could hear his words, but the ripple of the news passed from mouth to mouth, the cry growing louder.

"Attack!"

"An attack is coming!"

"Hours?" Lucas gripped the man's shoulder. "Impossible. They could not have kept secret an attack of that scale. The troop movements, the preparations...Impossible. Our intelligencers would have sent us word by now."

"So it's true, then." The man slumped in on himself, losing what little color he had still retained. "You have had no warning. We feared our messages weren't getting through. Even the compositions seem to have failed. I wasn't supposed to leave my post, but two had already tried to come in person, and yet no word had come back through the usual channels."

He gasped and swayed. He would have fallen if Lucas hadn't held him upright.

"This is too big," he said between labored breaths. "I had to try, or all of Ardann will be lost."

"Healers!" Lucas called from down in the mud. "Where are the healers?"

A purple robe appeared and knelt beside him. To his credit, Reese wasted no time asking questions, his whole focus on the patient.

"You and you." Lucas pointed at two burly soldiers. "Carry this man to headquarters."

Reese muttered a half-verbalized protest, but Lucas waved it aside.

"You can accompany them, Reese. We have no time to waste."

He stood and surveyed the crowd. His eyes fastened on the silver robes now dotted among the gray uniforms, even more approaching from further in the camp.

"Officers." Lucas shouted, his voice rising above all the other noise. "Gather your squads. All of them. Call every soldier to active duty. Triple the sentries, and await further orders from the general."

His eyes found me only steps away from him.

"Spoken Mage, you're with me. And you—" He pointed at the two soldiers who had managed to lift the injured man back to his feet. "Follow me."

Six more of the royal guard had arrived while he issued his orders, and they didn't hesitate to clear the path ahead of us, knocking people aside as needed. Lucas soon outstripped Reese and the soldiers with their wounded burden, but he didn't slow to their pace. At a signal, four of his guards dropped back to stay with them, while the other four surrounded him.

I raced beside him, inside their protective circle. All of my earlier doubts were thrust aside next to the enormity of this news. Lucas had called me Spoken Mage, not Elena, and it was in that role I responded. Even the memory of the gully attack could not deter me. If the enemy intended to attack this camp and my friends within it, I would fight to defend them.

We almost ran, taking the straightest path possible, and yet the news somehow managed to precede us. On every side I heard voices calling warning of an attack, and as we crossed through the double gates, the alarm bell began to sound.

Lieutenant Martin must have kept his word because the soldiers at the doors of headquarters made no attempt to hinder our passage. Or perhaps they were dissuaded from intervening by the aggressive posture of the guards who kept two steps in front of the prince.

We swept into the building, Lucas and me still not having exchanged any words, and straight to the command room. We met the general in the passage, on his way to the entrance hall. At sight of us he stopped and strode back in at Lucas's side.

"What is this talk of attack?" he asked, all business. "I have received no reports."

Lucas immediately relayed the message of the injured man, seeming to have memorized his exact words. The general's eyes narrowed and then widened.

"A full-scale attack? We haven't had one of those for—" He eyed Lucas and my white robes.

"Twenty years," said Lucas. "We haven't fought one off in twenty years. And that time we had enough warning to call all the able-bodied young mages in the kingdom to the front."

I tried to remember if I'd learned about that attack in school. Twenty years was before I had been born, although only just. And then I realized. That must have been the attack that resulted in our unusually small year group. Mages at the right age to be bearing children had been otherwise occupied that year.

I shivered. Twenty years was a long time. Why now?

"And you're sure this man was one of ours? An intelligencer, I presume?" The general frowned, clearly considering the possibility of a false warning, although I couldn't imagine what the purpose of such a thing would be.

"He's one of ours," said Captain Matthis, exploding through

the door and only just halting before he collided with us all. "I sent him out myself two years ago."

For one second the general stood in silence, absorbing the news, and then he roared for his aides as the command room erupted.

"The squads are assembling and awaiting your commands," Lucas told the general who nodded once before moving to the next person requiring his attention.

Lucas took a step backward and then another, as two aides pushed past him, too frantic to notice who they thrust aside. I grabbed his arm, ignoring the disapproving gazes of his guards, and dragged him to the side of the room.

"Do you believe me now?" I whispered urgently.

He frowned at me.

"A full-scale attack, and we heard not a whisper of it? The intelligencer himself said that they sent messages, that two tried to come in person before him. Are you still going to deny we have a traitor?"

Lucas frowned. "Kallorway—"

"What?" I cut him off. "Suddenly discovered every one of our message systems on their own? Worked out how to dismantle our communication systems? How to stop our intelligencers?"

He shifted uncomfortably.

"How did they do that, Lucas?" My eyes darted around the room. "Or did some of the messages get through only to be squashed on this end?"

In the background, the general barked orders into balls of power. Already answers were coming back. Advance scouts had been sent out, experienced mage officers with robes full of compositions.

The intelligencer had spoken the truth. An enormous army had already reached the far bank of the Abneris. Fear reflected in some of the younger officers' eyes, but the older mages had no time for fear in their frenzied efforts to direct our defense.

"We must stop them at the river," the general barked. "If they cross the river, the whole camp will be lost." He continued to shout orders, sending squad after squad to defensive positions on the riverbank.

"I don't know much about war," I murmured to Lucas, "but is it really wise to send them all? Shouldn't some remain behind as a last line of defense?"

The crash of the closing town gates sounded in the distance, punctuating my words.

Lucas hesitated, indecision on his face. I grasped a handful of his robe, pulling him down so that I could speak more quietly into his ear.

"You get more information than the rest of us. How are the intelligencers' reports received? Who has access to them?"

Lucas's eyes darted straight across the room to General Griffith.

"I knew it!" I whispered.

"The procedure changed after the attack on the gully," Lucas said, every word reluctant. "The enemy knew we would be there. Someone—or some working—must have tipped them off."

My eyes narrowed. So the top levels of command had acknowledged it—just not to me.

"What was the new procedure?" I asked.

"All reports go straight to the general, and all communication compositions are directed to him."

"And you still want to claim there's no chance at all he's a traitor? Maybe we should ask that intelligencer just how he was sending his earlier messages—and to whom."

Lucas hesitated for only the fraction of a second before striding back into the center of the room.

"General."

Griffith glanced our way, his gaze skimming over us and back to the aide beside him before he processed who had spoken and turned to face us.

"Your Highness? I think it would be best if you—"

"Where is the intelligencer?" asked Lucas. "Reese should have healed him by now. We need to find out how much more he knows, he may have valuable intelligence about the attack. And I would request that I be present when he is questioned."

The general frowned. "Fine. You may do the questioning yourself. Inform me of any valuable intelligence." He turned back to his aide.

Lucas's gaze swept the room, but the injured man and his entourage hadn't made it inside.

"Do you think they're at headquarters yet?" I asked.

"They should be." Lucas sounded grim. "Come on."

Together we hurried back out into the corridors of the mansion. The entryway now swarmed with soldiers, officers, and terrified townsfolk demanding answers. Standing on tiptoe, I unsuccessfully tried to scan the crowd.

"Can you see them? There are too many people in here, I can't see anything." I wasn't sure Lucas could even hear me over the din.

Lucas's hand snaked out suddenly, hauling a passing soldier from the crowd. I recognized him—or rather his bulging muscles.

"You," Lucas said. "Where is the healer and his patient?"

The man nodded, grunting something that might have been Lucas's title. "The purple robe insisted he needed somewhere quiet to work. We left them down there." He pointed back down the corridor. "Second door after the big room."

Lucas and I took off running. Sliding past the double doors into the former ballroom, Lucas pushed open the second door. I collided with his suddenly motionless form.

"Lucas, what—"

He stepped forward, and the question died on my lips. The small room was clearly sleeping quarters of some kind, perhaps for some of the general's aides, and it was empty. Empty except for the limp figure of the intelligencer lying on a cot against the far wall, his blood soaking into the blanket beneath him.

Lucas knelt beside him and then looked up at me.

"Dead."

I drew in a shaky breath, steadying myself against the door.

"His wounds, perhaps?" I suggested, but Lucas's shaking head silenced me.

"Where's Reese?" he asked.

"I don't know. I didn't see him. You don't think he…" I let my voice trail off, not sure whether I meant to accuse Reese or whether I feared for his safety.

"We need to speak to the general." Lucas wiped the blood from his hand and joined me at the door.

"But the general—"

"We don't have any proof, Elena." Lucas slammed his hand against the wall. "And we're in the middle of a full-scale attack. Do you really want to accuse our commander of treason right now? What if we're wrong?"

I looked away. If there was even a chance we were wrong…If it was someone else…

"And the general didn't do this." Lucas gestured at the body behind us.

"Not personally," I muttered.

He ignored me. "Griffith could be in danger for all we know. We need to get back to the control room."

I trailed behind him, my eyes darting from side to side as I waited for someone to leap from the shadows and attack.

But no danger sprang out at us, and back inside the control room, the chaos had noticeably diminished. Most of the mages had disappeared, leaving only a small handful of aides furiously scribbling at desks in a corner. They handed off their completed compositions to gray-clad soldiers—newcomers to this previously mage-run sanctuary—who ran them to the general. He did the tearing himself now, speaking into each ball of power before reaching for the next parchment.

The noise levels had lowered significantly, and the aides receiving reply messages now sat along one wall. As if even the few seconds it took to walk back and forth to their normal side room were too valuable to be wasted.

The general glanced up at us. "Still here, are you? Good. This is the safest place for you, for now. But have your guards draw up an evacuation plan. I've sent every available mage to the river, but if we can't hold them off, we need to get you out."

Lucas ignored the talk of evacuations. "He's dead. Our intelligencer is dead."

"What?" Griffith looked up, shock on his face. I examined him closely but didn't know him well enough to read if the emotion was real.

"And Reese is gone."

"Gone? Do you mean…"

Lucas shrugged. "I have no idea. I've seen no sign of him."

I tried not to imagine Reese lying dead in some room of the mansion. We might not have liked each other much, but he did spend his days saving lives. And he was Beatrice's relative. I didn't wish him dead.

"We must—"

But whatever the general intended to order was lost as Leila came tumbling into the room, shouting for the general as if she were not a lowly private. All sound in the room stopped as everyone turned to look at her.

"A townsman at the front door," she panted out. "He only just made it back into the town before they sealed the gates. He was down south searching for a strayed sheep, barely in range of the bells. He brought these."

She thrust out a small collection of compositions. The general took them off her with a hard look. These had no place in the hands of a commonborn soldier or the herdsman who had apparently handed them to her.

"He found an officer on the brink of death apparently." She looked white, and her voice shook. "He gave him these rather than risk them falling into enemy hands. And he had a warning, too." She looked confused and nervous as if she was passing on a message she didn't understand. "There's a breach team on its way."

An indrawn breath from General Griffith brought my head swinging back toward him. From the stunned look on his face, the news meant more to him than it did to Leila.

"A breach team," said Lucas quietly. "Perhaps we should have guessed." He met the general's eyes. "They must be stopped, of course."

A faint memory surfaced from armed forces studies. A breach team was a relic of the old wars when mages existed in greater abundance. A team made up entirely of mages, drawn from across the disciplines. Wind workers and creators to bring down buildings and walls, officers to fight any who might oppose them, and healers turned to the darkest of roles—assassins who knew every way a person might be killed.

Breach teams had been sent in situations just like this, with one purpose. To break through into the most heavily defended headquarters and assassinate those in command. With coordination and communication gone, our squads would soon break apart, chaos ensuring our battlefield defeat.

Griffith leafed quickly through the compositions in his hand.

"No communication workings left. It could be true."

I looked between the general and Lucas. Both men would surely be on the breach team's assassination list. And their approach only highlighted the truth of Lucas's earlier words to me. We could not afford to take out our leadership in the middle of battle. That would only be doing the enemy's work for them.

"We have to send a team to stop them," said Lucas. "They cannot be allowed to breach the town."

The general looked around the nearly empty command center.

"All my strongest squads and officers are already in the midst of battle. I have no one left to send."

I stepped forward. "Then it's a good thing not all the mages present are under your command. Not all of us with strength are fighting."

Lucas stepped up beside me. "Yes, we will go."

Griffith shook his head, the light that had filled his eyes at my words dimming.

"I cannot send a prince into battle."

"Then we will all fall. The Spoken Mage does not go without me."

"We're here, too," said an unexpected voice behind us. Clarence stepped into my line of sight with Araminta.

"What are you doing here?" Lucas asked.

"They called for all the squads to assemble, and Colonel Jennica assigned us to your team, remember," said Araminta. "We knew you had come here, so we followed."

"Where are the others?" I asked, sudden fear gripping me.

"With Captains Matthis and Carson, I think," said Clarence. "And Lorcan and Thornton must be with them, too. We haven't seen them here at any rate."

Terror washed over me. They were out there fighting, then.

"We have to go," I said. "There's no time to debate it. For all we know even a minute wasted here may turn the tide against us."

"I cannot—" repeated the general, but Lucas cut him off.

"You must."

Griffith growled. "Very well, for your own sake as much as mine. But take your guards and any of my soldiers you can find.

You!" He turned on Leila. "Gather up anyone you can find other than the door guards and go with His Highness."

Leila saluted before sprinting from the room. Griffith glanced around at his aides, his eyes latching onto Martin.

"And I'm putting you in charge, Lieutenant."

Martin stood to attention and saluted.

To Lucas, the general said, "He's the most competent one I have left. You may be royalty, but he has battle experience. Let him lead you."

Lucas nodded, and the general turned once more to Martin. Stepping close, he growled softly, "Whatever happens, keep the prince alive."

CHAPTER 22

*M*artin saluted again, and the five of us took off running. As we burst from the building, Leila appeared with four soldiers in tow, although only one I recognized. Tobias.

Ten of us, then. A squad. Plus four of Lucas's royal guards.

"This way," Martin said. "They've closed the gates, but I know a way out of the town."

He led us to where a few houses nestled against the southern wall. Signaling for us to wait, he slipped through the front door. What felt like an eternity, but could only have been moments, passed before he reappeared and waved us inside.

We filed through to a back room where an older man held open a cupboard door. He nodded grimly at us as we appeared and gestured for us to pass through into the storage space. Martin went first, dropping to his hands and knees and crawling through a hatch in the back wall of the cavity.

We followed one at a time, crawling through brief darkness before emerging on the outside of the town wall. Moonlight illuminated clear ground on the opposite side of Bronton to the camp. Martin pulled out a composition before eyeing my fellow trainees.

"I should have asked what compositions you have on you."

"This is a war camp," Lucas said. "We carry everything we have on us at all times."

Clarence and Araminta both nodded, their faces set into determined expressions, despite the terrifying circumstances. I knew they must both have far fewer compositions than Lucas. But then they'd been studying here for months without any action to drain their supplies. Hopefully they had enough.

"Good," said Martin. "But I'm assuming you don't have any homing compositions of your own?" He lightly shook the parchment in his hand.

I stepped forward and held out my hand. "Can I see?"

Martin hesitated. "It will only work for me."

I shook my head impatiently. "I just want to read it."

"Give it to her," said Lucas.

Martin glanced at him, and then handed the parchment to me. Griffith may have put the lieutenant in charge, but Lucas was still a prince.

I scanned the words. When ripped, the composition would send power sweeping through the surrounding area looking for enemy soldiers or workings. If it found either, it would send back a pulse of power to guide the mage to the spot.

"This isn't going to work," I said. "It's too broad. There's a battle going on, a big one, and it's going to confuse your working. The last thing we need is to be led straight into the middle of the fighting."

"A homing composition set to locate a breach team would obviously be more useful," he said, "but since there hasn't been a breach team in centuries, none of us exactly carry those on our persons."

"That's where I come in." I thrust his composition back at

him, already running over the words in my mind, revising and adjusting them.

"Not too much power," Lucas warned in my ear. "We don't know how many of them there might be, and we'll need you before the night is over."

I nodded, too focused on my composition to speak. A distant explosion shook the ground, and orange blossomed in the sky to the north of us.

"They're already fighting at the river," Martin said. "We need to move."

"Give her time." Lucas glared at the lieutenant.

But the last of the composition had formed in my mind, and I hurried to begin the binding words. I instructed my power to search for the breach team, overlaying the name with the sense of a group of Kallorwegian mages creeping through the night. And then I sent it rippling out from me with a final, "End binding."

The commonborn soldiers shifted from foot to foot, peering uncomfortably out into the darkness while we waited. The five mages stood poised, each of us facing in a different direction as we waited for the slightest sensation of power returning in our direction.

"They might feel it," whispered Araminta. "And know we're coming."

I bit my lip. Should I have tried to work a shield into my composition? Lucas had said to conserve power, and that would have been a complicated and chancy working...

"We'll just have to hope they pay it no mind," Martin said tersely. "With all the chaos going on tonight, no one would be surprised to feel odd surges of power rushing around."

I exchanged a glance with Lucas. We could only hope the lieutenant was right.

Somehow I had ended up pressed almost against Lucas's side, and he reached out under cover of the darkness to clasp my hand. We stood like that through the drawn-out moments of waiting, until a soft squeak from Araminta accompanied a steady thread of power arcing back in our direction.

"Does everyone feel that? Where it's coming from?" I looked around at the other mages. As soon as they all nodded, I severed the flow.

Martin started, staring into the dark and then back at me.

"Where did it go?"

"Conserving power, remember," I told him.

"Things operate a little differently when you're the Spoken Mage," said Lucas with a hint of both amusement and pride in his voice. "Much more efficiently, for one."

Martin looked intrigued, but he didn't stop to question me, leading us instead in the direction my power had indicated. Lucas dropped my hand, increasing his pace to run beside the lieutenant.

"We're curving toward the battle," he said, so low I almost didn't hear it.

"If the breach team did feel her working," Martin murmured back, "then they will have felt our location just like we felt theirs. I'm taking us around to approach their position from the rear. And don't worry, I'm taking into account the progress they must be making toward Bronton."

Lucas nodded once before letting his pace slacken enough that he dropped back to my side.

No more bright fire lit the sky, but we could hear the growing sounds of battle. Shouts and screams rent the night air, and the crashing sound of rising and subsiding water sounded over the top of it. I cast a nervous glance at Lucas.

"They'll be trying to clear a path through the river, and we'll be trying to turn it against them," he said. "They were no doubt intending to be safely through before we discovered their presence."

"If this is an all-out offensive, and they've returned to the old ways, they may have wind workers among them."

Wind workers specialized in all weather and were therefore the experts on manipulating water. The thought that it might be them who turned the river against our own forces made me shiver. I tried to see up north, but the darkness prevented me from making out anything more than occasional flashes of light illuminating a distant sea of dark bodies.

"Remember all of our seasoned officers do a year with the wind workers," Lucas said. "A necessity when your front line is dominated by a river."

My anxiety lessened slightly, but I still feared our mages might be outclassed.

A moment later, a southern stretch of the glistening river came into view, the water still frothing and tumbling from whatever gymnastics it had been forced to perform upstream.

"Look," yelled Araminta, pointing up the river.

I followed her finger and gasped when I made out figures moving in the dim light only a short distance from us. The moon sailed out from behind a cloud, bringing them into sharper relief. A blue-robed mage led a group of black and red clad soldiers from the river. They walked up from its bed as if the water did not exist at all, an invisible bubble holding it back.

Araminta's cry must have reached them because several turned in our direction. But a battle cry from upstream had them pivoting into formation, facing north. What looked like at least three squads of our own soldiers raced toward them, spears locked. Behind them ran a silver-robed man who sent fire balls flying toward the Kallorwegians.

The glowing spheres broke against an invisible shield, but the mage kept sending them. The final two crashed through the unseen barrier, although they fizzed as they did so. With a renewed yell, the commonborn soldiers poured through, clashing with the Kallorwegians.

For a brief moment we had all fallen motionless, spell-bound by the battle before us. But Martin urged us onward.

"Surely we must help them," protested Clarence.

Lucas shook his head, shoving our year mate back into movement. "No, we must stop the breach team."

He was right, of course, but it still galled me to turn and run as our fellow Ardannians fought and died. But far more would die if we couldn't incapacitate the breach team.

Martin led us southward away from the battleground but now curving eastward as well, back toward Bronton. We had circled the breach team and would come at them from the rear, gaining the much-needed element of surprise.

The town walls came into view in the distance as we passed along a line of boulders, a copse of trees to our right. Had we cut our path too wide? The breach team would nearly be at the town by now, and we needed to spring our attack before then.

Lucas once again moved up to jog beside Martin. "Shouldn't we have warning compositions going ahead of—"

Several thin whistles, followed almost immediately by a loud thwump and a sharp scream to my right, sent me diving to the ground. Leila and Tobias followed suit on my other side, hitting the dirt hard.

"Ambush!" Lucas screamed, as the sound of ripping parchment filled the air.

A surge of power rushed to form a shielded bubble around us. I turned on my hands and knees to attend to the downed soldier, but even as I watched, he spasmed and lay motionless, blood pouring from his chest. A direct hit to the heart. Leila peered over me and moaned.

Armed figures emerged from the boulders and trees on either side of us. Every single one of them wore a mage's robes, just as the townsman had warned. In Ardann, the solid black material would have indicated academia in either the University or the Academy. In Kallorway it promised death, and it concealed from us which specialty belonged to which mage.

Somehow they had known we were coming and had laid a

trap of their own. Several of them already had compositions in hand and spears of pure power hit our shield from every direction. It weakened, only just holding. Another lanced toward us, Martin tearing a composition of his own and activating another shield just as Lucas's working shattered.

I scrambled up and ran to Martin.

"Do you want me to shield or attack?"

This time several of the boulders uprooted themselves and catapulted toward us, colliding with the shield and dropping to the ground with thunderous crashes. Already our second shield was weakening. Both Clarence and Araminta pulled new ones from their robes, but there were four of them and ten of the enemy. This wasn't a scenario we could win.

When Martin didn't immediately answer, I turned to Lucas.

"Shield or attack?"

"Attack," he said after only a moment's pause. "We need your flexibility."

My mind bounced uselessly from possibility to possibility. No use aiming for their hearts here. Every one of them was a mage with the ability to properly shield themselves. I would burn myself dry before I broke through.

My eyes fell on three mages who stood between us and the thicket of trees. Blindly I grabbed at the closest arm, pulling Leila toward me.

"Get the others ready to run for the trees," I whispered, and she slipped away from me.

Whispering the binding words, I added, "Split the ground and send them falling." I weighted the words with a description of the three mages I wished to target, before finishing with, "End binding." My power raced toward the ground at their feet.

A localized earthquake erupted, gouging deep fissures in the earth and sending rocks and even the first row of trees jumping and falling. The Kallorwegians cried out, two of them falling to their hands and knees while the third staggered away from the attack. The two downed mages sent questing hands into their pockets.

"Now!" I screamed. "Run!"

I didn't waste time looking back to see if my team followed me, but I could feel them at my back as we burst through the tree line and into the cover of the trees, our shield dying behind us.

"Spread out," Lucas called. "Find shelter."

We scattered.

I threw myself behind a bush, Leila beside me. With a rustle, Clarence disappeared into the branches above us. He climbed faster than I would have thought possible for someone of his size.

An unnatural wind blew through the trees causing a thud and stifled exclamation from above me, although Clarence didn't plummet down through the leaves as I expected.

Tobias, thrown off balance by the force, stumbled into a shaft of light, and an arrow curved impossibly through the air to pierce his throat. He fell sideways and didn't move.

A stifled scream from beside me preceded a single sob from Leila. I turned my head away from the downed soldier. Another person I hadn't liked but who hadn't deserved death. I drew a deep breath as I tried to think what to do.

They had ambushed us, no doubt alerted to our presence by my composition. But we had to do more than hold them off. We had come out here to ambush them, and although we had lost the element of surprise, we still needed to take out every one of them.

Peering slowly around the bush, I saw that the three downed mages had all regained their feet. Two more had come to join them, and they formed a line five abreast, advancing toward the trees.

A ripping sounded above me, and leaves tore away from trees all around us, throwing themselves into the air and dancing on invisible currents. It obscured my view, but I still managed to make out a silver-haired, grim looking woman in the rear group reach into her robes.

She had only made it halfway through ripping her retrieved composition when another tearing sound above me caused a fiery cord to spring into being and wrap around her throat. She had time for a single, strangled scream before its burning length tightened, and she toppled to the ground.

For a brief moment our attackers stood frozen in shock, all their eyes on her, and then ripping sounded throughout their ranks, and a wave of solid power rippled into existence around them. Only now did I notice that they had previously been relying on a shield between the front row of mages and the trees.

Clarence had killed her. He had come up with a way to identify their wind worker, and then he had cut her down. How had he done it? A composition aimed at any enemy in the midst of activating a composition perhaps? I threw off the thought. I didn't have time to consider it now. I needed to follow his example. We all did.

The line of five mages stalked forward, reaching the first trees which had been damaged in my earthquake. As they kept coming, they spread out, one walking toward us, his eyes darting through the trees. I examined the forest around him, watching the way his shield did nothing to flatten the leaf litter and detritus at his feet. A limited shield, then.

Whispering my words as quietly as I could, I took my time with a binding, needing finesse rather than brute strength this time. When I ended the binding, a vine, bright with spring green, unwound itself from a nearby tree. Slithering along the ground, it reached its quivering length for the mage's legs.

Wrapping around him, it had made it to mid-calf before he felt its presence. With a yell, he tried to swipe it off, but it tightened, drawing his legs together and sending him crashing to the ground. His head smashed against a jagged rock, and he rolled once and didn't get up.

A crash on the other side of the copse told me that battle had been joined elsewhere, as well, but I couldn't see any of it. A sound at my side sent my arm flying up, my elbow aimed at the newcomer's face.

"Elena!" Lucas's whispered word reached my ears just in time for me to redirect the attack before it smashed into his face.

"Where's your shield?" I asked. "There should be power around you!"

"And give away my position?" He shook his head. "But forget about that. We need to get through the shield around them." He pointed at the four mages who stood to one side of the fallen wind worker.

A shout, and the sounds of a tussle erupted off to one side of us, but greenery blocked my view. Surely we needed to deal with the mages among us, first?

"Do you see the young one?" Lucas's eyes hadn't left the Kallorwegian mages.

I examined them again, despite the panic threatening to overwhelm me. One did indeed look younger, more like our age than that of the older mages who made up the rest of the breach team.

"Yes, I see him," I said.

"Well, I recognize him. Two years ago, our intelligencers sent back a portrait of the Kallorwegian royal family, and that is Crown Prince Cassius."

CHAPTER 23

"*W*hat?" I wobbled in shock and peered around the bush again. "The Kallorwegian crown prince? Here in Ardann? But why would they risk that?"

"Never mind why," said Lucas. "We can work that out later. He's the one we need to focus on. Without him, I'm betting this breach falls apart."

Leila leaned in toward us. "I could create a distraction? If it would be helpful."

I shook my head. "No, you keep out of sight. We should never have let the general send you. This is a mage's battle, and you'll only get yourself killed."

She frowned but didn't argue.

I refocused my attention on the crown prince and his three attendants. Now we knew why they were hanging back.

"Raw power?" I asked. "I could bombard them until the shields give way."

"No." Lucas spoke quickly. "We don't know how many they have with them or how much power they've put into them."

I nibbled on my lip.

"Each one can only contain limited power. There's no way

MELANIE CELLIER

anyone drained themselves to make a single shield composition. They'll be relying on quantity. So maybe Leila's right. We need a distraction. Something to make them forget to set new ones. Or to make them unable to do so."

One of Lucas's royal guards came shooting out of a dark space between two trees. His foot caught on the body of the Kallorwegian mage, and he went sprawling. A black robe fluttered as the man pursuing him leaped out into the open.

Lucas's hand dove into his robe, but he wasn't going to be fast enough.

"Shield him," I whispered, and power burst into life around the guard just as the mage's sword descended toward his neck.

The mage gazed around, his eyes attempting to pierce the gloom and discover who had protected the guard. The guard, meanwhile, had twisted onto his back, somehow releasing the dead mage's sword which had been trapped beneath him.

The mage looked back down at him, his eyes widening as he attempted to pull his own sword back up in defense. But there was no time.

The guard's sword speared upward. For a moment it seemed to slow as if encountering some barrier, and then it flew forward, faster than ever, to pierce his chest.

I didn't need to ask Lucas what had happened. The ripping sound in my ear had been enough to tell me that the guard's attack had been given extra power. They were down three mages now, but that still left seven.

A scream in the trees to my left that sounded all too much like Araminta, nearly sent me to my feet. Lucas's restraining arm held me down, however.

"I'll go," Leila whispered and was gone before I could protest.

"The prince," Lucas whispered. "We need to focus on the prince."

I drew a deep breath and tried to think.

"What about Colonel Jennica's trick? The illusion of the

attacking army. I bet you've been working on that since we saw her work it." He wouldn't have been able to resist the intricacy such a composition would require.

Lucas didn't try to deny it. His hand slid into one of his many internal pockets and returned with three compositions.

"All of them," I said before he could ask. "Use all of them. Let them think there's an army descending on every side. We need them to scatter."

Lucas hesitated for the briefest moment, glancing at the pieces of parchment. How much time and energy and training did they represent? But in another second, he had shaken off any hesitation, tearing them all through with a single movement.

A cacophony of sound instantly filled the air. The thud of pounding feet and the roar of battle cries accompanied the sight of soldiers pouring out of the landscape toward us from every direction.

I raised my eyebrows. They were better than I had expected. He must have put a lot of work into them. They even interacted with the environment in a natural way, coming at the Kallorwegians from the most logical directions.

One of the older mages shoved the prince toward the trees while the others fanned out, racing to take up defensive postures among the boulders.

"Don't lose him," Lucas hissed in my ear, and we both took off through the trees toward where the prince had disappeared.

Both of us abandoned any attempt at stealth in favor of speed, crashing through the leaves and branches that clawed at us. A shooting burst of power rushing toward us gave me just enough warning to scream, "Shield!"

The blow crashed against my shield, nearly unbalancing me enough to send me to the ground.

"Get a shield up. Now!" I screamed at Lucas, and he retrieved and ripped a parchment faster than seemed possible. Only when I felt his power spring up around him did I relax slightly.

A black-robed mage stalked out of the trees, his eyes fixed on both of us, a parchment in his hand. Lucas turned to meet him.

"Go!" he told me. "Find the prince. I'll handle this one."

I hesitated, but he shoved me, and I took off running again. Twice more a screaming wave of power gave me just enough warning to throw up a shield. For the first time I felt the beginning stirrings of fatigue. Two years ago I would have been exhausted by now, but the rigorous training had expanded my endurance, and I pressed on without pause.

The sound of the attacking horde had dissipated, and I could hear shouts from the direction of the boulders. More mages would be on us soon, and I didn't have time to waste. I flew through a gap in the trees just in time to see a black-robed figure step over the prone body of a gray-uniformed soldier.

He turned toward me, and I recognized the figure of the younger mage. Crown Prince Cassius.

I had no time to step back, out of sight, before his eyes found mine. A determined light sprang into their black depths. He stepped toward me.

I gasped my way through the binding words even while my mind scrambled to come up with a composition. In the end, I only managed to throw up a shield. I needed time to think. Now that I had found him, I suddenly realized that I didn't know if Lucas had intended to kill or capture Cassius.

"The Spoken Mage." His voice sounded almost reverent. "So it's true."

"Call off your attack," I said to buy myself time, although the words sounded foolish to my ears. Perhaps I could incapacitate him without killing him. Let Lucas decide his final fate. I glanced back over my shoulder, but there was no sign of my own prince yet.

"On one condition." He took several more steps toward me.

I stumbled back, his answer throwing me off balance again.

"Condition? What condition?" I hadn't expected him to take my demand seriously.

"I will call off this entire attack and have all my troops withdraw past the Abneris—as long as you go with us."

I sucked in a breath, my head spinning. "Go with you? Never!"

"Just think about it." He stepped closer, and I had to edge sideways around the small clearing to avoid him.

My mind ran through the countless terrible scenarios of what might await me in Kallorway.

"This whole battle could end right now," he continued. "No more lives lost. In exchange for just one person. Can you really refuse such an offer?"

"You're saying this is for me?" I asked. "This whole attack is for me?"

"We tried sending intelligencers after you when we thought you were unguarded in your home town," he said. "And then we tried a raiding party. Four whole squads and an ambush." He shook his head. "Each time you defeated us just demonstrated how valuable a prize you really are. So here we are. The entire Kallorwegian army as distraction."

I gulped. The breach team had never been after headquarters. They'd been after me. And I'd run straight into their arms.

This time when he stepped forward again, shock held me immobile. But a shout followed by a scream in the distance unfroze me. I spun toward the sound. Had that been Araminta? Leila?

"It can all stop right now," Cassius repeated. "I'll give the order as soon as you come with me."

My shield still burned around me, so when he tried to reach out a hand to me, it smashed into the barrier of my power. He pulled it back and shook it as if the contact had stung.

"Put down your shield. Come with me. And we can end this war."

"The war? I will never help Kallorway invade Ardann."

He shook his head, his eyes still fixed on me as if nothing else in the world existed. As if we were not standing in the middle of a leafy battlefield.

"My father hates Ardann, has hated you with a passion for all his life. He believes you Ardannians stand in the way of the rightful Kallorwegian possession of the entire southern half of the peninsula."

I frowned. None of this was news to me. And it hardly inspired me to sympathize with their cause. Cassius's voice dropped lower, and despite myself, my body swayed forward to hear what he had to say.

"Not everyone in Kallorway agrees with him."

I pulled back, my eyes searching his face as I tried to understand his words. This close I could see that his eyes weren't black but a dark, rich brown. And they glowed now with excitement and sincerity.

"Some of us—many of us—are sick of this drain on our kingdom, of the unnecessary loss of life. But some hesitate to rally around me because of my youth." He leaned toward me. "But with you by my side, no one would doubt my power. With you by my side, I could win the Mage Council to my cause."

"You would depose your own father?" I choked over the words.

He looked away, breaking eye contact for the first time.

"He would burn down both kingdoms for the sake of his pride," he said. "We owe our people better than that."

My mind whirled. Could it be true? Could it really be that simple? If I went with him now, could we end the war?

"Once I am king in Kallmon, you would be free to go where you pleased," he promised. "You could return to Corrin the next day, if you wished."

I trembled, fighting within myself. If I went with him now, my friends would think I had betrayed them. But when the war ended, they would understand. They would have to. *If* the war ended, that was. If I didn't find myself locked forever in some Kallorwegian dungeon or executed alongside their insane crown prince for an attempted coup.

I swallowed.

"It will only get worse if you don't help me," he said. "It's already worse than you realize."

My eyes raced to his. "What's that supposed to mean?"

"My father has been hearing rumors about the Sekalis. Rumors he doesn't like. He's getting…creative."

"What do the Sekalis have to do with this?"

He gave a short laugh. "I heard you were originally commonborn, Spoken Mage, but surely you know the vast might of the Empire? If they choose to involve themselves in this war…"

"The Sekalis don't care about the southern savages," I whispered.

"Don't they?" he asked. "I heard they invited an Ardannian delegation into their lands not so long ago. And, more importantly, my father heard it too. And so he told his mages he needed something new."

I could feel Cassius closing in on me, although he didn't actually move any closer. And though he didn't attempt to attack me, my energy still burned out of me into my shield, and I could feel my mind growing fuzzier.

"I heard you had an unseasonably warm winter last year," he said, watching me for my reaction. "Warm weather isn't good for green fever. I hear it even mutated—became a killer. Fighting it must have taken a lot of Ardann's resources. Which would have made it an ideal time to launch a large offensive."

"No," I whispered although my voice sounded weak. "That can't have been…"

My denial trailed away, and he remained silent, letting me absorb the truth of his words. The change in the weather. The mutation. The Kallorwegian attack just afterward. The only mystery was that it had never occurred to us that it might all be part of the same offensive.

This time the prince did step forward.

Dead. So many dead. I wavered, and he stepped closer again.

"Lower your shield and help me end the war, Elena," he whispered.

With a soft sigh, I cut off my power.

"You've made the right decision," he said, resting his left hand on the small of my back and trying to guide me back out of the trees toward the boulders.

But a small sound from back in the direction I had come made us both look around.

"Lucas," I gasped as he stepped forward into the open space.

"Elena!" he cried at the same moment as movement flashed in the corner of my eye.

A rock, held in Cassius's right palm, swung toward my head. My mind went blank, empty of words.

And then somehow Lucas was there, thrusting me out of the way as the rock glanced off his shoulder. He grunted in pain, wrestling with Cassius as the stone dropped to the forest floor.

I scrambled backward, trying to make sense of what was happening. I wanted to call out to Lucas to stop. To tell him that I had chosen to go with Cassius. But the rock. The Kallorwegian had lured me into lowering my shield, and then he had attacked.

"Separate them," I screamed, still too muddled to know what I should do.

The two princes shot apart, landing hard against trees on opposite sides of the clearing. Cassius fell backward against the body of one of our soldiers, and I remembered with blinding clarity who had killed the soldier. Cassius was our enemy.

I stumbled, almost falling, as I ran to Lucas, helping him off the ground. He recovered more quickly than his opponent who had become tangled in the dead soldier, and he whipped out a composition. A new mage burst from the trees behind Cassius as Lucas ripped it.

The Kallorwegian prince screamed, a brief sound of agony that cut off as he slumped against the ground. The new mage ripped his own composition, a shield springing up around both of them, before he dropped to his knees beside Cassius.

He placed his hand against the prince's chest, and I saw it rise and fall slightly.

"To the prince!" The mage yelled. "To the prince. Retreat!"

Lucas grabbed my arm and dragged me backward into the trees.

"He's not dead," I gasped, unsure if I felt disappointment or relief.

"Unfortunately not," said Lucas. "But killing him might have only inspired them to fight harder. We need them to withdraw."

I looked at him in confusion.

"That's a rather nasty composition of my own invention," he said. "The kind of injury that requires complex analysis and healing. Even if they have a healer among their team, they will require space, time, and quiet to heal him. None of which are to be found on a battlefield."

While he spoke, we had retraced our steps to our original position. From the bush where I had first hidden, I saw the black-robed mages emerge, the prince carried between them and a protective barrier enclosing them on all sides. They passed in front of the boulders, heading back toward the river.

But just as they passed in front of us, a rustle and a muffled curse sounded from the tree above me, as if Clarence had slipped and only just caught himself. One of the mages on the outside of the group looked over. With one arm he helped support the unconscious Cassius, but the other whipped into his sleeve and pulled out a curl of parchment. Gripping it in his teeth, he ripped it clean through, and then flung out the arm, pointing it at Clarence.

Before the rest of us had even realized what was happening, a bolt of lightning appeared and shot in the direction of his pointing finger. The tree exploded, fragments flying out in every direction, and the main bulk of the trunk began to fall directly toward me.

"Elena!" screamed Araminta, and then someone else pushed past her, diving at me and sending me flying.

The tree crashed to the ground, branches everywhere, some of its leaves still burning.

"Elena!" Lucas was at my side before I could take a single breath, drawing me to my feet, his eyes roaming over me.

"I'm fine," I said. "I'm fine. But Clarence. Where's Clarence?"

A soft mew of pain sent me crawling through the sparks and ash and remaining greenery. Wedged beneath the fallen trunk, her lower body crushed, lay Leila. I realized now who had gone flying past Araminta. Who had saved me.

"Leila!" I dropped to my knees beside her, tears welling up in my eyes.

She smiled up at me, her lips trembling.

"I couldn't let the Spoken Mage die, now could I?"

My hands scrabbled uselessly at the heavy trunk. I looked around for help, and my eyes fell on the burned husk of a body.

I screamed and fell backward, my hands flying to my mouth. My stomach heaved, and I barely kept myself from retching.

Clarence. Tall, bookish Clarence, who had never had any place in a war and who had still managed to take down the first of their mages. He had taken a direct hit. No healer could help him now.

Tears fell from my eyes unheeded as determination filled me. I might be too late to help Clarence, but I wasn't too late to help Leila.

"Elena."

Distantly I heard Lucas's voice speaking to me, but I didn't turn to him.

"Lift!" I screamed, too full of frustration and grief to take time with binding words or proper limitations. The tree trunk shot up as if lifted by a giant's hand and flung away from us, slamming against the boulders.

I crawled forward to cradle Leila's head in my lap. With the trunk lifted, I could see the extent of her injuries. And without the pressure, her blood now flowed freely.

My head spun, and I was glad I wasn't standing. I had no time for finesse, this healing would have to be all or nothing. This was exactly the scenario Thornton had warned me against.

But some things were worth it.

"Heal her," I said, just as Lucas shouted, "No!"

Power poured out of me into my friend, filling her body. The trees spun around me, and the noises of my companions sounded fuzzy, first loud and then too soft.

And still the healing continued to drain me.

I had already used too much power in this fight. I could feel it in my bones. When I blacked out this time, I wouldn't wake up.

But Leila, at least, would live.

Lucas slumped to his knees beside me. He pried my hands from Leila's face, although the action made no difference to my working.

"I love you, Lucas," I said softly.

"Don't say that!" he snapped. "You can't leave me."

I tried to muster a final smile for him, but the energy to do so eluded me.

"Take my energy," he said.

"It doesn't work like that," I managed to murmur.

"Nothing about you works the way it's supposed to. Try! Just try."

But even trying required energy, and I had nothing left. Centuries of testing had shown that compositions couldn't store power.

A lightning bolt flashed through my mind. My compositions

didn't work the way written ones worked. I didn't need to store it on parchment and then release it. As long as I didn't use a binding, my workings happened instantly as I spoke them. I didn't need to pull energy into a dead parchment, I needed to pull it into my living self. Everyone had been so focused on how I could increase my own energy limits, no one had ever had me try to siphon energy from someone else.

Blackness crept in around the edges of my vision as I distantly felt Leila's bones mending and skin knitting back together. I tried to pull words in front of my eyes, but the letters swam in front of me in a jumbled mess.

I blinked and forced the last shreds of my willpower to pull them into line.

"Take...energy," I whispered, clinging to Lucas's hands as the blackness grew, eating at my vision until all that was left was the bright of his eyes. And then even that began to fade as I felt the life draining out of me.

CHAPTER 24

*B*ut the green of his eyes didn't disappear. Instead his image grew stronger as fresh energy flowed into me from his hands. I could feel two energy flows now. One drained out of me as my power surged into Leila, and one, like a rushing spring, poured into me as my power drew energy from Lucas.

Hope sprang into his face as my back straightened, and I met his eyes, my own growing wide. The drain ceased, and Leila sat up. But still the well of energy from Lucas poured into me. The fog of exhaustion lifted from my brain and limbs. I felt tired still, but no longer near the point of collapse.

As I straightened, Lucas's shoulders slumped slightly. I abruptly cut off the flow of power, remembering the origin of my new energy. Lucas leaned forward, cupped my face in his hands and kissed me deeply.

When we drew apart, he was staring at me with awe.

"Elena, you just—"

I shook my head, not wanting to hear him say it out loud. I looked up and found Leila and Araminta watching us with similar shock and wonder on their faces. Leila offered me a hand, and when I let her pull me to my feet, she swept me into a hug.

"Thank you," she said, tears in her voice.

"Whoa." I laughed shakily as I staggered, my energy levels still low despite the reserves from Lucas. "You saved me first remember."

Araminta approached, and her eyes fell on Clarence's body. For a moment she stared at it, and then she gagged and turned to throw up in the bushes. I stepped toward her to help her, but she was already turning back to me, anger in her eyes. She held out a hand to me.

"Take mine, too, Elena."

"What?" I stared at her.

"Take my energy. Fill yourself up, and then go and make sure this is truly over."

"I don't…"

"Yes," she said, her gaze meeting mine without flinching, "you can. I just saw you do it."

I bit my lip and then reluctantly opened my mouth, and said, "Take half." At least that way I knew I wouldn't risk taking more than she had to give.

More energy flowed into me, buoying me up. My aches and pains disappeared along with the last of my tiredness. I felt as if I could run a hundred miles, as if I had just woken from the most refreshing sleep of my life.

"Wait," Lucas said. "All of you." He looked at each of the three of us. "This needs to stay our secret." He met my eyes. "At least for now. You've just worked out how to access almost limitless power. There are people who would kill for that."

I swallowed, averting my eyes from Clarence's mangled body. He was right. People were already killing for the power I possessed.

Leila and Araminta murmured assurances of their secrecy, but I couldn't stay to hear them. Energy burned inside me, set afire by anger, and it was time I gave it an outlet.

The other remaining members of our team converged on us,

but I took off without looking back, even as Martin's voice called questions to Lucas. I broke through the last of the trees at a run.

I didn't turn toward the river, and the fleeing Kallorwegians. If I wished to end this entire thing, I had a different target in mind. Running faster than I had ever run, I sped toward Bronton. When I reached the gates, I planted myself in front of them.

"Let me in!" I screamed up at the guards. "Let me through!"

I had no doubt their orders were to let no one through, but something in my appearance must have convinced them. After a long, slow moment, one gate inched slightly open. I slipped through the gap, and it crashed closed behind me.

"Spoken Mage," a guard said with a respectful nod.

"Spoken Mage," repeated another.

I didn't stop to speak to them, rushing past through the streets. The soldiers at the doors of headquarters likewise made no effort to stop me. I only slowed as I walked through the doors of the old ballroom.

Everyone in the room froze and stared at me.

"Out," I said, my eyes fixed on the general. "Everyone out."

Not one of them waited for his confirmation, scattering before whatever fire burned in my eyes.

"Griffith."

"Elena." He spoke calmly, but I could see a wariness in his eyes he'd never directed at me before.

"There was an ambush waiting for us."

"Where is Prince Lucas?" He looked behind me as if hoping Lucas would appear at my back.

"The third Kallorwegian ambush I have encountered this year. Tell me, General, Head of the Armed Forces, Devoras—how do they know so much about my movements? And how do we know so little about theirs?"

The general stared at me uncomprehending for a moment, and then enlightenment dawned on his face. And, swiftly following it, came fear. The sight of it filled me with a heady elation. Let one of them tremble for once. Let one of them know what it was like to be afraid before someone of greater power.

"I have been trying to work that out for some time," the general said slowly. "If you have any insights, please share."

Fury filled me that he would make so little attempt at an answer. That he didn't even attempt to explain away the fact that all intelligencer messages came through him. Or that he was the only one who had known of our mission against the breach team. Well, he and the handful of aides who had been in this room with him the entire time since.

"You claim you want what's best for this kingdom," I snarled at him. "You claim to want to see the war end. And yet everywhere you ignore the commonborn. You let them fight and die for you, and yet you brushed away the idea that they could be properly equipped or given positions of command."

I trembled so hard, I feared I might fly apart.

"At the end of the day, it doesn't matter if you're the traitor. You're still responsible for hobbling this kingdom. For propping up your own power while commonborn—and even mageborn—blood waters the soil. I would be doing Ardann a favor if I killed you right now."

The general took a step back, his fingers twitching toward his sleeve.

I laughed, an ugly sound.

"I promise you, general, you don't have a shield strong enough to stop me."

I could feel the strength coursing through me, filling me to bursting, begging to come pouring out. I could destroy the general, of that I had no doubt. And more than that. Since tapping into Lucas and Araminta's energy, I had gained a new awareness of the way it filled the core of every person I encountered. I could feel it filling the general now.

Take it all. That's all I'd have to say. *Take it all.* And my power would drain his energy dry. And maybe he even deserved it.

Maybe the kingdom would be better off without him as I had just said.

But still I hesitated.

My own anger scared me. It burned too brightly. Was this justice talking, or grief and rage? What was the use of learning to control my impetuous tongue, if I couldn't control my actions?

I forced myself to take a step backward. To take a deep breath. The general didn't move, didn't try to convince me, just watched me with cautious eyes.

A voice I didn't recognize sounded in the otherwise empty room, and my eyes flew to the corner where his aides had been receiving incoming communications minutes before.

"The enemy is starting to retreat," the voice repeated. "Should we pursue? Or withdraw and assess casualties? We need immediate orders."

The general and I exchanged startled glances, the shock cutting through my threat and the dangerous tension between us.

"Is this your doing?" asked the general. "When you burst in here, the battle wasn't going well for us. We were holding them back, but only just."

I said nothing. Another ball of power appeared with another voice requesting orders.

Griffith pointed to a composition on the table in front of him.

"I need to reply. To give them the order to withdraw. We've suffered enough casualties tonight."

His words snapped something inside me, and I raised a hand to my pounding head. Weakly I gestured for him to proceed. He ripped the composition, barking a rush of orders into the ball of power that emerged.

I stumbled away from him. What had I nearly done?

I had always resented the mageborn for using their superior power to rule over the commonborn—and yet I had nearly done the same thing. I had nearly appointed myself judge, jury, and executioner over a member of the Mage Council, no less. If I started here, where would it end? If having greater power gave me the right to remove those above me when I disagreed with their decisions, I could see only one eventual end: a crown I did not wish to bear, followed eventually—inevitably—by an assassination I didn't see coming. No one could rule entirely alone through nothing but sheer power—and no sane person would want to.

I wanted them to see there was a different way. And I had to start by showing them with my own actions. If General Griffith was a traitor, then he needed to be declared so by more than just me.

The general sank into a chair, the last of his orders apparently given. For the first time since I had met him, he looked old and unutterably weary.

After a moment he looked up and met my eyes.

"Two soldiers found Reese, by the way. He had been hit over the head and stuffed in a storage closet. He didn't see his attacker."

I slumped into another chair and rubbed a hand across my eyes. Energy still filled me, but it no longer compelled me to action. My grief had taken a different turn, and I now felt heavy and detached.

"I was at the front this last summer, you know," said the general.

I looked up and frowned at him, unsure of his meaning.

"Lorcan told me he meant to keep you safely at the Academy all summer. You can ask him for yourself. I never knew he let you go home for a week. I didn't even hear about the attack until a month later."

"But Captain Carson and Lieutenant Martin are your men. Lorcan didn't request them from you?"

Griffith shook his head. "No, Lorcan assigned them directly. All of my officers get regular postings away from the front. Both Captain Carson and Lieutenant Martin were posted to Corrin last summer. They would never have been available for the assignment if they had been under my command."

I frowned. It did make sense.

"But what about the intelligencer reports? They come only to you."

He sighed. "That I cannot explain. They should come to me, and yet I have received none for some time. It's been a quiet spring, though. I tried to tell myself no reports came because my agents had nothing to report..."

A sick feeling began to build in my stomach.

"You can work a truth composition, if you still doubt me. I won't try to stop you."

When I hesitated, he leaned forward, a sudden energy filling him.

"Do it! I want you to know that I am no more a traitor than you."

His eyes bored into me, and for a shame-filled moment, I remembered Cassius's hand on my back as I went with him willingly. But I pushed the thought aside and called up the words of a truth composition.

I spoke slowly, ensuring the working was tight and strong. Whatever the outcome, I never wanted to have cause to doubt it.

The general didn't hesitate once, and the glowing sphere of white light in front of me never darkened in the slightest. Mages valued their privacy, and only the Head of Law Enforcement could compel another mage to submit to a truth composition. But Griffith seemed to find the process fascinating rather than insulting, watching me almost as closely as I watched him.

"That you have energy left for such a working," he murmured when I ended the composition. "Remarkable."

I turned my face away hurriedly and let my shoulders droop. I had been foolish to let him bait me into such a powerful working. And yet, I had needed to know. And now I did.

General Griffith was not the traitor. The sick feeling in my stomach had spread, the tremble now back in my hands. How close I had come to killing an innocent man.

But another thought loomed over me, distracting me. If Devoras were as loyal as Lucas had always claimed, then there was no one person with the position and power to have colluded with the Kallorwegians alone. There must instead be a vast network of traitors—a whole family of them. My mind turned back to the moment when I saw my attacker standing among the Stantorns. I had let myself get distracted by the general, but it must always have been them.

Redmond, my composition instructor, perhaps, who had known about my visit to my family. Jennica, who had ordered us out on patrol. Even Reese, who could have turned his healing powers to evil, as the Kallorwegians had done, and then locked himself in that closet. The endless possibilities gave me the terrifying sensation that the walls of the enormous room were closing in on me. I hadn't left my enemies out there on the battlefield, they surrounded me at every turn.

Helplessness gripped me. I had just committed myself not to take the law into my own hands but instead to work within the system to bring lasting change. But could I do that if no one else would believe me about the Stantorns? Could I go back to the Academy and sit in Redmond's class as if nothing had changed? And if I did, how many more attacks would I have to endure before eventually one succeeded?

But neither could I act. Because what if I was wrong? What if I was not the only new development after centuries of unchanging power? What if Kallorway had discovered a game changer of their own—some new way to wield power and evade our defenses? Perhaps their intelligencers were part of that network—I knew they had smuggled in two new ones just in the time I had been at the front. For all I knew that whole attack had been feints within feints, and the intelligencers had made their way back here to Bronton, where no one was looking for them.

The possibilities weighed me down, exhausting me with a fatigue that had nothing to do with the physical. And the idea of all the twisty possibilities made me think of the green fever epidemic. I should tell the general its true origin.

But I couldn't bring my mouth to form the words. I couldn't tell him that I had stood within striking distance of the Kallorwegian crown prince and instead of attacking had agreed to accompany him to Kallorway. And most of all, I couldn't tell him that all this death and destruction had been so the Kallorwegians could get their hands on me.

I would tell Lucas, of course, and that would have to be enough. Let him decide who else should know.

CHAPTER 25

*W*hen the trainees assembled for the return trip to Corrin, we were a somber group. Already a small year, Clarence's absence felt glaring at every turn. Even Natalya and Weston had been shaken when the rest of my squad brought his body back into camp, Lucas at their head.

The other two trainee groups had mustered under Lorcan and Thornton when news of the attack broke. Our instructors had commanded them to join the single reserve squad guarding the camp. A few Kallorwegians had broken through, but the fighting had been light from what Coralie told me.

Every time someone asked me in an awed voice how I had succeeded in fighting off the entire Kallorwegian army, I told them instead of Clarence's bravery and intelligence, and how he turned the tide of our own small battle. It was all I could do, and it didn't feel like nearly enough.

Leila pulled me aside to whisper that my secret was safe with her, and for all her open, chattering ways, I believed her. She had thrown herself in front of death for me—I didn't doubt she could do this too.

Heat pressed at us from every side—summer had arrived. We

would be arriving back at the Academy only to leave again in a few short weeks. Well, for most students, anyway. I wouldn't be going anywhere.

Lucas had insisted that the Mage Council at least must be told what the Kallorwegians had been after, and also what they had done with the green fever. He hadn't told anyone about Cassius's offer to me, however, or that I had nearly accepted it.

It often haunted me at night, though. What would have happened if Lucas hadn't arrived at that exact moment? Was it possible Cassius's offer had been sincere, and he had tried to strike me out of fear that Lucas would change my mind? Perhaps he thought it easier to get me back across the border unconscious?

Lucas remained steadfast in his belief that Cassius had intended to kill me, but he hadn't been there to hear the crown prince talk. He hadn't looked into his eyes. And so, I wondered.

But even without the knowledge of my near treachery, the information that Kallorway wanted me badly enough to send their entire army as a decoy for my abduction meant I held no hope that Lorcan would let me out of the Academy for the summer. And that despite the fact that I was no longer a private in the Armed Forces.

Lorcan had insisted that Griffith discharge me for honorable service. The general agreed far more readily than I had expected —no doubt because after the attack, no one wanted me within striking distance of the front lines.

And Lorcan had informed us all of one other silver lining as well. After consultation with Thornton, he had declared the Battle of Abneris—as the soldiers had started calling it—sufficient to ensure a third year passing grade for all of us. There would be no exams at the end of our journey.

Carriages had arrived from Corrin for us, but they waited on the other side of the Wall. Colonel Jennica insisted that we walk the distance from camp to Wall, saying that while we might not

MELANIE CELLIER

have survived a full conscription, we had survived a major battle and should honor the traditions. I no longer trusted the colonel, but as we trudged slowly along the road, the jagged line of gray rocks approaching ahead of us, I found myself appreciating the time for reflection.

We had left more behind than we could afford to give. And yet we could have lost so much more still. And some things even had been gained—as Lucas's hand in mine attested. I had tried to protest, but he only gripped it harder.

"No more hiding," he said. "I nearly lost you, and I'm not wasting any more moments together."

Natalya's eyes narrowed at the sight, and her head leaned close to Lavinia's. I suspected I wouldn't like whatever backlash was coming from them, but after the battle, I couldn't seem to care.

When we reached the Wall, Lucas let my hand drop, however. This was something we each had to do alone.

One at a time, all ten of the other trainees approached the rocks and ripped a parchment—some big, some small. When my turn finally came, I stood there for a long moment, sensing the complicated tapestry of power enmeshed in the stones. And I felt something else, too.

The new awareness I had gained since taking power from Lucas and Araminta had remained. Now I could not only feel power in the workings of other mages, but I could feel the potential of it resting inside them, the energy that pulsed at their life core, and in the core of every commonborn as well. And I felt how easily I could pull their energy into myself.

Sometimes the sensation frightened me, and I had done no further experiments since my desperate attempts among the trees. But I felt some ghost, some whisper of that energy now. Drops scattered among the rocks. The blood left by the commonborns who survived mingled with generations of mage-born power.

I thought of their sacrifices and of the horrors they took away with them, like the ones that now traveled in me. And I knew what composition I wished to speak. But there was something else I needed to do first.

Pricking my finger with the tip of my knife, I flicked a drop of deep red onto the rocks. Ignoring a muffled murmuring behind me, I whispered the words of my composition so no one else could hear, taking my time to shape them. And when I finished the binding, each of the droplets, not just my own, flared, their own lingering energy fueling my power as I poured it into them. Death would await anyone now who tried to cross them.

I turned back to the road and found Lorcan watching me with a strange expression. I refused to meet his eyes, clambering into a carriage after my friends.

The camp had been too public, so it was in the carriage on the way home that I told Coralie, Finnian, and Saffron of my breakthrough and of the true purpose of the attack. For a long moment after I finished, silence reigned.

"I understand if...if you see me differently now," I whispered when the minutes stretched on. "All those deaths because of me."

"No," said Coralie swiftly. "You will always be my friend first and the Spoken Mage second."

"None of it is your fault," Finnian added, his arm wrapped tightly around Coralie's shoulders. "This war is the fault of a power-hungry would-be emperor. And you don't seem to fit that description at all."

I had to force the smile onto my face, awash with shame at the memory of how close I had come to starting down that path.

"And if you can't leave the Academy, then we'll just have to stay and spend some of the summer with you," said Coralie loyally.

Only later, when we stopped at a roadside inn for a meal, did she whisper that she had her own selfish reasons for wishing to cut her summer away from the Academy short.

"Staring death in the face might have made me realize that love is worth fighting for, but that doesn't mean I'm eager to meet Finnian's mother. Horribly cowardly of me, I know."

"It could be worse," I said, my eyes on Lucas who spoke to Lorcan on the other side of the room. "She could be queen."

"Yes, about that," said Coralie, following my eyes. "I don't envy you one jot. But I do expect a full account when we get back to the Academy." She paused to bend a serious expression in my direction. "A full account." Her face relaxed, and she giggled. "Plus a promise not to forget me when you're a princess."

I winced. "A princess." With everything else going on, I still hadn't fully processed that possibility or Coralie's words just before the attack. War might have had the same effect on her it appeared to have had on Lucas, but that didn't erase her earlier perspective or the uncomfortable truth behind it. If the mage-born couldn't accept me, I could never make a good partner in life for a prince. Our marriage would ruin the both of us.

The thought lent bitterness to the lingering kiss he gave me in the entranceway of the Academy when we finally reached home. A crowd had gathered, mostly trainees on their way to the midday meal, and I could hear their whispers swirling around us. But Lucas didn't hurry, gripping me with sure hands, his mouth firm and warm against mine.

When he at last broke away, I hoped he hadn't noticed the two salty drops that lingered on my lips.

"Tomorrow," he told me, his words a promise. "In the morning I will go to the palace to speak to my parents. I'll tell them of my intention to court you and demand they change the law."

If he saw the fear on my face, he didn't ask me about it, and for that I was grateful. Because despite my fear, I was far too weak to give him up.

I would just have to hope for the best. Together we were

stronger than we were apart. We had proved it again and again now, and it would have to be enough.

I had planned to spend the afternoon resting, but I suspected I would most likely spend it being interrogated by Coralie instead. So when the knock sounded on the door, it was no surprise.

When I pulled it open, however, the smiling face of the Academy's head servant greeted me.

"Welcome back, Elena. It's nice to see these suites in use again."

"All except one," I couldn't help saying, and Damon's face fell.

"I'm sorry," I said after an awkward pause. "I didn't mean...It's certainly nice to be back."

"Some things take time to adjust to," he murmured. "And some things you don't forget." He glanced down the corridor. "He always had his light on the longest, you know. I used to notice it whenever I did my nightly walks through the halls to check everything was well."

"He studied hard," I said. "He would have thrived at the University."

We both stood in silence for a moment.

"We've heard rumors of what you did," said Damon eventually.

"I promise you they aren't true."

"Aren't they?" He regarded me steadily. "Well, true or not, it seems to me it was a fortunate day for us all when you arrived here."

It was strange to remember Damon showing me to my room on that first day. How out of my element I had felt, and how foreign and terrifying everything seemed. The Academy then had been far from the safe haven that greeted me today.

"Oh," said Damon, holding out a sealed parchment. "This came for you by messenger from General Griffith."

I frowned down at it but swallowed my questions. Damon would not have read my private correspondence, even if he could. I took it with a murmured thanks and withdrew into my suite.

Coralie barged in several minutes later to find me still standing in the middle of the room staring down at it.

"What's that?" she asked, tweaking it from my hand. It only took her a moment to absorb the contents, and then she regarded me with a raised brow. Tossing it onto a small table, she collapsed into a chair.

"Well? Are you going to go?"

"I think when a member of the Mage Council requests your attendance at their mansion, it isn't really a request."

"We knew he had come back to the capital ahead of us," she reminded me. "All those reports for Their Majesties."

I looked away. How many of those reports had involved me? And now I was summoned to the central Devoras mansion. Well, their main Corrin home, at any rate. Their estate in the foothills of the Graybacks was far larger by all reports.

"I suppose I might as well get it over sooner rather than later," I said.

Coralie rolled her eyes at me. "I don't know why you look like you're off to your own execution. He probably wants to tell you you're getting a medal for valor or something."

Of course, my friend didn't know I had threatened the general's life and then accused him of treason. And that was on top of driving our enemies to launch an attack on the kingdom with my mere presence.

Coralie did however take appropriate interest in the discussion about what I should wear. She wanted me to choose my most elegant day dress, and I thought I would do better in my white trainee robe.

In the end I settled for something in between. And when I stood in my practical leather outfit—one I often wore under my robe—she gave me her unqualified approval.

"You were right in the end. It makes you look powerful. Like you're a fully fledged mage who just hasn't chosen a discipline yet. Everyone already knows you're powerful enough you could graduate tomorrow—no harm in reminding them of it."

Her words buoyed me until I stood at the wide gate of the general's Corrin mansion. I had expected to have to explain my presence to the gate guard, but at the sight of me, he immediately swung the gate open. And somehow that turned out to be even more intimidating.

Inside the fence, vast, well-manicured gardens surrounded a tall, elegant house of white marble. I could almost hear Finnian's laughing voice in my ear.

Someone's trying a little too hard to remind us all of a certain other building in Corrin, wouldn't you say?

His father's Callinos mansion was a much more relaxed red sandstone.

Drawing a deep breath, I marched up the gravel drive and knocked on the front door. It swung open as quickly as the gate had done, and I entered a cold, sparsely furnished entry. Every instinct told me to turn around and leave this unwelcoming place, but I forced myself to continue further inside. At least I didn't have to fear running into one of the twins.

"This way, My Lady," said a footman, appearing at my elbow so silently that I jumped.

He led me down a long hallway to a large receiving room decorated in icy blue satin. Inside the general sat on an uncomfortable sofa. When I entered, he stood.

"Welcome to my home. Thank you for coming so promptly."

I nodded at him cautiously, not quite ready to thank him for the invitation. He bade me sit and inquired about our journey.

"It was uneventful," I said.

"Excellent." He smiled. "The best kind of travel, then. I myself will be heading back to the front in a matter of days."

I smiled awkwardly, trying unsuccessfully to guess where all this small talk could be leading. The door behind me opened, and the general once more stood, so I followed his lead. When the new arrival strode into the room, I gave an internal sigh. Calix must have come straight here to his father after we arrived in the capital.

"Welcome, Elena," he said with a broad smile, as if we were friends. "How do you like my home?"

Only the seat behind me prevented me taking a wary step backward.

"Um, it's lovely," I managed to say which seemed to satisfy him.

"It's the finest house in Corrin," he said proudly. "Aside from the palace, of course."

I didn't bother to tell him that it was the first mageborn mansion I had seen inside the city.

We resumed our seats, Calix taking a high-backed chair beside his father, and the general smiled at me again.

"No doubt you have some slight suspicion as to why we invited you here today."

Wait…We? I looked between him and his younger son. Not one of my ideas had related in any way to Calix.

"To be honest? I haven't the faintest idea."

The general chuckled as if I had made a joke, but I could only manage a weak smile. I felt as if I had entered some alternate world where I was a mageborn and not the commonborn Academy-pariah-turned-Spoken-Mage.

"My son informs me that you celebrated your nineteenth birthday at the front," the general said. "I wish I had known so we might have hosted a celebration for you."

My eyebrows shot upward before I could stop them. That would have been a surprise.

"No doubt," General Griffith continued, "you are starting to think of marriage."

My face flushed. So this was about Lucas, then.

"I hardly think I need enumerate the advantages of this family," the general said.

So...not about Lucas?

"I believe our position and strength speak for themselves, and your three years at the Academy have given you ample opportunity to observe the virtues of my son."

Calix grinned across at me as if we had been best friends from the moment I arrived. A surreal feeling set in. The general couldn't possibly be saying what he seemed to be saying. Could he?

"Naturally my family would be honored to welcome you into our number—despite the oddities of your origins."

A change of tune for the mighty Devoras. Apparently I had finally won their respect with the only currency they truly valued —power.

Something of my horror must have showed on my face, because he added, "Of course there is no rush for an actual marriage. You will both wish to finish at the Academy first at the very least. Perhaps even finish your mage term at the front. A formal betrothal would be more than sufficient."

"I'm sorry, I don't think I understand. Betrothal? Between me and Calix?"

"Certainly, my dear. What else would I be talking of? Of course there is no question of love in the case—not yet at any rate —but that is hardly a necessity at our level."

Our level. I stared at him.

"Both my son and I have long admired your strength and determination, and we—"

"Would that be while you were voting for my execution, or while Calix was attempting to kick my ribs in?" I asked.

The general gave a strained laugh.

"My dear girl, this is exactly why you need us as much as we need you. You have much to learn, but I will give you this tip to begin with. In politics one must have the longest of memories while pretending to have only the shortest."

"I thought we were talking about a marriage, not politics."

He raised a sardonic eyebrow. "There's a difference?"

"My behavior was a misunderstanding," added Calix. "And one I can promise you won't happen again."

I slowly shook my head. No, it wouldn't happen again, because I would send him flying if he ever tried. But surely neither of them could think I would seriously contemplate marrying Calix of all people?

"You could do a lot worse than my son," said the general, and I tried to decide if his voice had an edge. How would he react when he understood that I would never agree to such a plan?

"I'm sorry, general." I stood up. "I cannot possibly marry your son. Not now, not ever. I am...honored by your proposal, but it is best we do not talk of it any further."

"Oh, sit down," he said, sounding more exasperated than enraged. "Calix, get out of here."

To my surprise, Calix amiably left the room without the smallest sign of discomfiture at being thus dismissed. Whatever the general was trying to accomplish here, his son seemed to be entirely in support. And that astonished me almost more than all the rest.

"I have to admit," Griffith said, "I had my doubts about the chances of such a proposal, but it was worth a try. My son understands the value of power as much as I do, and it would have been the neatest of arrangements. But no matter. There are other options, you know."

I slowly sank back into my chair.

"Other options?"

"Certainly." He leaned back, regarding me through hooded eyes. "I meant what I said, Elena. You still have much to learn in the ways of court. Not all power comes from compositions. The Devoras family is old. We are strong, and we are respected. If you were one of us, no one could ever question your place among the mages."

"I don't understand," I said. "I'm not marrying your other son, either."

The general gave a genuine laugh at that.

"No indeed. Julian is a less amenable son than Calix, and he has not had the opportunity to observe you up close. He doesn't realize the potential…"

"So what exactly are you suggesting then?"

"I'm offering to formally adopt you into my family. I'm offering, Elena, to make you my daughter."

$\mathcal{I}$ stood, sat, and stood again before striding to the fireplace against the distant wall. When I reached the general again, I stopped.

"You want to adopt me. You want me to become a Devoras." I had to say the words out loud to even begin to process them. Such a possibility had never occurred to me in even my wildest dreams. And if it had, it wouldn't be the Devoras family I would have looked to for acceptance.

I tried to wrap my mind around the idea of becoming a member of a family that I had hated.

"You know I'm not an orphan, right?" I asked. "I already have a family."

He shrugged. "Legally that is of no consequence. And you are past the age of eighteen, so their consent to the arrangement would not be required."

I winced at the thought of betraying them in such a fashion. Of rejecting them just as my parents had feared. What would Clemmy say?

A strange feeling crept over me. My family had shown me that their love came without condition. Clemmy loved me too much to make any protest. She would know that a legal document did nothing to change our relationship. And if I accepted the general's offer, then I would have a claim on all the vast resources this mansion represented. And through me, my true family might benefit.

Perhaps this wasn't an idea to be rejected out of hand, whatever I thought of the individual members of the Devoras family. At least I knew they weren't traitors. The memory of the general offering to undergo a truth composition made me pause. How long had he been planning this? No wonder he had wished to reassure me of his loyalty. I would never have considered allying myself with traitors.

"You know, Elena," said the general in a deceptively soft voice. "There are all sorts of advantages to being a member of one of the great families."

I sank into the nearest chair, stunned. A member of one of the great families. There were indeed many advantages, but only one that mattered to me. In the midst of my shock, I had forgotten what Lucas had long ago told me over a desk in the Academy library. Royalty were only permitted to marry other royalty or members of one of the great families.

The general watched me with an all-too-knowing look in his eyes. He knew about me and Lucas. He knew this was his trump card. No wonder he hadn't seemed thrown off by my refusal of Calix. He knew he had a lure I could not refuse.

And however it worked out between me and Lucas, the general still won. The Devoras family gained the only known Spoken Mage in history either way. If I one day became royalty, they only stood to benefit even more.

But try as I might, I couldn't actually think of any downside for me, either. Well, other than gaining Calix and Natalya as siblings. And it wasn't as if I intended to move into their house.

Callinos had already accepted me, and now Devoras was ready to do so as well. And beyond that—they would give me legitimacy in the eyes of all the mageborn. As a Devoras, I need not fear that I would have no place in court at Lucas's side. I might be considered a safe person to offend or threaten or ostracize, but a Devoras was not.

When I looked up, the general already had the gleam of satisfied triumph in his eyes. He was canny in ways I was only beginning to understand.

"Will you answer a question for me, General?" I asked.

"If I can."

"I know now that you are not a traitor, that you never were. So when I threatened you, during the Battle of Abneris, why didn't you defend yourself? And why have you not mentioned it since?"

For a moment I thought he didn't mean to answer, but then he sighed.

"I am not a young man, Elena. I had chosen the armed forces discipline before the threat of war became real. I was part of the forced march and subsequent battle with which we turned back the first incursion by the skin of our teeth. And I have been waging war ever since. Yours was not the first battle rage I have seen, fueled by grief and fear and anger. Such rages cannot be reasoned with. They must be either restrained or allowed to burn their course."

He regarded me steadily.

"That was not the first time I stared death in the face, and it will not be the last. But when you restrained yourself, you proved to me that while you weren't born a mageborn, you should have been. Control and power—those are the tools that will take you far in court."

There was something very disturbing about the fact that it took my threatening his life to convince him that I belonged among the mages. But did it really matter why, at the end of the day?

"Very well, General Griffith, I accept your offer," I said.

"Excellent," he replied. "I already have the legal documents drafted, they require only our signatures. I'll call for them now. And please," he paused as he reached for the bell that would bring a footman running, a wicked twinkle in his eye, "call me Father."

I almost ran back up the steps into the Academy. I had assured the general that I would not be calling him Father, and we had agreed on sir as an appropriate mode of address. The documents had arrived by that point, and it wasn't until I found myself back in the streets that I had been able to contemplate the change in my status.

All I could think of as I flew up South Road toward the Academy was telling Lucas. Everything had changed. The law no longer needed to be changed. No barriers at all stood between us now. With the legal status of a Devoras, I dared anyone to question if my strength was sufficient for the royal family.

But in the entranceway, I came to an abrupt halt, entirely distracted from my purpose.

"Jasper? Clemmy?" My siblings both came forward with large smiles, fighting over who got to hug me first. I met my father's eyes over Clemmy's head.

"Mother? Father? What's going on? What are you all doing here?" I would have been terrified to see them turn up so unexpectedly if I hadn't had Clemmy whole and healthy in the circle of my arms.

"We came up to the city for Jasper's graduation," my mother said, pride beaming from every line of her face. "A university graduate! In our own family. Seems too good to be true."

"Oh Jasper!" I turned to my brother. "I missed it! I'm so sorry."

He ruffled my hair. "Never mind. It was only a ceremony."

I rolled my eyes. "Only, he says…"

He grinned, and I grinned back.

"We're going out to celebrate," Clemmy announced. "Mother and Father have saved some coin, and we're going to the best restaurant in the city."

I glanced a little longingly at the stairs, but Lucas had said he wasn't going to the palace until the morning. I had time to spend with my family.

I let Clemmy tug me out the front door, chattering all the way down the street about all the things she had so far seen in the capital. Jasper kept pace beside us.

"I have some other news," he said.

I looked up, a smile and congratulations on my lips, but he didn't announce his betrothal to Clara as I had expected.

"I've taken a position."

"Oh." I raced to recover from my less than enthusiastic response. "That's wonderful. Tell me all about it."

"There isn't much to tell, really. It's as a palace official."

"Wait—what? I thought you were going to work for a merchant family?"

He shrugged. "Plans change."

We reached the restaurant, and I pulled him aside while my parents requested a table.

"Jasper, what do you mean? Why have your plans changed?"

"I've heard some rumors while you were away, little sister."

I groaned. "Not the rumor that I defeated an entire army on my own, I hope?"

"I have heard that one, actually, but that wasn't the one I had in mind. It's the one about you and a certain person who is so far above us that I can't believe I'm even having this conversation. Except it's you we're talking about, so somehow I'm not surprised at all."

I flushed and looked away.

"Oh, Elena." He sighed. "You know there's no way that's going to end well, right?"

I shook my head stubbornly.

"And this is why plans change."

"What do you mean?" I stared at him, my brows drawing together.

"When I started at the University, it was to protect one of my little sisters. And the best way to do that was to earn as much money as I could as fast as I could. But now she doesn't need me anymore." He threw an affectionate glance at Clemmy who bounced up and down at my mother's side, looking around the restaurant with wide eyes.

"Instead my other little sister needs me. And I can keep a better eye on her inside the palace than anywhere else."

"What does Clara think?" I asked.

He looked away, suddenly as interested in the restaurant as Clemmy. "She understands. And it may not be as high-paying as some other jobs, but I'll be able to save still. I'll earn enough eventually, if she's still..."

He bit his lip, still studiously not meeting my eyes, and I got the impression there was something else going on that he wasn't telling me.

"Oh, Jasper, no." What exactly had he given up for me?

"It's already done. There's no point talking about it further."

Our parents called to us, and reluctantly I let it drop. But I determined to find out the full story, and if Jasper was making sacrifices for me, to convince him to change his mind. I had just been pulled the last of the way into the complicated game of court—there was no turning back for me now—but that didn't mean my brother had to come with me. My family would have the prosperous and productive life in the commonborn sector of Corrin that they had always dreamed for themselves.

When everyone had eaten their fill, and the talk turned to their journey back to Kingslee, certainty filled me. I had just transformed from Elena of Kingslee to Elena of Devoras. It was time for my family's long chapter with Kingslee to end.

"You're only going back to sell your store," I told them. "And then you're coming straight back here. We're all going to spend the summer in Corrin."

"Yes!" Clemmy crowed.

Jasper frowned. "I haven't had the chance to save much money yet, Elena. I don't know how far the sale of the store will go, considering—"

I cut him off and told them all what I had just done.

"You're still my real family, of course," I assured them, suddenly nervous that they would be hurt by my decision after all. "It's just a legal thing. I no longer have any need to claim Kingslee when you all are leaving it. Elena of Devoras will be the same person. And it comes with an allowance. One I have no need of myself, since I'm still at the Academy."

The allowance had been a surprise, and I had tried to refuse. But the documents had already been signed at that point, and the general had merely regarded me with surprise.

"You are now my daughter, Elena. And I can assure you all my other children receive such an allowance. Just ask Natalya." Amusement had sounded in his voice, perhaps at the idea of his true daughter refusing his money, and it had felt churlish to keep pushing. Now I was glad I had acquiesced. Why shouldn't my family gain from my arrangement?

Their exclamations and the required explanations lasted all the way out of the restaurant and up the street toward the Academy since they insisted on returning me there. But my parents slowly drifted into silence, exchanging looks with each other that put me on edge.

I let Clemmy race ahead of us, Jasper going after her with an affectionate sigh.

"What is it?" I asked my parents. "Are you disappointed in me?" I worried at my lip. Should I have told them about Lucas and me? I wanted to wait until he had spoken to his parents, but it might help explain my decision to my family.

"I know you were afraid of losing me," I said, "but that isn't what's happened. Please believe me when I say that I would never truly wish to be a part of the Devoras world."

"I should always have known we would never get to keep you to ourselves," said my father quietly. "Or your brother. You're too special. But we are grateful for the claim we do have on you, whatever papers you may have signed. We want what is best for you, and we recognize we no longer have the experience to advise you as to what that must be. We trust in your judgment."

"Thank you, Father." I swallowed around a lump in my throat. "But what do you mean you should always have known? There was nothing special about me before my powers appeared."

My father looked at my mother, and she nodded. A stirring of unease shot through me.

"You're entering a whole other world now, Elena. Your mother and I realize that. And we've been talking. There's something we haven't told you. Something we probably should have..."

I stared at them, my wrung-out mind unable to come up with even a remote guess as to what they could be referencing.

"When your father and I were first married, we couldn't have children," my mother said. "We tried and tried, and I grew desperate. Your father said we should go for a holiday. That perhaps a trip might help. I didn't have any hope left, but I also had no energy to resist, so I went along. But it turned out the holiday was only a story for our neighbors. He had something else in mind."

She glanced at him, and he resumed the tale.

"I had heard distant rumors of someone who could help in such situations. My parents had worked hard and amassed a small fortune in gold from their profits at the store. They left it to me, and I could think of no more worthy use. So we went to this woman. A mad eccentric she was, in the end. But she sold them to us anyway. Two of them. A boy and a girl, she assured us."

"Two of what?" I asked, afraid of the answer.

"Two compositions," my mother whispered. "I ripped the first one as soon as we got home, and a month later I was pregnant with Jasper. I ripped the second two years later."

"I've never heard of a healing composition that produces pregnancies." I frowned. "Did she analyze you first, like Beatrice did with Clemmy? Perhaps she worked out something in you needed healing."

My mother shook her head.

"She wasn't…wasn't a normal sort of mage," my father said.

"What do you mean?" I asked.

He shrugged. "We don't understand mages like you do these days, Elena. I just know she wasn't the normal sort."

"But it worked," my mother said. "And that was all that mattered to us. And then Jasper turned out to have a mind like he does…" She shook her head in wonder before turning her eyes on me. "And then you…"

"We just thought you should know," my father added. "There's a reason you're both so extraordinary, even if we don't know what it is, exactly."

I stared at them, my mind racing. "Do you understand how important this is? That a composition might have made me like this? It seems beyond impossible, but perhaps the situation could be replicated!"

I frowned. "But Jasper can't compose. He's as unable to control power as the two of you. It can't have been just that composition. No composition has the power to grant an ability like mine."

I ground my teeth in frustration.

"Can I read them? The compositions she gave you?"

My mother shook her head. "We burned them as soon as we tore them. We had no use for them once they were used, and keeping words in our home any longer than necessary? No."

"Well, perhaps I can find this mage then? Ask her directly."

"I'm afraid she wasn't young when we found her," my father said. "There's no chance she'd still be around now with your brother already twenty-one."

"I can't believe you never told me this. Why did you keep it a secret even from me?"

My parents exchanged a final glance, and then my father leaned close to me.

"Because this mage woman…she lived in Kallorway."

Sudden understanding filled me. We had already been at war with Kallorway twenty-one years ago. Some might try to argue my parents' actions were treasonous. I could never take this story to Lorcan, so perhaps it was a good thing, after all, that they could tell me nothing of the woman or the composition.

When they said goodnight, my mother gave me a lingering hug, and I understood what her words didn't say. We had all been through a lot to create and protect our family. All of us had made sacrifices in our own way. And each of us had been forced to do our best in a less than ideal situation. Through it all, it had been love that drove us, and it was our love that would bind us together, no matter what.

As soon as they disappeared through the gate, I hurried to Lucas's suite, no one appearing to prevent me this time. I had even more to tell him than I had thought.

But when I knocked at the door, I received no answer. I turned away, trying to think where else he might be. Surely he would not have gone to the library? We had neither exams nor assignments to study for.

"You won't find him here," said a cold voice from the stairs.

Slowly I approached my new sister. "What do you mean?"

"Lucas is at the palace." Something nasty in her smile stripped away the buoyant joy that had carried me here.

"Oh really? He told me he intended to wait until morning."

"I believe," she said, her voice offhand, "that he may have had a summons from his parents waiting on his bed."

I frowned.

"It seems they got word he was showing some...undesirable tendencies, and they wanted him out of the Academy as soon as possible."

Outrage filled me. I didn't need her to spell it out to know where that word had come from. Lucas had feared that if word of our relationship became public, someone in Corrin would turn his parents against me before we could return, but the poison had come from someone with us at the front. Had she sent word through her older brother, Julian? I couldn't imagine she had done it through her father—not given his plans where I was concerned.

With effort I tamped down my emotion.

"Undesirable?" I loaded my voice with surprise. "You can't mean me. No one would call a Devoras undesirable, surely?"

"What do you mean?" A note of panic entered her voice.

"Why only that I also received a summons of my own this afternoon...sister."

"No. No, no, no. He didn't. Father wouldn't...I told him..." She stared at me with horror.

"Go ask him yourself." I shrugged. "He can show you the documents."

She turned pale and started down the stairs but paused only two steps down. When she looked back at me, her expression squashed any feeling of satisfaction.

"Well, it doesn't matter. Not where Lucas is concerned. You could be as much a Devoras as me, and it won't change a thing."

"What are you talking about?"

"You haven't heard? Another delegation arrived from the Sekali Empire while we were away. And the rumor circulating Corrin is that this time they're ready to propose a marriage alliance. Their oldest princess with Prince Lucas. It's supposed to be signed by the time we graduate. Not even a Devoras can compare to a princess with the might, resources, and soldiers of the Sekali Empire behind her."

I swallowed. An alliance? With the Sekalis? Impossible. And yet Lucas was gone. And Prince Cassius had alluded to something like this.

I swallowed, trying not to let my fear show on my face. Lucas's parents would never agree to his courting me if there really was an alliance offered. But he would still fight for me. I could feel his lips lingering on mine. I knew he would.

"If Ardann ally ourselves with the Sekalis," Natalya continued, "we would have Kallorway suing for peace within a week."

All my certainty crumbled into nothing. If Lucas could single-handedly end the war without a life lost, how could he possibly refuse? How could I ask him to do so?

I wanted to laugh although I felt no humor. I had just discovered I had access to limitless power—I had become the most powerful mage who ever lived. And none of that power was enough to get me the one thing I wanted.

Natalya turned and marched down the stairs, her departure turned into a walk of triumph. Coralie bounded up past her, grimacing at her back before slipping her arms around my waist and giving me a squeeze.

"You survived the general, I see! Don't let anything Natalya said get you down. I want to hear what the old codger wanted."

"I don't think you'll believe it," I said slowly, my mind barely functioning well enough to process her words.

"Well, try me, I'm the believing type." She led me up toward her suite. "Finnian and Saffron will be joining us any minute. Turns out they had some more cookies waiting for them, and they also want to hear what the general wanted with you. Then we're all going to write to our parents to ask for permission to stay on at the Academy for a while."

My family on hand, the best of friends—and cookies. It had the makings of a perfect summer. If only my heart wasn't in the middle of ripping in two.

Coralie continued to chatter about the various things she hoped to achieve over the summer, and my mind snagged on the word hope. Hope. That was what I needed to hold onto. If Natalya was right, I still had time.

All I had to do was find a way to end the war with Kallorway during our fourth year so that Lucas wouldn't be obligated to go through with the alliance. No big deal at all, in other words.

I rolled my eyes at myself and let Coralie pull me into her suite. As I flopped into one of the chairs, Prince Cassius's face again filled my mind. Perhaps it could be done. Perhaps there was a way.

"Cookies!" announced Saffron, entering the room with a large box carried ceremoniously in front of her. Finnian followed behind, sweeping Coralie into his arms and placing a kiss in her hair.

"How are you, light of my heart?" he asked.

"I only saw you five minutes ago," she protested.

"What does that have to do with anything?"

Somehow, despite myself, the smallest of smiles slipped across my face. Finnian had won Coralie over, and I had to believe there was a way for Lucas and me as well.

NOTE FROM THE AUTHOR

Finish the Spoken Mage series in book 4, *Voice of Life*.

To be kept informed of releases and of bonus shorts in the Spoken Mage world—including an exclusive bonus chapter of Voice of Power, retold from Lucas's point of view—please sign up to my mailing list at www.melaniecellier.com.

Want more fantasy, romance, adventure, and intrigue while you wait for the end of Elena and Lucas's story? Try *A Dance of*

Silver and Shadow, the first book in my *Beyond the Four Kingdoms* series in which twelve princesses must do a lot more than just dance when they get caught up in a dangerous and magical competition.

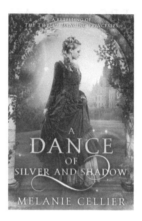

Thank you for taking the time to read my book. I hope you enjoyed it. If you did, please spread the word! You could start by leaving a review on Amazon (or Goodreads or Facebook or any other social media site). Your review would be very much appreciated and would make a big difference!

ROYAL FAMILY OF ARDANN

King Stellan
Queen Verena
Crown Princess Lucienne
Prince Lucas

MAGE COUNCIL

Academy Head (black robe) - Duke Lorcan of Callinos
University Head (black robe) - Duchess Jessamine of
    Callinos
Head of Law Enforcement (red robe) - Duke Lennox of
    Ellington
Head of the Seekers (gray robe) - Duchess Phyllida of
    Callinos
Head of the Healers (purple robe) - Duke Dashiell of
    Callinos
Head of the Growers (green robe) - Duchess Annika of
    Devoras
Head of the Wind Workers (blue robe) - Duke Magnus of
    Ellington
Head of the Creators (orange robe) - Duke Casimir of
    Stantorn
Head of the Armed Forces (silver robe) - General Griffith of
    Devoras
Head of the Royal Guard (gold robe) - General Thaddeus of
    Stantorn

ACKNOWLEDGMENTS

Voice of Dominion's first draft was considerably shorter than this final version, and it required more rewrites and new scenes than is generally the case for my books. So I'm more than usually grateful to my awesome beta readers and editors who helped me work out all the ways the story needed to be improved. I'm a verbal processor, so I'm particularly grateful to the many hours they collectively spent talking it through with me as I worked out what changes and additions to make.

To my developmental editor, Mary, and my beta team, Rachel, Greg, Ber, Katie, Priya, Marina, and Casey: I am constantly grateful to have your assistance. I promise I don't take any of you for granted!

My copyeditor and my proofreader also went above and beyond on this occasion, completing their work ahead of time and keeping my pre-order on schedule (and even before). I never write a draft without feeling gratitude for your expertise. Because no matter how many times you explain some of those fiddly grammar rules to me, I just can't keep them in my head. (I have to admit I've given up hope that I'll ever remember if it's *different from* or *different than*.)

My cover designer, Karri, continues to be a model of patience and skill as I bombard her with seemingly endless requests. New cover designs are only the start—there's also paperback covers, audio covers, title changes, and the list goes on. Sometimes it feels never-ending, so I'm always grateful to be working with someone of Karri's calibre.

My author friends continue to inspire, reassure, comfort, and entertain me—all essential things for the day-to-day survival of an author. Kitty, Kenley, Shari, Aya, Brittany, Diana, and Marina, I think my extroverted self would go crazy being stuck behind a computer all day if you weren't here with me—virtually, at least!

And this time I've saved my family for the end. Marc, Adeline, and Sebastian, your patience with me is astounding and always gratefully received. After every book I resolve to be more disciplined with my time for the next book, and somehow (so far!) life has always gotten in the way. I know my family bears the brunt of my long days when I'm drafting and then editing, and I'm so thankful for your flexibility. I hope one day I'll develop greater focus and be able to spend fewer hours shut up in my office away from you all.

And a final thank you to God, who helps keep all the ups and downs of the writing life in perspective.

ABOUT THE AUTHOR

 Melanie Cellier grew up on a staple diet of books, books and more books. And although she got older, she never stopped loving children's and young adult novels.

She always wanted to write one herself, but it took three careers and three different continents before she actually managed it.

She now feels incredibly fortunate to spend her time writing from her home in Adelaide, Australia where she keeps an eye out for koalas in her backyard. Her staple diet hasn't changed much, although she's added choc mint Rooibos tea and Chicken Crimpies to the list.

She writes young adult fantasy including her *Spoken Mage* series, and her *Four Kingdoms* and *Beyond the Four Kingdoms* series which are made up of linked stand-alone stories that retell classic fairy tales.

Made in United States
Troutdale, OR
12/21/2024

27112879R00192